# Pride, Prejudice *and* Cheese Grits

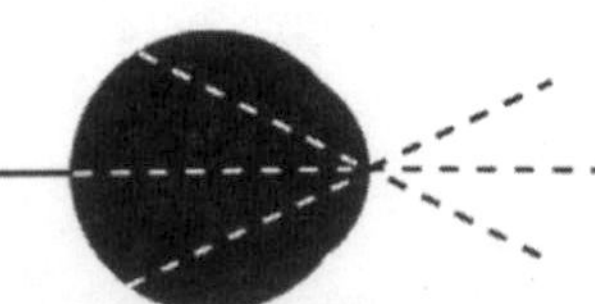

# Pride, Prejudice and Cheese Grits

JANE AUSTEN TAKES THE SOUTH
Book #1

Mary Jane Hathaway



Center Point Large Print
Thorndike, Maine

This Center Point Large Print edition is published
in the year 2014 by arrangement with Howard Books,
a division of Simon & Schuster, Inc.



The text of this Large Print edition is unabridged.
In other aspects, this book may vary from the original edition.
Printed in the United States of America on permanent paper.
Set in 16-point Times New Roman type.

ISBN: 978-1-62899-230-4

Library of Congress Cataloging-in-Publication Data

Hathaway, Mary Jane.
Pride, prejudice and cheese grits : Jane Austen takes the South /
Mary Jane Hathaway.
pages ; cm
Summary: "This hilarious Southern retelling of Jane Austen's Pride and Prejudice tells the story of two hard-headed Civil War historians who find that their first impressions can be deceiving"—Provided by publisher.
ISBN 978-1-62899-230-4 (library binding : alk. paper)
1. Historians—Fiction 2. Large type books. I. Title.
PS3608.A8644P75 2014b
813′.6—dc23

2014019468

For my sister, Susan,
who, when I first told her I was
writing a contemporary romance between
two Civil War historians in Southern academia
and it was based on Jane Austen's
*Pride and Prejudice*, didn't even laugh.

*I could easily forgive his pride,*
*if he had not mortified mine.*

—ELIZABETH BENNET

# CHAPTER ONE

Shelby Roswell rooted through her purse for the third time, tossing receipts and gum wrappers onto the cluttered desk. Those keys had been right in her hand a few minutes ago.

Squeezing her eyes shut, she sped through her morning in her mind, from unlocking her office until she arrived at her Introduction to the Civil War class. An image flashed through her mind—she'd dropped the keys onto the ledge of the old oak podium. Bingo!

Office hours didn't end for thirty minutes, but she'd just slip out. Hardly anybody came to visit this early in the term, anyway. She thought of how different it would look in another two months, when a line of students would be eager to haggle over their papers' grades.

The phone rang, a harsh trill that she could hear even when she was in the main office down the hall. Shelby puffed out an impatient breath and snatched the old black receiver.

"Shelby, it's Daddy," Phillip Roswell's familiar drawl sounded in her ear.

She loved how he called her office phone but never her cell. He didn't trust anything that tiny to work right.

"Your mama wanted me to remind you to come early weekend after next. She wants to introduce you around before the party."

"Hope springs eternal," Shelby muttered.

"Now, now. Just think how bored she'll be after she gets you married off."

"So, I'm her hobby?" she asked, laughing. Only he could make her see the humor in being considered a spinster at age twenty-nine. Shelby's mother spent more time trying to find her eldest daughter a husband than all the other mothers of Flea Bite Creek did for their daughters, combined.

"Now you got it. And I wanted to know how the new addition was working out," her daddy said, a smile in his voice.

She could just see her father, probably sitting in his study, feet propped on the corner of the antique desk, morning sun filtering through the diamond-cut windowpanes. He rarely left that room now that he was retired.

"Haven't seen hide nor hair. I heard they gave him an enormous office over in Agate Hall." She fiddled with a ballpoint pen, beating a staccato rhythm against her desk calendar. "And there was such demand for his classes that he's using a lecture hall to fit in the hundred or so who signed up." It galled her to admit that last bit. She was thankful to get the thirty or so kids she did.

"Well, as long as he stays out of your way, I won't have to come up there and have words with him."

Shelby snorted, imagining her mild-mannered Southern daddy having "words" with anybody. As the gentleman lawyer son of a gentleman lawyer, he didn't often resort to arguing. Power spoke for itself.

"I'm sure he will. He's far too important to deal with me. They've already had two receptions this week so people could meet him."

"Did you go?"

"Daddy, how could I sit there, smiling and playing nice? The review he did of my book was so mean, so low . . ." Her voice trailed off as she struggled to put into words what they both knew. It had not simply been a bad review. It had been a literary lynching in a national magazine.

"Why don't you have Arlen Beasley review it?"

Shelby sighed. An old family friend, Arlen would have nothing but good things to say. But no one would care to hear them either, since he was almost completely unknown.

"It's done. Ransom Fielding wrote *the* definitive series on the history of the Civil War. And the review came out in *NewsWorld*." She bit her lip and doodled in the margins of her calendar. Everything had been going so well. Her membership in the Southern Historical Society was almost assured, and she had nearly finished a groundbreaking article. But she had to bounce back from this catastrophe somehow. Her tenure application depended on it.

"No matter how many times I say that his criticisms weren't valid, nobody seems to listen. He didn't even have a problem with the work, just the way I wrote it."

"Why is he there teaching a college course if he's a writer?"

"Well, he holds a position up at Yale, so he definitely can teach a course. I know Finch was thrilled to have him join our department even for a year." Shelby nibbled her nail, a nervous habit she'd had since childhood.

"He should be thrilled to have *you,* brilliant girl," her father growled.

"You're like my own cheering squad. But I'd better get off the phone and go find my keys."

"Again? You remind me of your mother's aunt Kitty. She got so bad we had to hire a minder so she wouldn't set the house on fire."

"I don't think I'm that bad yet. But I could do with an assistant." Shelby eyed the teetering pile of research papers on her desk. Her housemate, Rebecca, liked to say Shelby used the EAS filing system: Every Available Surface.

"For Christmas, then. No more old books, just someone to keep your keys from walking off," he promised before hanging up.

Shelby sighed, wishing her Christmas present included going back in time and muzzling a man who seemed hell-bent on ruining her career.

After taking the stairs at a quick clip, Shelby was halfway down the first-floor hallway when she heard a voice drifting from the open classroom door.

"I understand we all want to be comfortable, but—"

The hallway echoed with the deep, unfamiliar voice. Shelby involuntarily slowed her steps.

"—even here, there must be a certain level of—"

The door was fully open, and as she came closer, Shelby could see the students packed solidly in the tiered lecture hall, every one of them riveted. A feeling of foreboding crept up her spine as she inched forward, her eyes finally confirming what her instincts told her: Ransom Fielding stood at the front of the room, and he seemed different from the man she'd glimpsed last week, striding across campus.

He was tall, but not gangly, with broad shoulders. His suit was well made, much better than what an average professor would wear, and he carried it with style. An almost too-handsome face was saved by severe brows, and his blue eyes flashed as he spoke. His intensity seemed to ripple outward.

"—the second day of class and there are still those of you who insist on disregarding my guidelines concerning classroom behavior."

The students seemed on the younger end of the undergraduate spectrum. Most of the girls were clustered down in the front three rows. The room was packed—nothing like the few rows she had filled earlier.

"—there in the red baseball cap, turned backward. Yes, you."

A kid halfway up the room paused midbite. He had a bag of chips and an orange sports drink on his desk, his notebook not yet opened, one foot propped on the back of the seat in front of him. He slowly swallowed.

"Come here and bring your food. No, just your food, not your books."

The student was somewhat lanky, and it seemed to Shelby that it took ages for him to get his foot down, gather his things and wander down the steps to the front. He stood to the side of the podium, shifting his weight nervously.

"Your name?"

"Tanner Keene," the boy said softly. He smiled tentatively and looked out at the class. There wasn't the slightest rustle of movement. No one stirred.

"Well, Mr. Keene, did you bother to read my class notes before this course began?"

The silence in the room was absolute. The boy cleared his throat. “I read a little of it, Professor Fielding. Your office hours, I think.”

“Ah, yes, office hours. Very handy to know for the day you will come to argue about the low grade on your midterm paper.”

There was a soft giggle from somewhere near the front. Shelby’s stomach churned. This man was like a grade-school bully, obviously enjoying himself.

“Did you read where I specifically state there will be no eating or drinking in my class? Because, Mr. Keene, it’s inconsiderate and distracting to other students, and to myself. More than that, *it is impolite*.”

These last words were spoken so clearly that Shelby flinched.

“I’m sorry, sir. I can throw it away.” The boy moved to toss the little bag and the drink into the trash near the door.

“No, you won’t throw it away. I think you should finish your snack. We will wait for you. All of us.”

Shelby felt Fielding’s words drop one by one into the room like pieces of ice down her back. The boy gaped at him.

“Go on. We’re waiting.”

As Fielding spoke, the words stopped making any sense, and all Shelby could think of was that review he’d written. Did he think humiliating people was funny?

Slowly, Tanner opened the little cellophane sack and withdrew a chip. He put it into his mouth and chewed, glancing up at the other students. Every crunch was magnified by the utter silence.

Shelby's eyes swept around the room. The students were riveted, most with fear, some with amusement. As Tanner chewed and swallowed, he again brought out another chip from the crackling cellophane bag. A few giggles sounded from the front rows.

Something stirred in Shelby, deep down where the words Fielding had written about her book had taken on a life of their own. *Just as a blind hog finds an acorn every now and then, so this author stumbles on a startling insight or two. The challenge is to find them in the fifty-six murky chapters that should have been cut to ten.*

It hadn't helped that she had never been considered willowy. Well, not never. One year in grade school she had been skinny, knock-kneed, with front teeth too big for her face. Since then, she'd grown some serious curves. Her friends assured her that curves were better than looking like a marathon runner, but Shelby still secretly wished God had gifted her with a lean athlete's body.

She moved to the door and knocked softly.

"—what we will do is—yes?" Powerful shoulders straightened with a jerk as she pushed open the door. His bright blue eyes widened, then narrowed.

"Excuse me, Professor Fielding. I believe I left my keys on the podium." Shelby strode forward and peered at the ledge of the wooden stand. "Yes, here they are."

There was the faintest waft of a woodsy smell as she reached under his arm. He was tall enough that she could grab her keys without having to bend too far. She glanced up at Fielding's face. His dark brows were drawn together. A thrill went through her that was only partly anger. He opened his mouth to speak, but Shelby turned away and stopped near the guilty student at the door.

"Oh, those look tasty! May I?" Without waiting for an answer she reached into the bag and grabbed a handful. Only a few were left, and Shelby managed to put them in her mouth all at once. She chewed thoughtfully, ignoring the sudden rustles and laughter from the students. A few crumbs fell from her lips and she brushed them from the front of her white shirt. The boy in the backward cap stood perfectly still, brown eyes wide, holding the empty bag in one hand and the drink in the other.

"These are so salty. Do you mind?" Shelby hated drinking after anyone else. Her sisters used to tease her that she would die of thirst in the desert rather than share a glass. But a fury was burning inside, and she wanted the bully to know that he would not win. Not here, not today.

She grabbed the sports drink and drank deeply, chugging the contents of the half-full bottle.

Peering into the bottom, she exclaimed, "Well, looks like that's finished."

She turned to leave, chuckles turning to laughter all around her, but paused midstep. On the board Fielding had written:

General Beverly crosses the
Ranawah Mountains after his
hometown of Oxford is threatened.

She read it twice, just to be sure. Had the country's most lauded Civil War scholar really made such a glaring mistake? Yes, he'd not only made it, he was *teaching* it.

"Oh, and by the way, Beverly was from Flea Bite Creek, not Oxford," she said in a clear voice. "I covered him in chapter three of my book about the Civil War battles in this area. I can loan you a copy if you'd like to read it."

Ransom Fielding had not moved. A muscle jumped in his jaw and the tendons on his large hands stood out where he gripped the podium. He seemed incapable of speech, but if he could speak, she had no doubt what he would say.

With a nod, Shelby strode toward the door. The last thing she saw as she walked through the doorway, amid another wave of raucous laughter from the students, was Mr. Finch, the head of her department. His balding head was a shade deeper red than his face, which bore an expression of deep disapproval. His knobbed hands were splayed flat on the desk, his entire posture one of shocked fury.

And to his right was Mrs. Greathouse, the head of the Southern Historical Society, who was currently reviewing Shelby's application for membership. A membership she desperately needed.

Gone was the polite smile from their previous, and only, meeting. Mrs. Greathouse's lips were now a thin, pale line of anger. From under her trademark silver crest of hair, her black eyes met Shelby's with a startling malevolence.

Shelby forced herself to keep walking, but her mouth had gone completely dry. Her professional woes had taken an ugly turn, and a bad book review was suddenly the least of her problems.

*Good opinion once lost, is lost forever.*
—MR. DARCY, *PRIDE AND PREJUDICE*

# CHAPTER TWO

Once Shelby was back inside her office, she closed the door and sat behind her desk, heart racing. The man was completely out of bounds! The damage he was doing to students! Pedagogy at its worst! And what was Finch doing there? With Margaret Greathouse? Shelby's thoughts whirled and beat against each other. She glanced at the clock. Not even eleven. Rebecca would still be teaching. She alternately paced the office and tried to sit down to work, but her emotions rioted within her.

When the fierce fire of her outrage had cooled to a simmer, she dropped her head in her hands and faced the facts. Her behavior had been completely unprofessional. She had allowed her temper to dictate her actions. And now she would have to apologize.

Just hours ago during her morning devotions she'd read the Bible verse about being "quick to listen, slow to speak and slow to anger," but a few hours later there she was, busting into Fielding's classroom, furious. The thought filled her with shame. *Lord, why can't you just put me on mute when I'm running my mouth?* But God didn't work that way. He let his children make their own messes—and clean them up. She groaned, grabbed her keys and headed outside. A walk would clear her head, help her find the words she needed to eat crow.

Shelby was deep in thought as she made her way down the narrow stairs to the second floor of the offices. She'd bought a small Civil War diary online and it should arrive any day. It would be a glimmer of happiness in her current situation. The sound of the departmental secretary's humming echoed out from the office. She tried to softly back out into the hallway. The woman could talk the ears off a jackrabbit and Shelby didn't have the time or the happy temperament to deal with her today.

"Shelby! There's something in your box!" Jolee's cheery voice rang out from the far corner of the high-ceilinged office. It was amazing how she always knew when someone came in, even though between her desk and the doorway was a few feet of blind hallway.

"Hi, Jolee. Just checking my mail." Shelby wandered over to the mail cubbies. Her small, white square was stuffed full. Slowly she reached out, extracting a cellophane bag of chips and a large orange sports drink, still cold from the vending machine. She carefully opened the white piece of folded paper that was under the drink and sucked in a breath.

You seemed ravenous.
Thought you might need a snack.—RF

Shelby read and reread the tidy, handwritten note.

"Isn't that nice? I tried to tell him that you didn't really eat junk food and I'd never seen you drink anything but water, Diet Coke and coffee, but he insisted." Jolee glanced up with a grin as she stacked outgoing mail next to her desk. Her bright blue eyes sparked with curiosity.

"Yes, very nice. We're . . . I'm sure we'll be good friends," Shelby choked out, warmth stealing up her neck. She gathered up her "snack" and waved a hand at Jolee, avoiding her inquisitorial stare.

He had thrown down the gauntlet, but she had no intention of fighting. She was a peaceful, Christian woman who was devoted to the Gospel of unity and love. At least, that's what she repeated to herself as she dropped the vending machine junk in the trash and strode to the front doors.

The morning sunlight smacked her in the eyes as she trotted down the brick steps and swiftly crossed the quad. The expansive grassy area dotted with students at any hour of any day was bordered by two enormous academic buildings and the library. The history building sat as something of an afterthought, holding down one small corner. Agate Hall loomed over the south end of the lawn, ten stories high and as characterless as a post office. All the important visiting professors got an office at the top of Agate. All the better to survey their temporary domain.

The elevator to the tenth floor seemed to take hours. Shelby nervously nibbled one fingernail and mentally rehearsed what she would say. *Please give me Your words,* she prayed. Rebecca often prayed she wouldn't get tongue-tied before a big presentation. That particular curse had never been Shelby's problem, sadly. *Don't let me say anything I'll regret later.*

The office door had a standard brown nameplate attached, white letters spelling out the occupant's name. She took a deep breath and knocked.

There was no response.

Shelby pushed the door the tiniest bit and peeked inside. A desk stood empty, papers stacked in tidy piles. The desktop computer hummed, and a cup of hot coffee gently steamed near the keyboard. She glanced back down the long hallway but saw no one.

Through the enormous window behind the desk, Shelby could see Chapman Hall in the distance. Being ten stories up made the redbrick building look even more humble, almost forgettable. Still better than having her office in a big gray box, she thought.

A comfortable leather armchair was in the corner near the door. Shelby perched on the edge of the cushion and gazed around. The office was large, but empty except for a few boxes near the door. Several books were stacked haphazardly, and she instinctively reached for the leatherbound ones at the bottom. The first was by Anthony Trollope. The next was *Wuthering Heights* by Emily Brontë. The third was *Pride and Prejudice* by Jane Austen. Shelby snorted softly, wondering whose books had been left behind. She slid them back and picked up a familiar, glossy hardback from the next stack.

"*A History of the American Civil War, Volume One*, by Ransom G. Fielding," it read in gold letters. She thought of her little volume on Thorny Hollow and resisted the urge to chuck the thick tome through the window. Instead, she flipped it open and read a few lines from the middle.

"Brigadier General Beauregard mustered a detachment from Garnett Hill, as ex-governor Wise attempted to fortify the troops and cross the intervening mountains." Shelby read the sentence again, a rapid-fire description. "Assisted by General Bragg, he confronted the Nationals in a heavy rainstorm, nearly penetrating the enemy camp within hours." The facts weren't glossed over with fine prose, but it wasn't dull and dry, either. She hated to admit it, but Ransom was an excellent writer. No wonder so many people enjoyed his books.

Shelby slammed the book shut at the sound of a throat clearing behind her. She rose from her chair, cheeks burning, and tossed it back on the stack. Ransom Fielding loomed in the doorway. His handsome face was unsmiling. In fact, he was positively scowling. She fought a sudden, insane desire to laugh.

"I figured you had just stepped out."

He stalked toward the desk and seated himself. She noticed his hair was a bit long, reaching his collar.

"Did you enjoy the book?" he said, eyes on his computer screen.

She wanted to lie. "It's well written." She wouldn't tell him she owned the series. It used to be within reach of her desk until two months ago, when she'd removed the five fat volumes and shoved them to the back of her closet at home.

"I have a good editor. And took a lot of writing courses." His tone was wary, waiting.

"I guess I need to sign myself up for one," she said, unable to resist. He had to know that she had read his review. It wasn't possible for him to think she hadn't.

Something flashed in his eyes—maybe anger, or remorse. "Always a good idea before you try to publish a book," he said.

There was a long silence as Shelby struggled against the words she wanted to fling at him.

He stood and walked toward her. She noticed deep lines, like commas, were around his mouth, even when he wasn't smiling.

"You wouldn't believe me if I told you that when they asked me to review a book on the Civil War history of Flea Bite Creek, I'd hardly heard of the place. I shouldn't have turned in that review. I was having a bad week."

Shelby tried to study him objectively, without taking in his perfect features or the intensity he radiated. Was it possible that he was actually remorseful? And that he thought a simple apology would cover it?

Completely possible, she decided.

"Well, your bad week became my bad year." Shelby was in no mood to be gentle.

He frowned. "There's a line, a description I shouldn't have used—"

" 'The blind hog'? Right, that was a special touch. Like the cherry on top."

He fixed her with a steady gaze. "I'm sorry."

She strode forward so abruptly that he almost flinched. "If you're sorry, then fix it," Shelby gritted out. "Print a retraction. Say. You. Were. Wrong." She shook her finger at him with every word.

Ransom's eyes narrowed and he didn't step back. "It was wrong to use that phrase, but the rest of the review was fair. The book was too long, too wordy. It was a mess."

"So it could have used a good editor. That was no reason to bury me." Shelby's eyes were flashing, her cheeks flushed with heat.

"I wasn't burying *you,*" he said, equal parts angry and defensive.

"So, as long as you don't know the author personally, it doesn't count?" He was so tall she had to tilt her head back to look him in the face. She could see the shadows under his eyes, the smooth darkness where he'd shaved. He met her gaze, his mouth opened as if he were going to retort, but didn't find the words. He focused on her with an energy that seemed to sear like fire. Her eyes dropped to his lips, and she felt a jolt run through her that was much more than anger.

Stepping back, she shrugged, feigning resignation. "What's done is done. If you printed a retraction, it probably wouldn't get any press."

"I wish—"

"Don't we all. Wish, that is." She felt suddenly weary, as if she had run several miles. Taking a deep breath, she said, "I came here to say . . ." Shelby tried to force her features into something like sheepishness. "I wanted to apologize for barging into your class." That was all she could muster. She wasn't sorry she had interfered with his "punishment."

Ransom Fielding crossed behind the desk and

angled into his chair. He said nothing, regarding her coolly.

After a few seconds, Shelby started to feel her blood pressure rise. She wondered if they were going to have an old-fashioned stare-down.

"All right." He drawled the words, left them hanging between them. It wasn't a question, but it might have been. It was almost impossible to hold his gaze without her heart pounding. She looked around the room, searching for a distraction.

"Better now?" Just the tone was enough to make her hackles rise. He moved to go back to whatever was on his screen.

"What?"

"Well, obviously this apology wasn't meant for me, but rather for you. Now you feel better, having done the very least required."

For a moment, she was speechless. "You deserve much worse than having someone interrupt your class."

"Interesting. So you came all the way to my office to offer an apology, yet you think I deserved worse."

Shelby's eyes widened. He was making her sound unhinged. "You humiliated a student. Having him stand by the podium and eat his lunch while you lectured is really beyond the pale." She couldn't speak calmly now. Her temper was rising by the second. She heard rushing in her ears.

"I make every student aware in writing and at

the first class that I brook no eating in class. He brought it on himself. The students here are completely uneducated in classroom etiquette." Ransom was still calm, but his jaw was tense and his hands clenched into tight fists.

"A simple reminder or a word would have sufficed. He was already embarrassed, but you had to hold him up for ridicule." She hated the high pitch her voice had taken.

"He won't do it again, and neither will any of the others." Ransom shrugged, as if that were the end of the matter.

"But at what cost? You've done real damage here. I'm surprised you've existed so long in this career with no pedagogical skills to speak of."

His voice was cold and angry. "I've existed this long because I'm a good historian and I can write, unlike some of us. Teaching is secondary. I am here to teach them what I know, and I can't do that with students wandering in at ten minutes past, clutching their fast-food bags and Big Gulps."

"I'd rather have a great teacher who can't write a decent book than a terrible teacher who can," Shelby bit out. "I'm not opposed to banning food and drink and tardiness, but what you did has instilled a fear in your students that will keep them from learning. And the worst of it is, you really didn't have to." He certainly could have commanded them with his reputation alone, and movie-star looks thrown in for good measure.

He sighed and pinched the bridge of his nose.

*I hope I'm giving him a headache,* she thought viciously.

"Perhaps when you've been teaching a few more years you will—"

"I've been teaching plenty long enough. If anything, I'll likely become more liberal in the classroom, when I don't have as much to prove. And I wasn't a student so long ago that I don't remember how it works, which professors were best. Mutual respect is what brings out true learning and thinking."

"Inspiring, really. And after you burn out from giving all your respect, time and effort while receiving nothing much in return, we'll talk about it again." He calmly stacked a few papers into a pile. "But for now, I have to go meet my aunt for lunch. She's scheduling the coming events for the Southern Historical Society and wanted my input. That's why she was sitting in on my class."

His aunt? She stared at him, hoping against hope. "Is . . . is Margaret Greathouse your aunt?"

He nodded, rising from behind his desk and crossing the room. He glanced at the large clock on the wall above the door. "If you'll excuse me, my office hours are over and I need to finish up here."

Shelby had no choice but to turn and leave. As she slowly made her way back down the elevator, she played his words over and over in her mind. That she couldn't seem to put that morning's verse into action when he was around was the least of her worries. A terrible feeling settled into the pit of her stomach. Dread and anger and something so shocking that she found herself whispering, "It was nothing, just nerves."

But deep down she knew that Ransom was a threat to her carefully planned life in more ways than one.

Ransom stared at the blank screen in front of him, his pulse pounding. He was used to women throwing themselves at him. But this one was fiery and angry and full of clever arguments, the opposite of an eager-to-please fan.

He dropped his head in his hands and closed his eyes. And so beautiful. That wild auburn hair, and huge hazel eyes that snapped with intelligence. He could hardly look at her without wanting to touch her. It had been so long since he'd wanted anything, he had almost forgotten what it felt like.

He had meant the snacks in the mail slot to show he wasn't without a sense of humor. The way she had crammed those chips into her mouth was one of the funniest things he'd witnessed in years. Those kids would never forget it. She had really done him a favor.

He winced, thinking of the review of her little book. It had been harsh, even brutal. But when he'd had second thoughts and called to withdraw it, the editor said they had already gone to press. For weeks he wanted to believe it hadn't mattered, that no one noticed. But it made the rounds, growing more and more famous by the week, as fiercely competitive academics feasted on it like vultures.

This year at Midlands was supposed to be sort of a vacation, time to write and do some research. He would teach his classes and let the little history department brag about the famous name they had on the rolls. He had hoped to apologize to her earlier in the term, but she never came to any of the department gatherings Finch had arranged. If he could convince her that he hadn't meant what he'd written, they could move on.

But once she was standing here, with her half apology, he couldn't resist the fight. What did she think, that he wouldn't see through it? That she wouldn't do it over again if it happened tomorrow? He knew her type, fearless in the face of tyranny. And that's what made him angry. He wasn't a tyrant. Not the way she made him out to be.

He had been so careful since Lili died. He went out with beautiful women, but kept his emotions clamped down hard. He never dated a woman who could carry on a real conversation, no one with spark. No one who could make him feel more than the mildest sense of pleasure.

He rubbed his hand over his face and groaned. Shelby had spark, all right. She was practically on fire. And he knew better than to get anywhere near that kind of woman.

*A lady's imagination is very rapid;*
*it jumps from admiration to love,*
*from love to matrimony, in an instant.*

—MR. DARCY

# CHAPTER THREE

"But don't you think the snacks are just a bit, you know, funny?" Rebecca shrugged one slender shoulder and tucked a silky strand of deep brown hair behind her ear. She slipped on a pair of oven mitts from the drawer and slid the pizza out of the oven onto the cooling sheet. The spicy diced-chicken-and-caramelized-onion pizza smelled heavenly. A bayou pie, as the locals called it, had never looked so good.

"Funny? Not at all. You're giving him the benefit of the doubt. If it were anyone else, maybe it could be a joke. But we're not talking about anyone, we're talking about Ransom Fielding. A man who apparently lives to humiliate students and colleagues alike." Shelby took some plates down from the cabinet and fetched the glasses. "Ice water or tea?"

"Water, thanks. I don't know, you two got off on the wrong foot and everything is going to be colored by that one bad episode."

As Shelby whirled around, her face flushed in anger, Rebecca held up her hands in mock surrender.

"One bad episode? He mocked me in a magazine that has a circulation of over a million!" Shelby opened the silverware drawer with a little too much force, rattling the forks. "I admit I shouldn't have gone in there." Her tone was bitter. "He's got a fearsome reputation, and whatever he chooses to do in the classroom is probably fine by the administration. I should be glad that he didn't go to the dean of faculty to complain. We could be having a meeting about it."

Rebecca rolled her eyes and laughed, depositing the mitts back in the drawer. As an English professor, she understood jealous colleagues and micromanaging department heads, and the silliness that happened high in the ivory tower.

"I need a do-over. How was I supposed to know his aunt is Margaret Greathouse?" Shelby grumbled as they sat at the table.

"You need to plug in to the gossip. Seriously." Rebecca frowned. "You can't expect to know what's going on when you stay at home all the time." Rebecca took a bite of the pizza and chewed thoughtfully. "What if, just consider the possibility, under that thorny exterior he really is just a nice Southern man?"

Shelby shook her head. "How many people do you know who act like that are actually sweet and loving *deep down?* That only happens in romantic literature."

"Not to harp on Jane Austen, but do you know why everyone loves Darcy?"

"Here we go. Austen has the answer for everything." Shelby laughed outright. There were no six degrees of separation for Rebecca: everything related directly back to Jane. "Um, everyone loves Darcy because he's rich and has a huge house?"

"Very funny. It's because he was sort of a jerk in the beginning, thinking he was above the rest of humanity. But after that first encounter, he really didn't do anything reprehensible. He was proud and a little obnoxious, but mostly he was shy." Rebecca took a sip of ice water and nodded sagely.

"Shy? I never got that."

"Mm-hm. Elizabeth is tattling to his cousin Colonel Fitzwilliam about the first time they'd met and how Darcy refused to dance even though there were plenty of available women. Fitzwilliam says that Darcy's not in a position to 'recommend himself to others.' She questions how that's possible, his being so rich and well connected. They're talking about his ability to make small talk and be charming."

"All right, but I don't think Fielding is shy. The man speaks at conventions and lectures to full college classes for a living. I think his true personality is what we've seen: arrogant and rude." Shelby wiped her fingers on her napkin and reached for another piece. Bayou pie was delicious, but it was messy. Her kitty, Sirocco, watched her hopefully from beside the chair, black tail swishing in a gentle rhythm.

"Maybe," Rebecca said, her tone implying she entertained serious doubts.

"You're determined to like him. He's handsome, rich and popular so you're not going to let his actions speak for him. But it still doesn't change the fact that we're talking about a kid eating in class. It's not like he was hurting anyone. It wasn't the right way to handle it."

Rebecca narrowed her eyes. "And your interruption was the right way to handle it?"

Shelby felt her cheeks flood with heat. "It seemed like it at the time." She picked at her plate, pushing the chicken from one spot to another. She knew she should be grateful to Rebecca—only your real friends tell you when you're being a hypocrite—but she didn't feel entirely thankful right now.

Rebecca leaned over and squeezed Shelby's hand. "Look, I'm completely on your side about the review. Every word he wrote about your book was wrong."

Shelby nodded. At least Rebecca remembered how awful that review had been, how much it had hurt to see Shelby's pride and joy cast in a negative light.

Rebecca continued, "But, I have to say that I find it extremely distracting when someone snacks while I'm lecturing. Plus, every now and then, they'll have something that smells incredible. There was a girl last week who brought a warm cinnamon roll. I thought I was going to die."

"You should have confiscated it. You could have stuck it in your bag and brought it home for me."

"It's not a bag, it's a Miu Miu tote." Rebecca waved a hand. "Anyway, don't bury poor Professor Fielding in the garden just yet. You never know what will happen."

Shelby sighed. "You're usually the voice of reason. But I'd bet my tenure that things are going to get uglier. I just have that feeling."

"Well, stay out of his way then."

"Yup. That's why I'm going to hang out with Aunt Junetta this weekend, so I'm nice and relaxed when I have to face the crazies at home."

"You're still going to that wedding on the twentieth? I thought you vowed no more forced socializing."

Shelby half shrugged. She wasn't sure she could really explain. A Southern girl was at her mama's beck and call way past the age most people were considered adults. If her mama wanted her to drive home, dress up, attend a wedding and stand around at a fancy reception thrown by old family friends, then Shelby had to do it.

“I may have been a little hasty to use the word *vow*. The Putneys have been friends of ours for generations. I should show up to their daughter’s wedding. And it’s not all bad. I get to see a lot of old friends. I just get tired of hearing the same old questions about why I’m not married. Sometimes when I’m in a room with all my parents’ friends, I start to feel like I’ve gone back a century or two.”

“Come on, you’d love to go back a century or two.” Rebecca laughed and poured herself more ice water. “Wow, this pizza is hot! I don’t remember it being quite this spicy. Did you change the recipe?”

Shelby frowned, considering her slice. “You know, when I cooked up that chicken, I was thinking about what Ransom did and I might have added the red pepper flakes twice. I was so mad I’m surprised it’s even edible.”

“Mmm, it’s still good. I’m just going to have to drink a whole pitcher of water. Anyway, Mrs. Putney usually has a good mix of people there, not just the old folks. Maybe I should go. I might just meet ‘the one’ and have a big ol’ Southern magnolia wedding.”

“Not likely. You’ll have your wedding in DC with all your relatives. But I can’t see you with a Southern man, anyway.” Shelby cocked her head, appraising her glamorous roommate.

“Because I’m African-American?”

“No, because you’re a Yankee.”

Rebecca laughed. “If I can live with *you* for years on end, I’m sure I could handle a Southern man.”

“Don’t even try to upgrade to a male version of me.” Shelby said. “There’s not a Southern man alive who’s going to cook for you, or discuss your Darcy obsession, or let you dress him in this season’s prettiest sandals.”

“True. But I could fake it well enough to get along with the right guy.”

“No, you couldn’t. Not even for five minutes.” Shelby started to clear the table. “You’re perfect just the way you are. The right guy will love you, North or South.”

Rebecca carried the rest of the pizza into the kitchen and got out the aluminum foil. “You know, for someone who doesn’t date a whole lot, you’re sure full of advice.”

“I don’t have a lot of time to goof around. I’m busy enough without dating half the town.”

“But goofing around is fun! We’re nice girls who go to church every Sunday. There’s no harm in going out on a Friday night, and some of the people I meet are a great change from my colleagues. They could really care less what journal just accepted my last article. Ross, the guy from that nightclub over in Oxford, he processes legal claims in a cube farm. And he thinks *my* job is boring.” Rebecca snickered, her lips twisted up in a smirk.

"I don't like to go out where it's too loud. What's the point of spending the evening together if at the end you still don't really know anything about the other person?"

"That *is* the point. If you don't talk, then you don't argue, and it all ends up a great success. Of course, we all know how much you love to argue."

Shelby put the glasses in the dishwasher and turned. "I don't love to argue! I really don't know how you can say that."

Rebecca raised her eyebrows and said nothing, letting an eloquent silence hang between them.

"All right, I do argue, but it's not because I love to ruffle feathers. It just makes me upset to hear people spout their ignorance. And they're as happy as a dead pig in the sunshine to keep on being ignorant."

"Ew, I hate it when you say that." Rebecca wrinkled her nose.

"I guess I'm like Darcy then, not really able to make small talk." Shelby set the coffeemaker for the morning. "That's it! I'm Darcy and I just need to find my Elizabeth."

"My friend, you couldn't handle Elizabeth." Rebecca laughed. "But let's go try on some outfits so you know what you're wearing to the wedding." She grabbed Shelby's hand and dragged her from the kitchen.

She let herself be pulled along. With her effortless glamour, perfectly arched brows and flawless complexion, Rebecca was the epitome of beauty. At one time Shelby would have throttled a horse to look like her, but that was in the past.

Mostly.

"Oh," she groaned, "I knew this was coming. At least make sure that I can sit without having to suck in my tummy. Otherwise, I really will be itching for a fight."

*A person may be proud without being vain.*

—MARY BENNET

# CHAPTER FOUR

Shelby popped a CD into the classic Jaguar's brand-new stereo system and headed out of town. The tense muscles in her shoulders gradually relaxed and a feeling of optimism crept over her. A weekend away, working and cooking at her aunt Junetta's, was just what she needed.

"I don't think the departmental deep freeze can last forever, Sirocco. Finch and his followers have to talk to me eventually." She reached over and smoothed her kitty's long, black hair and smiled as the cat responded with her usual *mmmmmrrrrp*. Rebecca made fun of Shelby's tendency to talk to the cat, but she was a good listener and it helped Shelby clear her thoughts. Plus, Sirocco never spilled a secret.

"But it will blow over. So he's written a bazillion books and is tenured at an Ivy League school, and I haven't and I'm . . . not."

A shiver went up her spine at the memory of Finch's face when he called her in to his office. *Your position is in jeopardy,* he'd said. Was it even possible? Rushing into Ransom's class had been a stupid decision, but it wasn't illegal or immoral or really harmful. She shook her head, trying to clear her thoughts.

"As soon as Fielding sees that everyone loves him best, he'll let it go." *But bullies never let go,* the little doubt in the back of her mind whispered.

The week since the day she'd stormed into his class had been quiet. As in, there was no one to talk to. Friends who used to stop to chat now walked by without a word. When she passed a group of colleagues, little whispers followed her. Ron DiGuardi was the only person who stood by her. They'd been friends since her first day in the department, when she'd walked into the department office and heard him giving Jolee a mini-lecture on medieval mendicants. He and his wife, Tansy, had welcomed Shelby into their family, and apparently not even departmental drama could sever that relationship.

Shelby turned up the stereo and tried to forget, at least for a little while, the wreckage she'd left behind. She was determined to spend the weekend reading, writing and painting, something that always made her feel better and now might soothe her wounded pride. The Thorny Hollow region had a charming name, but no one wanted to live there, not really. The longtime residents seemed to have given up the fight against the creeping kudzu, preferring to hack out small plots of grass around their modest homes. One convenience store, sitting at the end of a dreary main street filled with shuttered boutiques, was the total shopping experience available unless you wanted to drive to Oxford. Shelby's parents had one of the few truly beautiful homes, but it was just beyond the city limits, as if it, too, preferred to keep its distance. But Shelby embraced the town wholeheartedly, even the dreary little library with the dark basement for the children's section. She had spent countless hours there as a child, not minding the spiders that spun webs in corners no one bothered to clean.

In record time, she pulled into the long driveway of her aunt's ranch-style house. Aunt Junetta came out at the sound of the car tires in the driveway.

"Shelby, dear, let's get you inside and get started on some pies," Aunt Junetta said, a huge smile on her softly wrinkled face. She had one of the most extensive Southern-recipe collections in the county and wasn't afraid to use it. Shelby breathed in her aunt's freesia perfume and let herself be hugged to within an inch of her life. She felt the ache of tension in the pit of her stomach loosen. She leaned back and gave Junetta a kiss. "Let's definitely make some pies. And I've got a few paintings I want to work on in between research."

"Oh, I can't wait to see them. You're such a talented girl, Shelby." Junetta tucked Shelby's hand into the crook of her arm and led her toward the house. "I'm in awe of you."

Shelby laughed outright, but couldn't fight the wave of happiness that flooded through her at Aunt Junetta's words. "You're going to give me a big head."

"Never. You're the most humble person I know. Besides your daddy, of course."

"I agree with you there. I want to be just like him when I grow up." Shelby was teasing, but her voice caught a little on the last word.

Aunt Junetta turned her around, looking her right in the eyes. "You don't need to be anybody but yourself, hear?"

Shelby's throat went tight. Being herself wasn't working out so great. She nodded, eyes down.

"Now, let's get inside and start cooking. I missed our talks." Aunt Junetta tugged Shelby back across the gravel driveway and through the open door.

Smiling at the natural intersection of visiting and cooking, Shelby let herself be drawn into the warm, familiar kitchen. A little bit of space and a weekend might just smooth out the departmental drama. She tried to believe it, even as the nagging worry told her that her wish was too big to come true.

Saturday morning dawned clear and bright. Shelby could hear Aunt Junetta moving around in the kitchen. Shelby lay in bed, stretching out under the heavy quilts, and let every muscle in her body relax. A loud clank of metal against the old enamel sink made her jump. She frowned, listening to her aunt's movements. She seemed slower, less sure of herself than a few months ago. Shelby swung her legs out of bed and slipped into her robe. Maybe they both needed a restful weekend.

She padded into the kitchen, sniffing the air. "Bacon and cheese grits, my favorite!"

Aunt Junetta smiled over her shoulder. "You've always been a grits girl. Your daddy liked them well enough, but not like you. Every time you visited when you were little, you'd ask me to make cheese grits."

"Well, I never got any at home." Shelby perched on a stool and grinned. "Mama says she'd rather eat cracklins than grits any day, and she hates fried pigskin more than any other person I know."

"Even your Yankee friend?" Aunt Junetta loved Rebecca but she always remembered where Rebecca called home.

"Even her." Shelby let out a soft laugh, remembering the time she'd brought home some cracklins for Rebecca. It wasn't the flavor that bothered her. It was the fried pigskin part that had her shaking her head.

Sliding a plate across the counter, Aunt Junetta served two generous spoonfuls of cheese grits and a side of bacon. "Do you mind if we eat at the kitchen table? I hardly ever eat in the dining room unless I have guests."

"Of course not. And look at me, in my robe and slippers! I'm not one to insist on formal dining." Shelby took a bite of the cheese grits and closed her eyes in wonder. She savored and then swallowed. "I've missed this. Talking to you in person. Eating good Southern food. I wish I had come to visit sooner."

"Oh, honey, you had a busy summer." Aunt Junetta sat on the stool beside her and lost her balance for just a moment. Shelby reached out a hand to steady her. "Thank you. These stools are getting too high for a short, little old lady like myself."

Shelby nodded, but said nothing. Her aunt had always been so agile.

"After breakfast, I think you should take advantage of the sunlight and go paint. You can set up your easel on the covered porch. It's not too cold out there and the light is real good."

"You know, that sounds wonderful." Shelby took another bite of cheese grits and smiled. Whatever else was happening in her life, at this moment everything was pretty close to perfect.

Shelby stood back and surveyed her work. The late-afternoon sun was slanting through the porch screens, lending a golden hue to everything it touched. Her two small watercolors glowed brightly. In July, Shelby had driven the back roads of Flea Bite Creek, snapping photos of old barns and abandoned cabins. Something about the way the doors hung open, as if waiting for their last owners to return, was beautifully sad.

"Oh, these are real fine." Aunt Junetta stood in the doorway behind her, hands clasped together. "You get better and better every year."

"Remember my friend Tansy DiGuardi? The one married to Ron, who teaches in my department? She owns an art gallery and she brought in a watercolor artist last month for a weekend class." Shelby felt as if the weekend was the best part of her summer. So many fun people, so much laughter and learning new skills.

"Honey, I don't care how many classes you made me take, I could never paint like that." Aunt Junetta slipped an arm around Shelby's waist and hugged her tight. "And it makes you happy. That's the very best part."

Shelby smiled, but wondered if Aunt Junetta had noticed her mood when she'd arrived last night. Aunt Junetta would never pry, but she seemed to sense something was amiss. Shelby knew that when she told her about the departmental trouble, Junetta would be there to listen. Shelby just couldn't face that conversation just yet. Soon, but not yet.

After church on Sunday, they spent the afternoon looking at old pictures, and Shelby marveled again at how Aunt Junetta could remember stories her grandmother had told her fifty years before. As the day wore on, they settled in to make one last meal together. Preparing the pork medallions, cheese biscuits and collard greens, with peach pie for dessert, was like a balm to Shelby's wounded pride.

The doorbell rang just as they were setting the food on the table, and Shelby ran to let in their guest.

"It's so good to see you, honey!" Bessy Arbogast, Aunt Junetta's best friend for forty years, gave Shelby a hug, a kiss and a quick once-over. "Well now, aren't you the prettiest thing on this side of the Creek?"

"Don't let my sisters hear you," Shelby warned.

"Hmph. They may be pretty, but they don't have your sweetness. And that's what a good man is looking for, let me remind you," Bessy said, bustling around the kitchen.

After a soul-soothing meal and a few hours of heartwarming conversation, Shelby reluctantly gathered up the dishes. It was only a matter of time before she was headed back home to a mess that wasn't as easily sorted.

"Shelby was just telling me about the article she's working on for one of her historical journals. It's a real old-fashioned Southern mystery." Her aunt spoke over her shoulder as she filled the sink with hot water. "Tell her about the initials, dear."

"Well, I'm studying the history of this area, as

you probably know. It turns out a woman named Susanna Caldwell was rebuilding the schools in the valley here and over Thorny Hollow way after the war. The state just didn't have the money to spend on rebuilding the schools, so she took it upon herself to make sure there were grade schools and high schools big enough to meet the needs of the county. And everything had to be segregated, so she had twice the tasks, like coordinating with the Freedmen's Bureau and the state to get their teachers certified. But she never names her main benefactor. There's a pretty good paper trail all the way up to her, and then in her diaries she just mentions her benefactor with the initials MJ. Seems he really wanted to remain anonymous, but I don't know why. But if I can find out who he was, I'll fill in a piece of history that has puzzled scholars for years."

"That so? Those diaries can be real interesting. My great-great-grandmother kept one, and it's full of information about when they forced her family to board the Union soldiers. She wasn't too happy to cook for all those Yanks," Bessy said.

"Honey, I don't know why you don't just move in here with me and teach at our little college in town." Aunt Junetta handed Shelby another antique Tennessee Blue Ridge plate to dry, her hands trembling slightly as she held out the heavy china. "I sure would love having you here all the time."

“I know, but the community college here doesn’t offer the classes I teach. Also, I’m right on course for tenure right now. If I moved, it would get ugly.” Shelby tried to soften her words because she knew her aunt was lonely, widowed ten years and her only son rarely visited even though he lived only a few hours away.

“What’s tenure?” Bessy asked, reaching for a dry dishcloth.

“It’s an important promotion. Like being hired again. You can teach there for seven years, but if you’re denied tenure, you have to leave,” Shelby explained.

“Well, if that doesn’t work out, you should definitely move in with Junetta. Just think of all the fun we could have! The Winter Pie Festival is coming up and I bet we could take some top prizes. Georgia-Anne Dodd was ready to spit fire when you wouldn’t give her the recipe for that chocolate bourbon pecan you made last year,” Bessy said, placing the cut-crystal drinking glasses back in the simple hardwood kitchen cupboard.

Shelby carefully wiped the front and the back of her aunt’s dinner plate. She smiled, but inwardly she shook at the thought of not making tenure. All those years of work would be wasted. This is what she was sure God had wanted her to do with her life. How could she leave everything behind to spend her days making pies and quilting? But it wouldn’t happen, she told herself fiercely.

Ransom Fielding wasn't important enough to throw out the rising star of the department.

Or maybe he was. She sucked in a breath and tried to focus on the conversation at hand.

"You know, this weekend was just heavenly. I made more progress on my article than I have in the last month. Of course, I've probably gained more weight than I would have in a month at home!"

"You've got a long way to go before you have to worry about your hips. You just get prettier and prettier each time I see you. Now me, I should have given up on pie a long time ago, but without Mr. Arbogast here to impress . . ." Bessy trailed off with a sad little shrug. Her bright blue eyes clouded with tears.

Aunt Junetta dried her hands and gave Bessy a squeeze. "We miss him, too," she said quietly. "When my Jimmy went home to Jesus, I thought I would die before I found anything good in the world again. But he wouldn't have wanted me to sit and mope. So, I got myself back up that spring and started canning right on schedule. Did me a world of good."

Bessy's lip trembled a bit but she took a deep breath, wiping her eyes. "I'm so glad we're friends, Junetta. I don't know where I'd be without you."

"Probably home in bed! Now, we've got to let this mess go until morning or Shelby'll have to spend another night." Aunt Junetta's gray hair was disheveled from the heat and the effort of washing so many dishes.

"No, Auntie, we're almost done. Look, another glass and we're finished."

"All right, but leave that biscuit sheet for me to do tomorrow. I don't know how you can keep awake on those long drives."

Shelby glanced at the clock and was surprised at the hour. "I'll be fine, don't you worry."

Her aunt peered out the kitchen window, a slight frown creasing her brow. "It seems downright airish tonight. I just wish you'd buy something new, instead of running around in your daddy's old car."

"But it's a classic Jag and I wanted that car before I even graduated high school. When Daddy finally got something newer, I thought Christmas had come early!" Shelby smiled, and began to gather up her purse, overnight bag and Sirocco in her carrier.

"Classic or not, you don't want to get stranded in the dark."

Another squeeze for Aunt Junetta made Shelby want to store the hug somewhere safe inside, where she could bring it out when she needed it most. She could feel her aunt's shoulder blades through her thick sweater and winced. She felt so fragile.

"I've got my phone, and if anything happens, I can call for help. It's just an hour. I'll be home in no time." Shelby turned to Bessy. "Mrs. Arbogast, you take care and I'll see you next time I come down." Shelby gave the older woman a tight hug. She was the opposite of Aunt Junetta, pillowy soft and smelling of baby powder.

"Honey, take care, too, and you let us know when you find that nice man we're all praying for. I can't wait to bake some cheese straws for your wedding!"

Shelby laughed and shook her head. Bessy always made it sound as if Shelby's wedding were right around the corner.

Two hours later, she was only halfway home.

She shivered and flipped on the car's high beams, but the visibility was still only a few feet. Her hands were clenched around the wheel. The black fluff ball on her lap purred contentedly.

"Don't mind me, we're just going to drive off the road into the canal any moment now, Sirocco," she muttered.

Shelby licked her lips and tried not to panic. She recited a verse to herself, about letting "all who trust in You rejoice." She did trust. She was just scared silly at the same time. Thank goodness her father insisted she keep an old sleeping bag and emergency gear in the trunk. It probably housed more spiders than she cared to imagine, but it could be a lifesaver if the Jag broke down in this weather.

And her cell phone was dying.

Where was technology when you really needed it? But it was her fault for leaving the car charger on her aunt's table. It had been that kind of month. Mistake after failure after disaster. She tugged the top of her nubbly old sweater farther up her neck, chilled even though the heat blew full force into the car.

The Jag swerved a little and Shelby's thoughts snapped into the present with a sharp breath. *Was that ice? Or a gust of wind?* She didn't know which was better, but she decided it was time to pull over.

"Just you and me, girl. When it clears up, we'll keep going." Shelby's heart dropped into her shoes. An ice storm, in the dead of night, in an old car, on a deserted highway, with a dead cell phone. She felt like the first victim in a bad horror movie.

She pulled over carefully, trying to feel for the gravel at the side of the road. The red Mississippi clay was worn smooth in spots and she didn't want to slide down the bank. Satisfied she was out of the way, she put on her emergency lights and settled back. Her shoulders were knotted with stress and she worked to unclench her hands. She was going to trust God from the side of the road now, instead of driving bulldoggedly through the storm.

Sirocco raised her head with a *Mrrrp?* and

Shelby stroked her back. "Just a few minutes, till it gets better."

She rubbed her fingers through Sirocco's fur, feeling the vibration as the cat purred. A gust of wind spread sleet across the hood, and she wiggled her toes inside her black boots. She hoped they didn't have to stay here all night. The idea of sitting along the side of the road in the pitch dark was scarier than trying to drive home.

Bright lights flashed into the rearview mirror. A car slowed, pulling up behind her. She grinned at the sight of the Good Samaritan, just like in the parable. The windshield wipers made a squeal as she forced them back into action. A good-size pile of sleet was under each one.

She waited patiently for the other driver to make his way over. Finally, the dull clunk of a door's slamming shut, and a dim shadow passed through the lights shining in her rearview. A sudden shiver of unease traveled up her spine and she wiped at the window frantically, trying to clear the condensation. Sirocco stood, shook herself and left for the backseat. "Right, make me face them alone, you traitor," Shelby whispered, glaring into the dim interior of her car. Shelby turned her head back to the window and let out a shriek.

A shadowy figure was close, leaning down and shouting at her window.

*I hear such different accounts of you as puzzle me exceedingly.*

—ELIZABETH

# CHAPTER FIVE

Shelby cracked the window, her heart hammering, the old handle protesting in the cold. Icy rain stung her face as she squinted to get a good look at the man.

"Are you all right?" the dark shape was asking in a loud voice.

"Yes, I'm so sorry to make you stop—I was just taking a break, and I'll be going now." She nodded reassuringly at the stranger. His overcoat was pulled up around his chin, and under his dark, floppy hat she could hardly see anything except his nose. Little pieces of ice clung to his shoulders and arms, sparkling in the dim light.

There was a long pause. Shelby's stomach flipped over as he stared silently, his face in shadow.

"I can give you a ride. I don't think you should drive on this ice without all-weather tires," he said, as if coming to a decision.

He'd checked her tires? Shelby fought her fear by reminding herself she was inside, and he was outside.

"Thank you, but I can't accept a ride from you." There, that was direct. She smiled a little, hoping to look confident but friendly. Or at least as if she knew some self-defense.

He straightened up for a moment. He gazed toward his car, as if he was thinking, then leaned down again.

"And why not?" His voice wasn't particularly friendly now.

Wasn't it obvious? She wished she could see his face. Shelby felt like rolling the window up and speeding away. Well, trying to speed away.

"Because," she said slowly, "you are a *stranger*. I am a woman *alone*. It would not be prudent for me to get into *your car*." Shelby knew he was trying to help, but insisting on giving her a ride was scaring her.

Somewhere between his coat collar and his hat, she saw movement, something like his lips quirking up. "I'm a . . . Oh, that's all? Stranger danger?"

Shelby nodded mutely, wincing when a piece of ice hit her in the eye. Who said "stranger danger" anyway? The rain was pelting through the crack in the window, and the top of her head was cold and wet. Sirocco made unhappy sounds in the backseat, where the heater didn't quite reach.

"And of course, you could bring the attack cat," he said.

As if on cue, Sirocco crept up to the front and stuck her nose into the window, paws on the wet door. Shelby impatiently batted at the fluff of her tail and plopped her in the passenger seat, where she continued to peer toward the deep voice.

"I don't think I'll be able to get her out of the car in this weather, period. My car is fine, I'm going to start driving now. But thank you for stopping to make sure we were okay."

*Now, get out of the way before I run over your foot*. She put her hand on the window handle, hoping he'd take the hint. Something about his voice was familiar, it seemed to her, the longer they talked . . . or shouted. It was hard to hear over the rain.

The sleet was gathering in little heaps inside the window, near the door handle. Shelby shook her head and ice fell off her hair onto her sweater. She had kept her voice polite, but she was gritting her teeth.

"You got a cell phone?"

Shelby's eyebrows rose up under her bangs. Why would he ask that? Maybe he *was* a murderer. She gestured to the phone on the seat next to her. At that moment, to her horror, it beeped the low-battery sound.

"Run out of charge?"

Shelby sighed dramatically. The man was impossible! "Yes, it ran out of charge—I left my aunt's house far too late, I didn't know there would be a storm, and my cat is mad at me. I was dry and warm, at least, and now I'm wet and cold.

I do appreciate your stopping but I'm not in any need of assistance."

And that should do it. Just roll up the window. But a Southern upbringing runs deep, and she just couldn't force herself to do it.

"Wait here," he said, and trudged back through the wind to his vehicle. Shelby rolled up the window and waited, berating herself for every second that passed until he returned.

When he reappeared out of the darkness, he motioned for her to crack the window, and he slipped a thin, black phone through the inch at the top.

"Take this. It's charged and will last till Spartainville."

Shelby didn't reach for the phone. "And what will you do if you get stuck and I have your phone?"

"I have OnStar." He glanced meaningfully at the dash of the old Jag. "I'll follow you and we can stop at the Piggly Wiggly there on Beau Bridge Road."

He was holding down his hat with one hand. "It's getting wet," he said, his voice dropping an octave.

Shelby reached up and took the thin flip phone, drying it off quickly on the edge of her sweater, the side that wasn't already damp and cold. "Thank you," she sighed.

The brim of his hat dripped sleeting rain and he raised a hand to wipe his face.

Shelby had a brief flash of something, recognition or déjà vu. She opened her mouth, wanting to ask where he was from, but he disappeared from view, retreating back into the rain, and she started her car, slowly pulling back into the roadway.

Sirocco meowed pitifully and circled, looking for a warm spot in front of the heater.

"I swear he was going to drop that phone in my lap. At least we can call for help." She glanced at the phone and almost drove off the road when it rang.

She should let it go to voice mail. But what if he had someone else in his car and he was using that person's phone to get ahold of her? She reached out tentatively and flipped it open.

"Hello?"

After a sharp intake of breath, a woman asked quite loudly, "Hello? Who is this?"

Shelby thought for a moment, then flipped the phone shut.

It rang again, but she had already known it would. He would have to take care of it. Shelby ignored it, or tried to, as it rang and rang. Tucking the thin phone under Sirocco's blanket, she sang loudly to herself as the cat glared.

"Sirocco, they say no good deed goes unpunished, and here's proof. That woman didn't exactly sound like the understanding type."

*You expect me to account for opinions you call mine, but which I have never acknowledged.*

—MR. DARCY

# CHAPTER SIX

They made steady progress until finally the highway signs announced Spartainville. Shelby let out a deep breath and said a fervent prayer of gratitude.

The Piggly Wiggly parking lot was deserted, the store windows completely dark.

Shelby waited as the Good Samaritan pulled up alongside her. He drove a newish SUV, the cream color smeared with mud and dirt. Her ancient black Jaguar seemed to shrink in comparison.

"Gas guzzler," she whispered to herself, although deep down she knew her car probably had worse gas mileage.

Again the dull thud of a door's slamming shut, and a tall, shadowy form made its way to her side of the car.

She rolled the window down and said, "Thank you so much for the phone and the escort." She held the phone out halfway through the crack and felt her smile slide from her face in shock.

He was wearing the brimmed hat again, and his collar was still turned up to his ears. But what was hidden out on the highway was illuminated now in the sickening pumpkin-orange glow of parking-lot lights. Underneath the hat was none other than her nemesis, Ransom Fielding.

"Why did you stop?" she blurted.

"You had my phone," he said, eyes narrowing.

"Yes, I know that—" She let out a breath of exasperation. "But why did you stop when I was on the side of the road?"

He didn't respond, but only raised his eyebrows. He took the little cell phone and slipped it in his pocket.

"Right, of course. You didn't know who was in the car," she said.

"It wouldn't have mattered. It is what a Southern gentleman does," he said clearly, and turned to go back to his vehicle.

"Wait—" she called out, and unrolled the window a little more. He stopped and swiveled to face her.

"Your girlfriend called. She doesn't sound too happy about another woman answering your phone in the middle of the night."

His brow furrowed and he seemed about to speak, but Shelby rolled the window all the way up and angrily started the wipers.

"Unbelievable," Ransom muttered, slamming the car into gear. He stretched his neck and rolled his shoulders, attempting to ease some of the tension. Of course she couldn't just thank him. And he rose to take the bait. All of his good intentions weren't worth squat when he let her affect him that way.

She'd acted as if he were the sort of person who wouldn't help someone in need. He was a good guy, a lot better than those church-going types. In fact, he was probably a nicer person, with all the fund-raising he did and that small percentage of the proceeds from his book sales going to help orphans in Africa.

Why did he even care what she thought, anyway? That was the real question. Ransom whipped off the dripping hat and flung it to the side of the car, then slammed on the brakes, seeing the red light at the last moment.

He rested his forehead on the wheel and let out a long breath. It was time for Plan B: avoid her. Forget trying to be friends, or even apologizing for his part in that stupid departmental feud. Finch had taken it up as his personal cause, trying to freeze her out even after Ransom had made it known she didn't bother him. Well, she didn't bother him academically.

Ransom lifted his face and smiled grimly as the light turned green. Anyway, time to stay the heck away from her. And no more stranded motorists.

*You appear to me, Mr. Darcy,*
*to allow nothing for the influence*
*of friendship and affection.*

—ELIZABETH

# Chapter Seven

After a night filled with dreams of ice and strangers and an office door that wouldn't unlock, Shelby had never felt less ready for a day of teaching. All she wanted to do was pull the quilt back over her head and never come out again, but Sirocco was howling for her breakfast. With a deep sigh, Shelby relinquished her hold on the idea of staying in bed forever.

She stood in the shower and cranked the spray as hot as she could stand, willing her muscles to relax. An unrelenting dull throb was near the crown of her head. Every movement felt as if she were fighting through mud, and she wished with all her might she could call in sick. But she wasn't the type to give up so easily.

Once the smell of brewing coffee had filled the tiny yellow kitchen, she sat in the sunny spot next to the window and gazed outside, sipping the scalding liquid. Her Bible study for the morning was about letting the Word "dwell in you richly, teaching and admonishing one another." She smiled a little at the teaching part, and at how she tended to "admonish" more freely than she needed. But to dwell richly? Shelby closed her eyes and let the words settle in her, imagining them taking root. And across her field of vision swam Ransom's face, shadowed and stern, rain dripping from the brim of his hat.

Shelby rubbed her eyes and wished for the twentieth time that she were sitting across the table from Rebecca so she could spill all the torrid details, but she wouldn't be home from her trip to DC until late in the afternoon.

The storm had passed as quickly as it had arrived; just a bit of frost was left over in the shady places of the lawn. The sky was clear and the lightest blue, perfect for walking to campus. The thought filled her with dread. How many of her colleagues would ignore her today?

She slid on a pair of deep blue wool slacks and a creamy white shirt, tiny blue flowers embroidered at the cuffs. It was simple and understated, but the fabrics made her feel feminine. She decided not to fuss with her hair; instead she let it fall in soft curls past her shoulders.

The sidewalks bustled with students as she strode through the last block before the academic buildings. The bike racks were full and the bookstore doors were in constant motion. Friends hugged and exclaimed over each other while a middle-aged man tried to maneuver around them while carrying a large cardboard box. Despite the chill in the air, little groups of people gathered here and there to chat.

Shelby felt her spirits rise as she made her way closer to campus. All the bustle and noise reminded her of everything she loved about the place.

Midlands wasn't half as large as some of Mississippi's state universities, or even a quarter as large as University of Georgia in Athens, with its tens of thousands of students and an on-campus bus line. But Midlands' reputation for offering a first-class liberal arts education brought students from all over the nation, and the world.

Stepping past a group of young men who had stopped to compare schedules, Shelby looked up at Chapman Hall. Its graceful entryway was framed by stone steps curving outward toward the grassy quad, where students would sit and read in the sunshine. The double front doors were heavy, carved oak with large inset glass panels and covered with a wrought-iron overlay. The carved marble around the doors and above the entrance declared the name of the building. There were older and prettier buildings, but Shelby thought Chapman Hall was perfect for the history department. Stately and charming, adorned without being flashy, the whole building exuded dignity.

Shelby ran lightly up the front steps and pulled

open the door. It was dark inside and she stood for a moment, letting her eyes adjust. Her head pounded softly from the exertion and she rubbed her temples. As she quietly slipped by the department office she could hear Jolee in animated conversation. She passed Finch's office, noting the door was closed but the lights were on, and she could hear someone speaking. Strange, he was never here on Mondays, or really anytime he didn't have to be.

Stepping inside her office, she let out a sigh of relief. This was more than her refuge and workspace. It was a sign of the grit and determination she had to make it in the academic world. In this place, academic prowess only counted for so much; the rest was show. And Shelby had learned at her mother's knee the importance of making an impression.

The first year after she was hired as a teaching fellow, she mustered up the courage to ask Finch whether she could switch her tiny basement office with the janitor's closet, which was an enormous room. The ceiling was at least ten feet tall, the windows stretched from a few feet above the floor to near the ceiling, and beyond them was a large oak whose limbs gracefully arched up into the sky. Finch had waved a hand at her impatiently and told her to sort it out with Marcus, the janitor. Shelby almost danced out of the building that day because she knew Marcus would jump at the chance. The basement was the only area that was carpeted, and since the old building had no elevator, he had to lug the vacuum cleaner down the stairs every morning.

She found an antique braided rag rug in the local secondhand shop, bought a comfortable chair for guests, and set up a whole wall with floor-to-ceiling bookshelves. The only drawback came a few days later. Finch popped in, took a long look around and sniped, “If people didn’t know better, they’d think by the size of this place that *you* ran the department.” She had kept a straight face, but that’s exactly what she wanted. Finch would retire in a few years and she hoped to be one of the youngest departmental heads ever.

In the late afternoon, when the shafts of bright sunlight filtered through the oak leaves and she watched the movement of shadow and light play across her desk, Shelby knew true contentment.

Today the office seemed darker than usual, even though the sky was clear. The morning light was watery and cool. Shelby shivered and checked the thermostat. With the tall ceiling and windows, it certainly was hard to keep the office warm. She only needed to make copies of the syllabus and wasn’t planning to stay long, so she didn’t turn the heat up higher.

Shrill ringing issued from the desk phone.

“Shelby, it’s Katie.” On the other end of the line the usually clear voice was ragged and hoarse.

"Katie! You sound terrible. Are you sick?"

"I caught an awful bug from my roomie. I'm going to have to cancel our meeting tomorrow."

Shelby's heart sank. As Katie's adviser, she was responsible for keeping her thesis on track. Katie had already missed two appointments this semester, and Shelby had been forced to create a schedule and have Katie sign it.

"I understand. Call me as soon as you're well enough to come in and talk. We need to go over your detailed outline again and make sure you're progressing. You only have a few more months to bring it all together."

There was a loud sigh on the other end of the line. "I know that. I've been working really hard on it, I promise, but I can't come in when I'm on the verge of death."

"Just get better. We'll talk about it then."

After hanging up, Shelby sat frowning at her desk. She understood what it was like to be sick and probably stressed-out, too. The last few months before the master's thesis deadline are all work, work, work. But what had happened to the bright young girl she'd met three years ago? Katie had been so excited to research Thorny Hollow to tell the world about its rich history. She said her grandmother had a house somewhere near Natchez. It wasn't on the register of historic homes, but probably should have been, by what she'd said. Shelby needed to have a face-to-face meeting with Katie, and soon. But right now, she had classes to prep.

Deciding not to remove her coat, she grabbed the syllabus and headed down the hallway to the department office.

"Shelby, honey—" Jolee's face lit up as she saw Shelby walk into the mail area.

"Hi, Jolee. How's the new term going?" Jolee was a little high-strung, but she was the perfect office secretary. She never mislaid a paper or let a copier run out of toner.

"Oh, girl, you'd think we were Grand Central around here." Jolee shook her head of gray curls and waved her arm behind her at a large stack of boxes. "These arrived on Friday, but you know Mr. Fielding's office is in a completely different building. Now we have to get them sent over to Agate Hall."

Shelby peered at the pile and grimaced as the painful throb in her skull intensified. He must have brought his whole library.

The secretary leaned close and whispered, "He's sure a tall drink of water! Ron DiGuardi told me he's a widower and that's probably why he doesn't smile much. Ron said he lost his wife in a terrible car accident."

"That so?" Shelby didn't want to remember what Fielding looked like, and she really didn't want to spend any part of her day discussing why the man didn't smile.

Jolee continued in a normal tone, obviously a little disappointed in Shelby's lack of enthusiasm. "Then Marcus got his key stuck in the lock of the front door on Thursday and we had to call a locksmith to get it out. I've been telling Professor Finch that we need a new front lock. That costs a mint. Now they had to put in some cheap replacement until the order comes in."

The machine whirred comfortingly and the copies slid with a whisper into the bottom tray. "We have to go to lunch when things calm down around here. In a few weeks?" Shelby gathered up her copies and gave Jolee a hug.

"You betcha." Jolee beamed, returning the squeeze.

Shelby was almost directly across from Finch's office when the door abruptly opened and Ransom Fielding stepped out.

A word faded on his lips. His eyes widened when he saw Shelby, then narrowed as his gaze wandered lazily down to her toes and back again.

She was struck again by how tall he was, and how different he looked in the sun-filled hallway. His white shirt was open at the collar and his skin looked tan in contrast. Shelby struggled to shift her gaze to his face. Not even ten hours ago, they had been arguing in a dark parking lot, an ice storm raging around them.

"Miss Roswell." Something indefinable in his deep voice made her heart stutter in her chest.

*Elizabeth, having rather expected to affront him, was amazed at his gallantry.*
*—PRIDE AND PREJUDICE*

# CHAPTER EIGHT

George Finch followed Ransom through the door and said, "Shelby—glad I found you. We were discussing some departmental issues in here." The smell of stale cigars and cinnamon gum wafted into the hallway.

Shelby felt her mouth drop open. She had already apologized, sort of. Was Ransom so vain that he had to ruin her career even more than he already had?

Her shock turned to anger and she closed her mouth with a snap. Fine, let him try. She wouldn't go down without a fight. She barely registered that Finch was speaking again.

"—delivered Ransom's boxes to our office. They should have been sent to Agate Hall. But Ransom suggested a weekly roundtable discussion on Civil War history research methods."

His words seemed to filter in from a distance. Weekly discussions? Suddenly, his visit to Finch made wonderful sense. Shelby felt her panic fade away, replaced by relief so strong that she fairly beamed. "That sounds like a great idea. But I thought you were just teaching the one class?"

Fielding's eyebrows rose. "Just one this term, but winter and spring terms I'll have three classes. You didn't know?" He cocked his head a little and looked to Finch for some explanation.

Finch blustered, "Of course you knew. We've been discussing it all week." His balding head turned pink as he gave her a stern look.

Did he really expect her to know what was going on when her colleagues wouldn't even acknowledge her? But her job was safe—of course, she'd be working in the same department as Ransom Fielding for a whole year, but she'd deal with that later.

"Well, that's excellent news." Shelby grinned and then held up her papers. "Just making copies of my syllabus. Better go put them away."

"Wait a moment. These boxes need to be taken to Agate Hall." Finch was still going on about those darn boxes.

Shelby made an effort to concentrate. "Well, let's see. The courier system should run tomorrow morning. We can have them moved then."

"But I'm sure he would like them delivered today. Isn't there a hand truck or two down in the janitor's closet? A few trips with Jolee and you'd be done."

Shelby's eyes widened. Did Finch mean he wanted *her* and the *secretary* to move those boxes?

She stared at him for a moment in silence before Fielding said, "There's no need for Professor Roswell to take them over. Tomorrow is soon enough."

Was it her imagination or did he seem angry? His eyes had narrowed in something like disgust. Well, he could just get the hand truck himself.

"*Assistant* Professor Roswell wouldn't mind at all," insisted Finch.

Shelby felt a rushing in her ears. She knew that she wasn't part of the good ol' boys' club, but if Finch thought he would score points with Fielding by making Shelby carry over his stinking boxes, he'd better think again.

"I won't even be in the office today. I have other errands. They can be delivered in the morning by courier." Ransom's voice was ice-cold, the words clipped and final.

With that, he nodded curtly to Shelby and shook Finch's hand. His mouth was set in a grim line as he turned, walking briskly down the hallway.

Finch glared at her for a moment, his watery eyes locked on her face. "Shelby, you understand that if there's any conflict or friction at all, between you and Ransom . . . Well, let's just say it's a very important coup, departmentally and for this university, to have him here. We'll keep him happy at any cost." With those dire words, Finch then turned on his heel and left her standing in the hallway.

*My feelings are not puffed about with every attempt to move them.*

—MR. DARCY

# CHAPTER NINE

Shelby numbly continued down the hall, her stomach churning. How dare Finch threaten her? Of course she knew that having Ransom Fielding come for a term was important. The department and the university would get much-needed good press. But Finch had once said that *she* was the best new hire they'd had in years. She thought this was where God wanted her to be, teaching at Midlands, being close to home. Shelby had never felt so small and so unappreciated. She shut her office door softly behind her.

Finch's threat echoed in her head, over and over, and the room suddenly felt like a sauna. She started to slip off her blue wool coat, but in her anger only managed to get her hand caught in the sleeve. Furiously, she yanked on the other arm. Now the other sleeve was half inside out.

There was a light tap at the door.

"Come in," she snapped.

Ransom Fielding pushed open the door and stood still, taking in the scene. He made a small noise in his throat that could have been laughter.

Her face flamed as she yanked on one sleeve and then the other. How ridiculous she must look, trapped like a little child in her coat—she wanted to shriek in frustration.

Wordlessly, he strode across the room, leaned down and grabbed one sleeve, deftly peeling it off. Then he freed the second one, straightened them both and shook the coat back into shape.

Shelby had stopped struggling when he grabbed hold, but she hadn't started moving again. Her brain seemed to have shorted out. As he leaned near, she smelled something deep and foresty, and clean on top of it all. Part of her yelled to snap out of it; another just wanted to nestle her head into his chest and breathe deeply. As he stood inches away, she could see how his black hair had the slightest curl and his jaw was shadowed with stubble.

He turned and went to hang her coat on the rack beside the door.

Shelby shook her head and beat the nestling part of herself into the background.

"Thank you," she said, her words so cold they meant the opposite. She carefully wound her way around her desk and sat down. She folded her hands and waited.

He took a deep breath and seemed to steel himself. "I want you to know, I thought that his request was inappropriate," he said quietly. He didn't seem as angry as he had just a few minutes ago. In fact, he seemed downright comfortable.

"Fine." Shelby didn't blink and certainly didn't smile. Then, the meaning of his words sank in. He was offering her some measure of dignity that her own department head had denied. She sighed. "That's good to know." She rubbed her eyes and leaned back in her chair. "Please have a seat."

Ransom shook his head. "I need to be going. If we're going to be working together, at least in the same department—"

"Yes, I just got this lecture. And honestly, I really don't see any problem with you being here for a whole year. I'll stay out of your classes from now on, I promise." And then as an afterthought: "As long as I don't have to move your boxes from building to building."

To her surprise, he smiled. "Agreed. No moving duties." Two dimples had appeared with the smile; the blue eyes that seemed so cold and severe were softened.

She struggled to ignore how her heart thumped. "And I should thank you, again. In the daylight. For your help last night . . . even though I wasn't stuck." She bit her lip, wishing she could hit the rewind button. He must think she was incapable of making simple statements.

At this, Ransom laughed outright, a deep chuckle that made a light shiver run down her back. "That's as good a thank-you as your apology."

"What I meant to say—"

"That's all right. You're welcome." Ransom slipped his hands into his pockets and rocked back on his heels a bit, still smiling. "All right, so let's agree to—"

"Disagree? I don't think we've ever had a real conversation. How about we just agree to live in peace?"

"Exactly. Make love not war," he said, nodding.

Shelby opened her mouth to say something, but was momentarily sidetracked by his turn of phrase. She wasn't a prude, there was no reason to blush at a simple cliché, but Shelby felt, to her horror, a blush start from her neck and work its way up. She desperately searched for a new topic but the harder she tried, the more her embarrassment grew.

Ransom's eyebrows had practically risen to his hairline and he opened his mouth to say something, but Shelby cut him off.

"I need to get some work done, so . . ." She gestured toward the teetering piles on her desk, her hands spread out.

"Of course. I'll see you around." He slipped out, quietly closing the door behind him.

Shelby groaned and laid her head on her desk. Had all the stress finally broken her? Maybe it was time to get out. Maybe she needed more of a social life. Every time her mind flitted back to the moment he'd said "make love," her face burned.

Something about those words coming out of his perfect mouth. She put her cold hands against her hot skin and wished she could make it all go away. But he seemed to be here to stay, so she had better get used to it.

Outside, halfway across the grassy campus, a wide smile spread across Ransom Fielding's face. This term was getting better by the moment. She wasn't so dangerous. More goofy than femme fatale, after all. If he could keep Finch from making them mortal enemies, they might actually be able to get along.

*Laugh as much as you choose, but you will not laugh me out of my opinion.*
—JANE BENNET

# CHAPTER TEN

"I can't believe you blushed!" Rebecca's peal of laughter filled the car. Her flight from DC had come in a little late, but they were finally on their way home.

Shelby massaged her temple with one hand, the other gripping the wheel, and grinned ruefully. "I blame pheromones. He smelled delicious."

"When did you ever start believing in pheromones? You're the least romantic person I know," Rebecca said, raising an eyebrow.

"Probably right around the moment I had my head under his arm," Shelby said, laughing. "Anyway, it's over and I'm sure we'll stay out of each other's way from now on."

"We have to invent some way to keep throwing you in his path. Life has been so boring and we never even noticed."

"My life is exciting enough without him, thank you. My mother has called me three times this week to make sure I'm still coming to the wedding. My sisters are coming down, too, so we'll all be invading the Putney estate at once."

"Wow, both of them?" Rebecca grinned. She knew how Shelby's two sisters enjoyed those parties, often having one too many Orange Comforts and ending up making spectacles of themselves. Shelby's mom never seemed to mind, especially because her daughters received so much attention from the eligible bachelors that way. Last year at the Ashleys' estate, Ellie had gone swimming . . . in her clothes. Her pale pink silk dress was practically see-through, and she had plenty of admirers by the time Shelby had convinced her to head on home.

"Seems so." Shelby cringed inwardly. "I need to reassure my mother that I'm not going to end up unloved and surrounded by hundreds of cats. And then Sunday afternoon we're going to my cousin Lucy May's sip and see, so I won't be back until evening."

"Sip and see?"

"A baby shower after the baby's born. So everybody gets to hold the baby."

"Well, the important thing is to make sure you have really great shoes." Rebecca peered innocently out the window at the scenery. "I did find a few things . . ."

"I knew it. Did you spend the whole weekend shopping?"

"Not at all. There was dinner and church and a nice lunch with my mom in there, too. Honestly, you could meet someone really interesting at the reception"—Shelby interrupted Rebecca with a snort—"and what would they think if you were wearing that purple dress from three years ago?"

"I like that dress, it's comfy. And I sincerely doubt I will ever meet anyone *interesting* at one of these parties. Almost everyone is my parents' age, or else I've known them my entire life."

"Well, I just picked up a few things while I was shopping for myself, and I just know they'll be beautiful on you." Rebecca brushed her perfect bangs away from her eyes and smiled at her skeptical roommate.

Shelby pulled the Jaguar gently to a stop in front of their little house. She sighed, thinking how Rebecca looked amazing just rolling out of bed, while it took several hours just to tame Shelby's mass of curls into something that didn't scare the neighbors.

"I'm not prepping until the day before. I have a ton of work to do. I was hoping to spend a few hours this week at that little county library in Weston. The genealogist told me there are some letters there from around the right time," Shelby said.

She popped the trunk and handed Rebecca her carry-on bag. Shelby could see Sirocco in the window, her eyes bright and tail curled around her feet.

"I don't know how you can spend so much time

reading through those old papers. The writing gives me a headache. I'm ever thankful that most comparative literature studies are of the printed word."

Shelby unlocked the front door and greeted Sirocco with a scratch. Rebecca plopped her carry-on by the couch and headed for a cold Diet Coke. "You want anything?" she called from the kitchen.

"No, I'm good. And those letters aren't the worst of it, really. The diaries are probably the hardest to read because a lot of people were writing for themselves. They abbreviate everything." Shelby slumped into the couch, stroking Sirocco's back as she curled up on her lap. "But the usual pension records, wills, marriage certificates just won't cut it for this article I'm writing. I need to know who was helping Susanna Caldwell build those schools after the war. She didn't travel, and she didn't have a lot of influence. I'd bet my aunt Junetta's prize pecan pie that her benefactor is a big fish."

Rebecca settled down on the love seat and tucked her feet up underneath her. "You've been chasing Caldwell's people for a long time. Don't you ever get worried you've found everything there is to find?"

Shelby rubbed Sirocco's head and didn't answer for a moment. "I do . . . I am. But it's not enough, what I have right now. It's a good article, a good story, but I want something that makes everyone sit up and take notice—of her and me. Maybe I'm stubborn and think I can pull this off. But I don't want to give up." Shelby frowned for a moment. "My daddy says, 'If you can't run with the big dogs, then stay under the porch.' I guess I'm not willing to stay under the porch."

Rebecca reached over and squeezed Shelby's hand. "I'm praying for you. If anybody is going to find that mysterious Mr. J., it'll be you. I wish I could help. Now, if you need a comparison between Austen's domestic comedies and Mrs. Gaskell's industrial novels, then I'm your gal!"

"I know you are. But I have faith, I really do. He's out there and I'm going to find him."

"I bet you will." Rebecca stood up to admire a small picture propped against the salt and pepper shakers. "Hey, is this new?"

"Aunt Junetta's gazebo and koi pond. Of course, the trumpet vine isn't blooming right now. I added that for effect." Shelby came to stand next to Rebecca. "Did I tell you I registered for another art class? Donovan Shankel is doing a series on watercolor landscapes."

"Good for you. I can't believe how talented you are. Why didn't you major in art?" Rebecca picked up the painting and peered at it closely.

"Because I didn't want to go through the starving-artist phase."

Rebecca laughed and placed the painting back

on the table. "Sometimes I wonder if I shouldn't have gone into something with more job security. The tenure process is giving me gray hair."

"I know. But it's going to happen, for both of us. This is the year that everything will come together. You'll publish that book on the Austen miniplot and I'll uncover the Mr. J. mystery, we'll both get tenure, we'll get huge raises and be invited to speak at all the big conferences—"

"Find rich husbands—" Rebecca blurted.

"Get skinny thighs—"

"Go on *Oprah*—" Rebecca waved her hands in the air.

"Learn how to make perfect pie crust—"

"Journal every day—"

"Make our mothers happy—" Shelby giggled.

"Get over my dog aversion and run the New York Marathon—" Rebecca threw herself backward on the couch.

"Exactly! Lord willing and the creek don't rise, we're going to get there."

The next Tuesday dawned as normally as the day before, but by noon Shelby felt as if the world had shifted on its axis. The life she knew was becoming more and more unrecognizable, even as she fought to keep it the same.

She headed for the department office to check her mailbox first thing in the morning. As she passed George Finch's door, he called out to her, "Come on in here for a second, Shelby."

She stepped inside and suppressed a grimace at the heat. He must keep the temperature near ninety. And why did it smell like cooked cabbage?

He peered through his murky glasses from behind a desk piled with paper stacks ten inches tall. His short gray hair stuck up on one side, as if he'd just rolled out of bed. Shelby wondered for a moment about Mr. Finch's wife. Did she mind if he wandered about that way? The glasses, the uncombed hair, the stoop and the perpetual squint from reading too much tiny print made him seem mentally imbalanced.

"You need to turn in your evaluations from the summer course you taught."

"I gave them to you two weeks ago. They were in a manila envelope, marked with the class number on the front." Shelby frowned, trying to recall exactly when it was.

"No, no, you didn't. I've looked everywhere. You must be thinking of last year. I have to have them for your tenure review. Anything missing could cause some big problems." He paused and fixed her with a glare. "Are you sure there weren't some negative student comments in there? Something you want to hide?"

Her mouth dropped open in shock. "George, if I wanted to hide negative comments, I would have just removed those few and turned in all the rest. Why would I hide them all when surely you would remind me that they had to be turned in?" Shelby was shaking with fury.

"Well, I don't have them. You need to figure out where they went and turn them in before the tenure review process starts next month. Let me just say that they would look more favorably on a few negative comments than all your class reviews gone missing." With that he picked up his pen and started scribbling.

Shelby turned and walked slowly back to her office, her pulse pounding in her ears. Finch had never before lost anything important. The last five years of evaluations, for every class, every term, even the summer courses, had been filed on time.

She sat at her desk, a feeling of dread creeping over her. Did he really lose them? Could he be hiding them to punish her? She shook her head and hugged herself. Finch, as cliquish and power hungry as he was, wouldn't be dishonest. He wouldn't set her up to be denied tenure. Not for a departmental feud, not when she had worked so hard these past few years. Her stomach twisted as she realized that he just might. She dropped her head and whispered an anxious prayer. Those missing reviews would be one more black mark on her ever-darkening record.

*It is your turn to say something now, Mr. Darcy. I talked about the dance, and you ought to make some sort of remark about the size of the room, or the number of couples.*

—ELIZABETH

# CHAPTER ELEVEN

The evening was starting out on a decidedly low note. The wedding had been perfectly romantic, and Shelby had wiped a few tears from her eyes as she watched old family friends make a commitment to love, cherish and forsake all others. But the wedding was the easy part of Shelby's obligations. Now it was time for the reception, and Shelby wished she could have come up with some excuse to head back to Midlands.

"I think you should just stay home if you're going to look so sour." Ellie carefully adjusted her dress and glared at Shelby.

Shelby's mother, thoroughly inspecting each girl as she came down the stairs, checking hair and accessories, glanced at her sharply. "Ellie! Shelby looks lovely. And can't you find something else to wear? That looks like military canvas that's been remade into a party dress." The dress was a strange olive-green color, with a tight bodice, a tiny bow at the waist, and a skirt gathered at several points above the hem.

"Yes, Mother, that's exactly what it is." Ellie rolled her eyes and tugged at her top again. "At least I'm not wearing something from five years ago."

"Not that it matters, but Mama just bought this dress," Shelby said lightly. She had already found something perfectly nice in Rebecca's closet, but once she'd arrived, her mother had brought out her purchase. It certainly wouldn't have been her first choice for a wedding reception. A floor-length, gold-colored silk, it made her feel strangely exposed as it clung to every curve. Maybe because it was sleeveless or had a deep neckline, but Shelby itched to throw a cardigan over it. She touched the emerald solitaire at her throat and wondered how long the reception would take.

"Shelby, why don't you wear that diamond pendant I bought you?" her mother asked, fussing over her oldest daughter's hair.

"Because it might have been mined by poor Africans without access to proper health care, Mama," Ellie said snidely.

"Africans? What on earth do you mean? I bought that on Myrtle Avenue in Marlon Harlow's jewelry shop." Her mother continued attempting to smooth one rebellious curl back into Shelby's updo.

Shelby tried redirecting the conversation. "Let's all focus on having a nice time, shall we?"

Ellie smirked. "I'm going to focus on having a *great* time. Why don't you sit with someone you can get along with, like old Mr. Forrester? He's into Civil War stuff. You all can talk about battles or something." Ellie impatiently checked the clock and peered up the stairs for her sister.

"Loren Forrester would also prefer the nation went back to before women had the right to vote. So, no, I don't believe we'll have a lot in common," Shelby said, wishing the evening were already over and she was headed back upstairs.

"That Jennie Anne. I don't mind being late, but I don't want to miss half the party!" Shelby's mother checked her own hair again in the foyer mirror. Though she retained much of her youthful beauty, the deep lines around her eyes belied her true age. Although she could spend hundreds on miracle creams, Florence Roswell would never have work done. It wasn't proper. She turned and said, "Shelby, you're looking so lovely. You'll turn every head at this party."

Jennie Anne appeared just in time to hear Mrs. Roswell's comment and snorted. "Sure she will, as soon as she picks a good fight!"

"Enough! Let's get there already!" Shelby waved her hands in the air and the family trooped out the door.

Shelby glanced back and saw her father, sitting

in his leather chair in the study window, feet propped on the edge of the desk as usual. He met her gaze and pulled a face, which made her giggle. She wished that she could stay behind, reading and talking about things that had happened long ago, the way she had when she was little. But those days were gone. She suppressed a sigh and got behind the wheel, trying in vain to block out the sound of her sisters squabbling in the backseat.

The grand rooms of the Putney mansion were liberally dotted with three-foot-high vases of white and pale pink cabbage roses, and their heavy scent hung like an invisible fog. Deep green ivy strands wound around every post, down banisters and along mantelpieces, contrasting perfectly with the silvery wallpaper. Shelby thought of the last time she was here and the particularly fine cabinet she'd noticed in the downstairs bathroom, probably from the Civil War era, and made a mental note to find it sometime this evening. If she could get away from her mother, that is. Her sisters were granted leave almost immediately, but Mrs. Roswell seemed to sense that Shelby wouldn't engage in small talk unless she was forced.

Wealthy and influential families filled the room to capacity, but the air remained cool. Shelby's arms were covered in goose bumps from the chill, and she gazed toward the seventeen-foot ceilings, decorated with stamped copper trays that gleamed in the light. An elaborate ceiling medallion anchored the brass chandelier. With one wall covered in floor-to-ceiling windows, the heating costs must be astronomical in the winter. Shelby snagged a pepper-crusted shrimp from a passing tray. The Putneys always had Brightley Inn cater their parties, and this wedding reception was no different. Their Cajun blackened seafood and fresh salsas were famous around the region, and Shelby was grateful for the delicious distraction. She saw her cousin Langston across the room and waved. Langston's husband was as tall and handsome as ever, blond hair smoothed back, eyes just the same shade as his wife's. They were the all-American couple until you saw them with their beautiful new baby, adopted from China. Langston had never looked so happy; she positively glowed. She motioned to Shelby that they would come over in a few minutes and Shelby nodded, smiling at the chance to see so many friendly faces.

"Shelby, it's so good to see you!"

She turned at the sound of her name and saw Caroline Ashley, looking willowy and ethereal despite the heavy dress she wore. Shelby hugged her old friend tightly, trying not to crush the navy taffeta roses that trailed down the deep neckline of Caroline's dress. "How are you? I want to know everything. And not over all this chatter." Shelby waved her hand toward the guests milling in an ever-contracting circle. "I'm not heading back until tomorrow. We should have lunch."

Caroline's perfume was light and floral, a perfect match for the reserved young woman. "Great idea! You can tell me all about life in the big city."

Caroline laughed lightly, but Shelby knew Caroline felt left behind. Her mother had insisted that she come home right after she received her journalism degree and get serious about looking for a husband. After an internship at the *Washington Post*, Caroline had moved back to her tiny hometown of Thorny Hollow, a few miles from Flea Bite Creek, and now she let her mother run her life.

"Are you still working on your novel?"

"Sure. It'll never be finished, though. Three hundred pages on the Russian Revolution and counting. My hero has loved and lost and loved some more. But it keeps me occupied."

"I'd love to read it sometime." Shelby meant it sincerely, but Caroline smiled faintly.

"If I wrote half as well as you painted, then I'd be famous by now."

"It's just a hobby, something I enjoy."

"As I said, pretty nice hobby. I have the oil painting you gave me, the one of the magnolia tree at the edge of our property, right over my desk. It's my favorite thing in the whole room."

"Thank you," Shelby said, suddenly overwhelmed by the compliment. She had never been comfortable about sharing her paintings, but it seemed even odder to receive such praise when her real work was going nowhere. All her research was yielding nothing. Maybe she should have majored in art after all.

Caroline smiled and turned to acknowledge a tall man approaching them. Shelby thought his shock of white hair made him look a little like Mark Twain, or maybe it was his seersucker suit.

"The famous Shelby Roswell! I greatly enjoyed your last article in *Southern History Quarterly*!" His voice was loud but pleasant, with a strong accent. Georgia was her guess.

"Thank you. This is my friend Caroline Ashley."

"I'm Jacob Stroud, physician by training but historian at heart." He extended his hand to both of them. "Very fine work tracking the Schumachers through the end of the war. Jewish families are so rarely represented in Civil War articles."

"There weren't all that many, so it does take a bit of digging, to be fair. Most of the remaining families went North after the war ended."

"You mentioned Aaron Schumacher in your article. Is that the Aaron Schumacher who lost a leg at Shiloh?"

"Yes, how did you know?" Shelby asked, surprised.

"See, I collect antique surgical equipment." He leaned forward, bushy white brows twitching in his eagerness. "My wife thinks I'm plum crazy, but I bought a whole set of amputation saws at auction a few years ago, and there were diaries and logs included. They were the tools of one Dr. Peabody. After reading your article, I looked for Aaron Schumacher, and he was entered as having a leg removed above the knee."

"Very interesting! I found his name in the recorded requests for prosthetics. The wealthy are easier to follow that way. There's more of a paper trail."

The elderly doctor nodded excitedly. "I probably have the handsaw that removed your man's leg. The teeth are bent in a few places. Those amputations weren't easy, you know."

Shelby glanced at Caroline's face and fought back a laugh. Her eyes had gone wide, a look of horror replacing her pretty smile. Shelby felt a little sorry for her and hoped to find a way to end this conversation gracefully.

"Poor men, it's a wonder anybody survived the shock."

"This Dr. Peabody, he was a good doctor. Gave them two bullets to bite on, one for each side, so they didn't dislocate their jaws. The bullets were still in the kit, teeth marks all over 'em," Mr. Stroud went on, oblivious of Caroline's growing discomfort. "At least with a limb, they had a chance. Those torso or head wounds, those were something awful. They just didn't know enough about infection at that point. Most wounds festered and killed the patient by sepsis," he said, winding up for a long discourse. "This set came in a velvet-lined box and had a foreign-body probe, a metacarpal saw and a bone scraper. They used that one to remove necrotic tissues when—"

"I think I see Frank Marigund!" Caroline's voice was high and a little strangled. "I'm sorry to interrupt, but I should go say hi. It was nice to meet you!" She bolted toward another group of revelers with short, hurried steps, hobbled by the long dress.

Dr. Stroud coughed uneasily. "It seems I've let my passion for the war overrun my good manners, yet again."

Shelby put a hand on the doctor's arm. "Don't worry, she doesn't appreciate the more gruesome aspects of Civil War history. She spends her time immersed in writing great literature, where the hero is always wealthy and noble and hardly ever needs an amputation."

Dr. Stroud laughed, but a light pink flooded his cheeks.

"Now, there are some beautiful roll-up surgical kits on display at the Lincoln Memorial University Museum. Have you been there? They even have the glass vials with opium pills," Shelby said.

"Dr. Stroud."

The deep voice behind her sent a message to her mouth, bypassing her brain, and she faltered. Slowly turning, Shelby widened her eyes in disbelief.

Ransom Fielding, impeccably dressed in a charcoal-gray three-piece suit, stood a few feet away. Her father wore three-piece suits, but on him they looked genteel. On Ransom the suit was heart-stopping. A sapphire-colored silk tie set off the patterned handkerchief in his pocket and matched the blue pattern woven through the vest. In a flash, Shelby understood Rebecca's obsession with fashion. This was one of the most beautiful suits she had ever laid eyes on.

And the man wearing it looked devastatingly handsome with his dark hair smoothed back and angular features softened by the slightest smile. His gaze traveled from somewhere near the emerald solitaire at her throat over the silky curve of her hips to her sandals and back. Some indefinable emotion flickered in his blue eyes.

"Ransom! Great to see you here. Have you met Miss Roswell? She's quite an expert on the field maneuvers."

At the sound of Stroud's voice, Shelby realized she was gawking. That unnamed emotion she'd seen had probably been amusement as her mouth hung open.

"You could say we are acquainted. I've taken a

sabbatical at Midlands." Although the band was in full swing and the guests chattered happily, his deep voice cut through it all easily.

"Well, isn't that just perfect." Dr. Stroud beamed at the two of them and clapped Ransom on the shoulder. "We'll have to have dinner together, all three of us. Won't that be—"

"Shelby, dear! There's someone I want you to meet."

Shelby had been so intent on Ransom that she hadn't noticed her mother advancing. She started and released a breath she hadn't known she was holding.

"Excuse me, Dr. Stroud. It was wonderful to meet you." Shelby searched through her clutch and gave him her card. "I'd like to see your diaries and records sometime."

He seemed to swell with happiness. "Anytime, anytime! I'll send you an e-mail this weekend and we can arrange something."

"And, Mr. Fielding. See you back at Midlands," she said, lifting her chin and trying to appear dignified. She fought to keep the image of their last conversation from her mind, but she could feel a blush creeping up her cheeks.

"Miss Roswell, it's always a pleasure." His lips quirked up in a half smile, and Shelby was struck by the tiny laugh lines around his eyes. She wondered what he looked like when he really smiled, then hated herself for wondering.

"Shelby, honey, he's waiting." Her mother's fingers were pinched into Shelby's elbow, and she maneuvered Shelby back into the crowd, whispering the whole way. "You can't waste your energy talking to Ransom Fielding. He's already made up his mind about you. And don't spend your time on old men like that Stroud. His wife told me he spends thousands a year on ancient junk that nobody wants."

Shelby bit her tongue, wanting to point out that if *nobody* wanted it, it wouldn't sell for thousands.

"Now, Mrs. Whiting says there are more celebrities here than at the Governor's Ball, by at least a dozen." Shelby's mother's eyes glittered feverishly, scanning the room for men with high potential.

Shelby took a breath and hoped they would be able to stay out of Ransom Fielding's way.

"Here we are." Her mother planted Shelby firmly into another circle, populated with conservatively dressed men and beautifully made-up women. "Honey, meet David Bishop. He's from Jackson and he's down here helping Marion Dartmon find a vacation home. Come here . . ."

Shelby knew when her mother thought she'd found a good catch: she got extra-grabby.

"Pleased to meet you. How's the house hunting going?" Shelby asked brightly.

"Very well," David Bishop said, and self-consciously patted his hair. It was an odd style for a man in his forties, gelled and parted in the middle, military short on the sides. It sort of reminded her of the daguerreotype of society men in the 1900s. He was trying to grow a mustache . . . or maybe that *was* the mustache. “We’ve found some really excellent possibilities. Now it’s just a matter of convincing the owners to sell.”

“You mean, accepting a lower offer?” asked Mrs. Roswell eagerly.

“No, actually, these houses aren’t even on the market. We pick out a few we like and then approach the owners with an offer,” he said, smiling primly.

“Really? I didn’t know that was a common practice in real estate,” Shelby said.

“My clients do things a little differently.” He inclined his head and smiled at Shelby’s mother, who nodded enthusiastically, still gripping her arm.

Shelby was distracted temporarily from the pressure of her mother’s fingers. David’s tie was a bright purple, and the pattern that Shelby had at first glance thought was paisley was actually miniature dancing rabbits. With top hats and canes.

“And is that usually successful then?” she asked to keep the conversation moving.

“Oh, you’d be surprised. Everyone has a price,

that's all I can say." Here he let loose a high giggle, and Shelby felt her eyes go wide. "And let me tell you, the commissions are out of this world."

Shelby gently pried her mother's hand from her elbow. At that moment they heard Marion herself calling, "Florence—" Shelby's mother beamed with pleasure as she was summoned to Marion's little circle of revelers. Florence turned her head at the last moment and gave Shelby a wink.

Groaning inwardly, Shelby rubbed her elbow and tried to get some circulation back in her fingers.

"And commissions aren't the only perks," Bishop said, his voice dropping to a whisper. "I receive much more under the table, tax deferred, so to speak. And I was invited to the Governor's Ball this winter."

She forced herself to remain still as he leered toward her, his eyes bloodshot and the pupils dilated.

"Now, Shelby, I think we could really be good together."

She nodded absently. Then the words registered with a thud. What on earth had her mother told him?

*You could not make me happy and I am convinced I am the last woman in the world that could make you so.*

—ELIZABETH

# CHAPTER TWELVE

"I've been trying to find someone like you." David Bishop appraised Shelby slowly. "I understand you don't want to appear too forward, but your mother tells me you can be very persuasive. You see, there are times when I sensed that a woman's touch would have brought success somewhat sooner."

Shelby's face felt frozen in horror. It seemed the talent for persuasive speech that her mother so admired had completely left her.

"You might wonder what's in it for you? First of all, of course, is me." Another giggle escaped his thin lips. "I've been known as a most eligible bachelor in Jackson. I'm not promising anything, you understand," he added in an undertone. "We'll just have to wait and see how everything progresses. But I'm sure you'll enjoy mingling with people you normally wouldn't have had the chance to meet. You'll have doors open all over the South when you're known as my girlfriend."

Shelby blinked at him. Did he really think she was a social climber? And wanted to be his *girl-friend?*

"I helped Catherine DeLilo buy her last two houses." He stroked his upper lip. "Two weeks ago she saw a gorgeous antebellum mansion over in Galveston. She called me right away and I went straight to her lawyer's office. He sent them a letter letting them know who wanted their house and asking what they'd sell for."

"And did that work?" Shelby hoped they'd veered back into real estate permanently, at least until she could get away from the corner in which she was trapped. Over his head she could see Ransom Fielding by a long window, listening intently to a petite blonde who waved her hands as she spoke and whose short, sequined dress sparkled in the light. His face bore a small smile that didn't seem quite natural.

"Well, not at first. It had been in the family for generations. There was a lot of sentimental value attached to it. But when I'd seen that it was falling apart—you know how those old places are—I told them we'd be restoring it to the original pristine condition, probably get it on the Historical Register. I told them we'd keep the family name on it."

She dragged her focus back to David, her interest piqued. "Which house is this? Which family?" Maybe he was disgusting and smarmy, but so many Southern mansions were falling into disrepair. If he was helping to save them, he couldn't be all bad.

He waved a limp hand. "Oh, well, you see, once the sale went through, plans changed a bit. The front portico was falling apart, and the balconies weren't even safe. The bathrooms needed renovation, so we had all the old fixtures replaced. And the place had the ugliest wallpaper I've ever seen. It must have been a hundred years old. But the new owners fixed it right up, and it's a beautiful beach house now with everything opened up. Perfect for parties in the summer."

Shelby nearly choked. She glanced at her mother a few feet away, deep in conversation with Marion Dartmon, and fought to control her voice as it trembled with sudden anger.

"Well, thank you for"—what should she call it? A proposition?—"thinking of me, but I just am so busy with my research. I wouldn't be able to travel as much as you needed. You'd really want someone to be able to be there with you."

He tutted. "But, you're a teacher! How hard can it be to get a day off or two . . . three at the most? Maybe twice a month?"

"Well, it's actually rather hard to find substitutes at the college level, unless you have a class assistant, and most of my classes are small, so—"

"Can't somebody else just read the material to them?"

Shelby fought back a laugh. “That’s not exactly how I teach my history classes. There are—”

“History. I never understood you people who can’t let go of the past. You’d have us all living without electricity and sewing our own clothes.” His voice had taken on an ugly tone.

“This just won’t work. But thank you anyway. I’m sure your clients are . . . awesome.” Shelby cringed inwardly. That word seemed to slip out when she was at a complete loss for anything better to say.

“Oh—I see you’re very career oriented. Well, getting Margaret Greathouse’s attention would help you immensely. She and I are very good friends. She could get you a better job, where you wouldn’t have to teach. Probably running a museum or even soliciting donations for her projects.”

Shelby suppressed a snort. She already had Margaret Greathouse’s attention, thank you very much. “I like my job. I really do. I’m not there because I can’t find anything else.” She felt her face warming as her voice edged higher.

“I can’t imagine that it’s so fantastic that you’d turn down something with her, not to mention a pay raise.” With that he gave her a significant look, from head to toe, as if her salary were written on the front of her gown.

Shelby knew she didn’t have cutting-edge style, but for once she was deliriously glad her mother had forced her into something expensive.

“I don’t believe my salary is any of your business, and moreover, I consider teaching to be more of a calling than a profession.” With that Shelby started to move away, her heart pounding furiously. Out of the corner of her eye, she saw Ransom lift his head, brows lowered, as if he had noticed her sudden movement. She fought to control her expression and hoped her face didn’t look as tight and angry as it felt.

David Bishop sniffed and said, “I suppose you’re right. The woman I need at my side would have to intuitively understand good society. You wouldn’t be comfortable at all.”

Shelby stopped and swiveled to face him. “You’re right, I wouldn’t be comfortable, but not because I don’t understand good society, as you put it. I wouldn’t be comfortable with shady legal dealings and tricking people out of their homes,” she spat. With that she strode across the room to her mother, wishing with all her might that Ransom Fielding weren’t watching, that he were miles from the drama she had just created.

*Mr. Wickham is blessed with such happy manners as may ensure his making friends—whether he may be equally capable of retaining them is less certain.*

—MR. DARCY

# CHAPTER THIRTEEN

Shelby heard a few whispers behind her and knew their conversation hadn't gone unnoticed. Probably her ticked-off expression said a whole lot, too.

"Shelby—what happened?" Her mother's perfect upswept hair seemed to spring a few frizzy strands in Shelby's imagination.

"Mama, everything's fine." She smiled brightly. "He invited me to some parties with him."

"Oh, honey—I'm so happy." Her mother grabbed both arms now.

"Mama." Shelby tried to free herself. "Mama, please. I said I wasn't interested."

Mrs. Roswell gasped, Marion Dartmon gasped, and Shelby could have sworn someone behind them gasped.

"Why?" Shelby's mother's voice contained a tiny note of hysteria.

"Well, it's just not my thing, being toted from

party to party as the trophy girlfriend." Shelby decided it was best to be clear.

"What do you mean your 'thing'? A party is a party!" Now there was more than a note of hysteria. "You've probably offended him!"

Her mother peered nervously around the room, searching for David Bishop, until she found him in the opposite corner holding court with a group of elegantly dressed older women.

Shelby glanced over and could tell by his expression that he was not talking real estate. A tall, thin woman who resembled a stooped heron, all long limbs and sharp features, returned Shelby's look and didn't smile.

"Mrs. Dartmon—help!" Shelby's mother turned to her with a soft shriek.

Mrs. Dartmon, for her part, didn't immediately get up and move away from the leper colony they were becoming. She gently cleared her throat. "Shelby dear, I think there still might be time to go, quickly, and apologize."

"Apologize? I only said I wasn't really interested in being his trophy girlfriend, and we have zero in common anyway."

"In common? Listen to her—he's a man. You're not going to have a whole lot in common. Mercy, Shelby—you're going to give me a heart attack." Her mother's face did indeed look very red.

"Shelby." Mrs. Dartmon was on her feet now and moving carefully around to Shelby's other side. A cloud of expensive perfume enveloped her. "You should go and apologize. You don't have to say what exactly you're sorry about. That's a little trick I use." She smiled encouragingly.

"Oh, so I can't say I apologize for him being an absolute idiot? A raging liar? A cheat? He told me how he promises to get a house on the Historical Register, then turn it into a vacation home like yours." Shelby couldn't help how her voice had risen. Her hands trembled and she refused to glance in Ransom's direction, knowing he was probably watching.

Mrs. Dartmon's pale eyes opened wide. "I can see there was more to this than politely refusing an invitation." She pressed her lips together primly and moved toward a group of curious onlookers. The group enveloped her immediately, anxious to hear every detail.

Shelby rubbed her forehead. "Mama, I'm sorry. I don't want to ruin your party." She wished that they had never come, wished desperately that Ransom weren't witness to the entire debacle.

"If you were really sorry, you'd go over there this minute and be nice," her mother hissed, lips quivering.

"I can't, Mama. I mean, I can be nice, which I think I was, considering. But I won't go beg forgiveness for turning him down."

Sudden tears shone in her mother's eyes. "You're just like your father," she whispered. "His career was so promising and then there was all that trouble, and he wouldn't run for office again. It was so humiliating—whose side was he on?"

Shelby groaned inwardly. Her father's political career had ended with his support of busing students out of the inner city and into the white schools. Her mother had never gotten over his refusal to just let "those people stay with their own kind."

"Mama, please don't cry. Let's go home." Shelby couldn't resist one last glance in Ransom's direction. His head was bent to hear the blond woman's chatter, but his eyes were turned on Shelby, the small smile gone.

Her mother nodded, and two large tears dripped down her smooth cheeks, carrying a pale gray line of melted mascara with them.

Shelby tucked her hand into the crook of her mother's arm and walked her toward Mrs. Putney, who had stopped flitting from group to group in order to observe them more clearly. A sudden silence preceded their arrival. The elderly woman's deep green gown shimmered with tiny beads sewn around the neck, her earlobes dotted with tasteful diamonds.

"Mrs. Putney, my mother isn't feeling well and I'd better get her home."

"Of course. I wonder what could be the matter, dear—And your sisters will stay? I know that at least one is out near the pool . . ." Her flat gray eyes narrowed with undisguised mirth and she let the rest of her sentence trail away meaningfully. Shelby chose not to respond. There wasn't any way she could convince her sisters to come home now, with the party half-over.

"I think she'll feel better once we get home." Shelby moved her silent mother toward the door and guests stepped aside for them, faces curious.

"Are you leaving?" A low voice shocked a gasp out of her. Ransom bowed his head near hers, eyes filled with concern. "Did something—" he started to ask, glancing from Shelby to her mother.

"My mother isn't feeling well," Shelby said quickly. If she had to repeat the horrible conversation, she was sure she would die of humiliation. A woman her age practically pimped out to the highest bidder.

Her mother moaned and wiped her eyes. Shelby was momentarily thankful for her theatrics and hoped it was enough to persuade him.

"Can I help you both to the car?" he started once more, reaching out and touching Shelby's hand, but she shook her head. She tried to smile, but it felt brittle and cold.

"We'll be fine," she said, steering her mother out the door and away from his helpful hand.

There near the door was Mr. Bishop himself, back turned and arms crossed. He didn't spare them a glance. As they hit the hallway, Shelby heard loud ripples of conversation break the unnatural silence behind them.

In the car, Shelby tried to apologize once more, but her mother waved a hand.

"Don't, please. Just leave me be."

Shelby was left to her own muddled emotions on the long drive back. Ransom's cautious words, his concerned tone, the touch of his hand—they all played on an endless loop in her mind.

*An unhappy alternative is before you,*
*Elizabeth. From this day you must*
*be a stranger to one of your parents.*
*Your mother will never see you again*
*if you do not marry Mr. Collins,*
*and I will never see you again if you do.*

—MR. BENNET

# CHAPTER FOURTEEN

The ride back home was painfully silent, her mother wiping her eyes every few minutes. Finally, Shelby rounded the corner and they started down the long driveway, winding past the old elm tree near the pond. Its long limbs shone pale over the dark water. The Roswell family home seemed solid and welcoming, with its modest but stately pillars. Her daddy had left the front light on and Shelby noticed the paint peeling a bit on the porch railing. The rose garden at the east side of the house looked shaggy and overgrown in the shadows.

Mrs. Roswell revived enough to open the passenger door and stomp up the flagstone steps.

"Phillip! Phillip, come down here," her mother shrieked as they entered the house.

Shelby sighed. Her father was still closed away

in his study. He didn't seem particularly unhappy, but her parents existed in different worlds. Without their children, Shelby wondered if her parents would speak at all.

"Phillip!" her mother called once more, then marched to the living room and threw herself on the couch. "Oh, my head! You've given me a migraine. Get my pills, hurry!"

Shelby wearily retrieved one of the small white prescription pills from her mother's medicine cabinet. When she returned, her mother was already in full swing.

". . . and then she refused him! Said they had nothing in common! It was a nightmare and I was humiliated! See what all your ideas have done? All your notions about careers!" Her mother spat the words and grabbed for the pill that Shelby handed her with a glass of water.

Phillip stood there, holding a newspaper in one hand and rubbing his chin with the other. He was a tall man, his frame getting thinner as he aged. His shoulders were still broad and strong but his hair shone almost pure silver in the lamplight. The scent of liniment cream wafted toward her and she sensed that he was, like the old house, gradually falling into disrepair.

"Shelby?" His deep voice was serious, measured.

"Yes, Daddy?" Shelby looked at him levelly, daring him to side with her mother.

"Were you impolite to this young man?"

"No, Daddy. He's a Realtor who schemes and steals away historic homes, and he propositioned me. He thought I would be his girlfriend in exchange for being introduced into the *right* circles." She wanted to mention his glassy, bloodshot eyes, but didn't.

"And you wanted her to respond how, exactly?" He turned toward his wife. His tone was mild but the tendons stood out on the backs of his hands. Nobody messed with Phillip Roswell's girls.

"One or two parties wouldn't hurt! She doesn't have to marry him. Nothing permanent. What's the harm?" Her mother bolted upright and gestured wildly. "All I do is work and work to find these girls some suitable husbands and it's just thrown back in my face. I give up! Spend your life being that Rebecca's roommate. What do I care?" With that she threw herself back on the couch, lay an arm across her face, and started to sob. Her mother always referred to Shelby's best friend as "that Rebecca" when she was angry.

"Shelby, honey. I understand your feelings. And I suppose I must say . . ."

Shelby straightened her back and looked her father in the eyes, unafraid. She knew he was the most traditional of Southern men, concerned not just with politeness or protocol, but the *rightness* of the matter.

"I hope that no daughter of mine will sell herself, for money or power . . . or a good party." He finished his sentence with a deep sigh that Shelby understood. How they both wished they could avoid the scene that was sure to follow.

"Oh! I knew it! You have to go and make it a capital case!" With that Mrs. Roswell gathered herself from the couch and ran to the bedroom, slamming the door.

Phillip shrugged and retreated back to his study, patting Shelby lightly on the shoulder as he passed. There was no victory celebration here.

Shelby trudged down the long hallway toward the back staircase and swung open the kitchen door. A chill draft wound its way around the dark space and she flipped on the overhead light. She tried not to see the cracks on the ceiling that grew wider every year. Fixing a cup of hot raspberry tea, she slipped off her high heels and slowly ascended the creaky, old staircase. She ran her hand along the highly lacquered railing, feeling the scratches and dents under her fingertips. Her room was the smallest, but the brightest during the day, with three windows. One window faced the front of the house and the two others overlooked the rose gardens. Shelby turned on a small lamp and slipped out of her dress and into some comfy jeans and a T-shirt. Slowly taking the emerald solitaire from her neck, she nestled it in the worn velvet of a battered jewelry box. She settled into the window seat, blew on her hot tea, stared out into the darkness. She had done the right thing, she was sure. But it didn't take away the sting of her mother's words, or that her social life was in shambles, again. She took a sip of tea, letting the burning liquid sit on her tongue. There was nothing else to do but wait for her sisters to return home.

*My dear Lizzy, do not give way to such feelings as these. They will ruin your happiness.*

—JANE

# CHAPTER FIFTEEN

"I don't see why you had to have a fit at the poor man. He was trying to do you a favor." Jennie Anne stretched across the end of the couch, her long, tan legs dangling off the side. Her highlighted blond hair was coming loose from its upsweep, but the escaping tendrils made her look even more fetching. The fitted cream dress she was wearing looked as fresh as it had been five and a half hours ago. The party had been a success, with so many young men to tease that she didn't know where to start. Now, close to midnight, she'd finally found her way home.

Ellie was still MIA. Shelby could only hope she was with a stubborn group of revelers, refusing to leave.

"I didn't have a fit. I just refused him, and his tiny ego couldn't take the blow. I wouldn't expect you to understand, but there's no need for me to be introduced at every party from here to Savannah."

Shelby checked her watch for the third time and

thought about trying Ellie's cell phone again. She wouldn't answer until she was ready, but she had to know that Shelby was calling her. As Shelby sank into the armchair next to the couch, the thought of driving back to retrieve Ellie sounded more and more appealing as the minutes ticked by.

"Well, it sure wouldn't hurt. You're the one who's always complaining about how cliquish your department is. You don't think making good connections would help?"

"I admit it's like the ultimate popularity contest run by geeks, but I don't think hanging out with David Bishop would make any difference. And even if it did . . ." Shelby raised her hands. She honestly didn't know how to explain it to Jennie Anne. Her sisters seemed so eager to be popular, it didn't seem to matter how they accomplished it. She got up from the armchair and peeked out the curtains at the long drive. They could see car lights coming half a mile away, but tonight there wasn't a glimmer in the blackness.

"You remember Evan Marchand?"

"Hooey, yes! That man doesn't have the decency to die." Jennie Anne's face wrinkled in a pretty pout.

"Okay, remember when he asked you to go with him to that big party at the Glendale Mansion? And you said no because you thought he'd asked you just to make himself look good? You were offended because you were sure he couldn't stand you."

At this, Jennie Anne swung her legs off the arm of the couch and sat bolt upright. "No! I turned him down because I knew for a fact that he wouldn't look twice at a girl who wasn't interested in his creepy reenactments. The man spends all his free time sewing special outfits so he can play dress-up with other Civil War weirdos. They go lie in ditches pretending to be dead and get their pictures taken. He says it's not a good weekend if he can't go 'bloat' with his buddies."

Shelby suppressed a grimace. "So he has a hobby. He's a dentist and they have a lot of stress. Maybe that's his way of feeling normal on the weekends."

"Normal?" Jennie Anne waved her arms around. "The guy sleeps in muddy ditches, spooning with other men, for fun. The first time we talked about his little hobby, he showed me his brass buttons." She cocked her head. "You want to know about his brass buttons, Shelby?"

She didn't, really. "Fine, I'll bite. What about his buttons?"

"He got new brass buttons but they were too shiny for his uniform, so he put them in a cup of his own pee and let them stew awhile. That makes them look authentically aged, he said. He told me this after he put one in my hand!"

Shelby couldn't restrain a laugh. "Oh, well, that's . . ."

"Nasty, that's what that is. And plus, at that

brunch where we met, he kept telling me what he would and wouldn't eat because it wasn't available during the Civil War. He gave up Granny Smith apples five years ago because they didn't exist in our state then. That man is plain weird."

"Okay, so Evan really wasn't your type and you knew you weren't his. But if you thought that going out with him would open doors for you, to the *best* families, would you do it?" Shelby was sure she'd gotten her point across.

Jennie Anne examined one pale pink, perfectly manicured finger. "Probably. Actually, yes."

"But you just said you can't stand him!"

"I can't. But if he got me a rich Cahill boy? I'd put up with him for as long as it took. I'm not going to live in some old house forever."

Shelby's jaw dropped. "You mean this house? It's not *old,* Jennie Anne. It's historic. There's a difference."

"Whatever you say. This place is crumbling to bits, and when I get married, I'm going to have a custom-built home, right on the water somewhere. All granite countertops and steel appliances, the newest of everything. I'm sick of using that old claw-foot bathtub. I'm going to have a whirlpool Jacuzzi, sunk right into the master suite."

"You know, your great-grandparents bathed in that tub."

"Exactly! I don't want a tub that held their wrinkly old behinds. Everything is going to be new, new, new." Jennie Anne threw herself back on the couch.

Shelby regarded her sister quietly. Sometimes she seemed so much younger than her twenty-one years. How had someone who had been raised in the thick of history turned out so dismissive of it?

"I understand what you're saying. But it doesn't make you feel . . . connected to this house, to know that for generations your family has touched these same objects?"

"Um . . . no. Not really. I know you and daddy are always going on about Great-Grandpa Parker or Great-Aunt May, but it just doesn't mean much to me. They're gone. I'm here now."

With that, Jennie Anne yawned and rose from the couch. "I don't know why you're waiting up for her. She'll find her way home, with or without your nagging. So stop calling her and go to bed."

Shelby peered back out the window. "I can't. If anything happens . . ."

"If anything happens, you're not going to know it until the morning anyway." A final flip of her highlighted hair and Jennie Anne disappeared down the hallway toward the stairs.

Shelby leaned her forehead against the cold window. She closed her eyes and let out a long breath. Not everyone connected with the past the way she did, obviously. But to call this beautiful home "crumbling" made her inexplicably sad.

She opened her eyes and saw light bouncing

slowly down the lane. *Finally,* she thought, and strode to open the front door. She walked down the short flight of steps from the wraparound porch to the grass and waited for the car to appear from the last bend of elm trees. A taxi eventually pulled up into the circular drive and stopped. The driver quickly opened the back door and helped Ellie out.

"You family?" The man seemed irritated, his harsh voice carrying clearly to Shelby.

She stepped forward. "I'm her sister. Is she okay?"

"Sure, she's fine. My backseat ain't, though. That's gonna cost you another fifty for cleaning."

Ellie giggled and weaved toward Shelby. The pretty flowered wrap dress was wrinkled and stained. There was a definite odor of "after party."

"Just a moment. Ellie, go inside. No, here, watch the step. One more, there. Now, just sit for a second."

Shelby went inside and grabbed her purse out of the kitchen. After paying the taxidriver, she maneuvered Ellie up the stairs and into the shower. Finally, tucked in bed and smelling much better than she had when she arrived, Ellie drifted off to sleep. Shelby sat for a few minutes at the end of her bed, watching her youngest sister and wondering if any of her forebears had once been in her shoes.

*You wish to think all the world respectable and are hurt if I speak ill of anybody.*

—ELIZABETH

# CHAPTER SIXTEEN

Now where were those keys? Shelby let out a deep sigh in frustration.

Oh, she had dropped them by the sugar bowl after putting groceries away. Snatching them up, she wondered how late Rebecca had returned from her party last night. It had been a week since the disaster at the Putney estate. Of course, Rebecca had missed the entire episode so she felt free to venture out. Shelby never wanted to go to another party again.

"Rebecca!" Shelby called softly at her housemate's bedroom door. "Are you up yet?"

There was a groan and the door swung inward.

Shelby choked back a laugh. "Oh, girl. It's going to take more than night cream and some cucumbers to fix that mess."

"Don't rub it in. I kept telling them I needed to get up early, but the party just went on and on. It was almost one and people were still arriving! I don't know what kind of party it is when you show up at one in the morning."

"Apparently a good one. Did you have fun? Meet lots of nice folks?"

"They were a little on the young side. In fact, they seem to get younger every year. I bet they don't have to get up at the crack of dawn, either." Rebecca yawned and rubbed her puffy eyes. But even on her worst day she was stunningly beautiful. "I did meet someone who didn't mention Facebook every other word. But he was from out of town."

"How far out of town? Like Oxford?"

"Like Florida." Rebecca lifted one shoulder in a small gesture of resignation. "He was home visiting, but lives in Miami." A little smile played around her lips. "I don't want to get my hopes up. But he's different. He told me he's part of a Bible study for singles and that he has complete faith that the right girl is out there, that it's all in God's hands."

Shelby grinned. "Now, that's a perfect pickup line. But a Southerner who lives in Miami? What does he do over there?"

"Um, well, that's the odd thing." Rebecca chewed her lip for a moment. "He's a computer programmer. You know, those people who write code for a living."

Shelby's eyebrows shot up. "A cube-farm inhabitant? I thought you said you couldn't think of anything more boring."

"It's weird, but the way he described it all, it

almost sounded fun. And he doesn't live in a cube, he runs his own software business." Rebecca smiled uncertainly. "Probably nothing will come of it. But he has my number."

"You never know. Anyway, I'm going in early to see if I can make any headway on that article," Shelby said.

"Text me later and we'll go to the Grind. The barista, Zoe, told me they're having a special on chai tea."

"Will do," Shelby called as she grabbed the leather satchel she had inherited from her grandfather. She paused, running her hand over the buttery-soft material worn smooth, and a dream flickered out of her subconscious. Just impressions, fragments from last night, but she remembered the joy at hearing his slow drawl. *I miss you, Poppa,* she thought, giving her fingertips a kiss and pressing them to the satchel on her way out the door.

Four hours later the optimistic start to the day had slipped into dreariness. Her morning class was less than enthusiastic, and two students succumbed to sleep halfway through. Shelby tried not to take it personally. They certainly had more going on in their lives than her history class. *I bet no one sleeps in Fielding's class,* she thought, then ruthlessly shoved the spiny thorn of jealousy back into the dark.

A knock at her office door yielded Finch, his tie askew and murky glasses covered with water spots. He didn't bother to sit, just cracked the door and leaned in.

"Tomorrow they're tearing out the leaky windows on the third floor," said his disembodied head.

"What time will that be?"

"Oh, nine or so. I think that's what we told them."

"I have class right below that area. Is there any way to change it?"

Finch heaved a sigh and half shrugged. "Shelby, you know those workmen always come late. And if they're on time, I'm sure you can handle a little background noise."

Background noise. Shelby was sure it was going to be dusty, earsplitting and exactly at nine. Finch had known about this for days and told her at the last minute, leaving her no choice but to carry on as planned. She'd thought the morning couldn't get worse, but she was wrong.

William, a doughy boy with a wide-open face, dropped in to chat about her Tuesday class. He loved history, but only if it concerned anything before 1500. Shelby pulled and teased tidbits of family history from him until she got a clear picture of sharecroppers, businessmen and small-town government officials. It was a losing battle to convince him his more recent ancestors were just as laudable as his tenuous European claims.

"I've saved enough for a trip to Scotland after graduation. I'm gonna visit the McDonnahugh Castle and see where it all started," William said.

"What about visiting your great-grandmother's old boardinghouse? It sounds like it was an important stop for Confederate soldiers making their way back home."

"I suppose. She told my grandma stories about the starving and barefoot men, piled in heaps in the parlor. They would each get a cooked potato and a thick slice of bread. It was sometimes their first meal since they got dumped from their regiment." He paused. "You know, I don't like being part of the losing side. My Scottish relatives are kind of nobility, they've been there for centuries."

As the door closed again, Shelby laid her head in her hands and wished she could fast-forward to five o'clock.

Shelby stretched her arms and tried to refocus her thoughts on her papers. A sudden knock at the door had Shelby on the verge of letting out a primal scream, but she settled for a terse "Come in!"

The door swung slowly inward and Ransom Fielding stood framed in the doorway. He was wearing his usual expensive suit and silk tie, unnervingly handsome. His expression was wary as he glanced around her office.

Shelby fought back a laugh. Of course he was here. The worst morning in the term wouldn't have been complete without him.

*I never saw a more promising inclination; he was growing quite inattentive to other people, and wholly engrossed by her.*

—MR. DARCY

# CHAPTER SEVENTEEN

"I'm sorry to disturb you." Ransom seemed uncomfortable, although he stood very still, his eyes now fixed on her face. He cleared his throat. "Ron DiGuardi suggested I ask you for help. He's the medieval-history professor?"

"Right, I know Ron. We're friends." Shelby hated the edge in her voice but Ransom was talking about Ron as if they'd never met, when Shelby had worked with him for years.

Ransom continued, wariness in his eyes. ". . . any information you might have on Susanna Caldwell. My students have expressed more interest in her than I was expecting."

She didn't get to teach the class, but she got to do his research? She wanted to send his gorgeous self back to his office empty-handed.

Ransom seemed to take her hesitation as confusion. "She was at the forefront of rebuilding the schools, hospitals and medical training—"

"Yes, I know who she was," Shelby snapped,

and immediately regretted it. Giving him the information while being nasty about it was beneath her. "I'm sorry. It's been an odd morning. Let me see what I can find." Rising from her desk, Shelby crossed to the bookshelf and carefully lifted out several archive boxes.

He moved a few steps closer and peered at the papers she laid gently on the desk. She felt him somewhere close over her shoulder and willed herself not to glance back.

"These are just facsimiles. The originals are in Charleston." She carefully sorted through the sheets of handwritten pages. "There is a lot of nitty-gritty information on who donated what and where, but there are some first-person accounts also."

Next she held out a small leather diary. "This has several pages of accounts on the rebuilding of the Mississippi hospitals. The diarist was a lumber-mill owner but also garnered some contracts with the government. He met with Susanna a few times. He has a good description of her no-nonsense style." Shelby allowed herself a small smile.

Fielding slowly took the diary from her hand. "I'll make copies, but I'll have to read through the diary first to find—"

"Here, I can show you where." Shelby deftly opened the little book, flipped through the stiff and yellowed pages. After inserting some slips of paper, she handed it back. “You can make some copies in the office.”

“You have an excellent memory.” He seemed genuinely impressed.

She glanced up and met his gaze. A thrill coursed through her, chased by irritation. Why did she even care what he thought? He’d made his opinion perfectly clear when he destroyed her book sales with a flaming review. It was a little late for flattery.

“When I heard the class was being considered, I didn’t know they had already chosen an instructor, and I started some research.” Shelby didn’t care if that was picking a fight. It wasn’t fair that he got the class just because he was famous. Her research looked as if it was leading to a pretty important article, one that might seal her tenure, but that he’d been handed the class still rankled.

He held the little diary in both hands, turning it over gently, and cleared his throat. “I hope your mother is feeling better?”

Shelby gritted her teeth. Of course he didn’t want to talk about the way he could just walk in and get the choice classes. He wanted to know how her crazy mother was doing.

“She’s fine. Just a headache.”

He started to speak, then seemed to reconsider. “I noticed you talking to David Bishop.”

Shelby looked him in the eyes, which meant

craning her neck, since he was close enough to make his six-foot-plus seem even taller. “Yes, we were introduced.”

“And what did you think?” His tone was light but he hadn’t dropped his gaze.

She tried her best to ignore the fizzing in her blood and focus on his words. Some part of her brain that kept her safe and sane was yelling for her to step back, to drop her gaze. But she couldn’t. “About what?”

“Did you feel you had a lot in common?” His voice was still casual, but the tiniest flicker was in his gaze, as it dropped to her lips as he spoke.

She almost laughed. “Not really, no. Personally or professionally or otherwise. If you really need to know.”

He didn’t smile but dropped his eyes to the leather diary. “I don’t mean to be rude. But he has a reputation—”

Letting out a sigh, Shelby interrupted, “I know, he’s a great catch. Thank you for your concern. My mother seems to think I’m incapable of finding myself a husband. But the last place I’d find one is at one of those parties.”

He tilted his head. “And exactly where is the best place to find oneself a husband?” His deep voice was slow, teasing.

Shelby felt the heat start to rise in her cheeks. That tone, those eyes. “Oh, probably at church. That’s where my parents met.” Of course, she hadn't met anybody there yet, but there was time for that. Lots of time.

He blinked and then nodded. "Always a safe bet."

She motioned toward the diary. "Is there anything else I can help with?"

"No, this is fine. I'll be right back." He turned and disappeared through the doorway.

Shelby stared into the space he'd left behind. Why was everyone so concerned about her finding a man? Did she have a sign over her head that read SPINSTER IN TRAINING? She was happy alone . . . or single, she should say, because she didn't feel alone. Or lonely. Until maybe just recently, right around the beginning of the term, when he showed up.

She shook her head. There was no reason for her to feel that way. And he was still an ogre. An apology only went so far. And the way her heart thumped when he looked in her eyes made her want to slap herself.

The crack about her parents meeting at church was true. But they weren't exactly the happiest couple, either. There was no mistaking his reaction when she mentioned the C-word. He wasn't someone who thought you should find your future spouse at church, that was for sure.

Shelby rested her forehead on her palms and tried not to think of anything. Not her class of sleepy students, not the construction slated for tomorrow, not the students chasing castles, not

Katie's lack of progress. Especially not Ransom, or the emotions that flickered over his face.

"All right?"

Shelby jumped. For a man as powerfully built as he was, Ransom moved quietly. He stood in front of her, holding his copies.

"Oh, fine. It's just been a long day so far, and it's not even over yet. Office hours weren't particularly productive." She tried to project lighthearted ease, as if the last few minutes had never happened.

"Some days I want to bolt the door," he said matter-of-factly, handing back her diary and pages, his fingers brushing hers.

Shelby laughed. "I love my students, I really do, but some days . . . Yeah, bolting the door sounds like a good plan. I was trying to keep my spirits up with the promise of a treat, but it wasn't working."

"Treat? Like chocolate?"

"A mocha, actually. Don't tell Jolee, she thinks I don't drink much coffee anymore. There's a great little place, the Daily Grind. Maybe you've seen it. Excellent coffee."

"I haven't been in there yet. Thank you for your help." He paused, looked down at the sheets in his hand. "Ron DiGuardi was right. He said you would help me out if you could. I wasn't so sure, but he knows you pretty well." With that he turned and left.

Shelby sat still, emotions battering against each other. Ron was the best professor she knew, and a great human being. She was humbled at Ron's faith in her. He made her want to be a better person, to live up to his expectations.

After a while she went to close the door and sorted through another tall stack of documents she'd copied from the little library in Noxubee County. There were lots of letters, some newspaper articles and a few sheets of government deeds.

She managed twenty minutes before there was another knock, this time not so hesitant.

"Come in!" *And please don't stay long,* she wanted to add.

"A thank-you." Ransom handed her a Daily Grind cup that issued tiny wisps of steam. The bittersweet smell of roasted beans filled her office.

"You didn't have to . . ." Her voice faltered.

"I wasn't sure if you liked it hot or iced, so I asked the barista. I mentioned your name, that you went there all the time. She made your usual: caramel mocha, single shot, with whipped cream and a little straw." He wore an expression not unlike that of a triumphant warrior returning home. His dark hair was ruffled from the wind but he hadn't made any effort to smooth it down. The total effect was breathtaking.

Shelby choked back a laugh. She knew Zoe

worked this afternoon. The bubbly, flirtatious blonde would have been on high alert when she saw Ransom step through the door. The campus rumor mill was probably hitting high gear at that very moment.

"I'll let you get back to work."

She raised a hand in a mute farewell as he closed the door behind him. Shelby took a sip and scalded her tongue, but didn't really notice.

Ransom couldn't help the self-satisfied smile that crossed his face as he went down the front steps. His long, quick strides carried him across the quad in seconds.

He'd been right to make friends. Plan B was doomed from the start. It was too small a department to think they would never run into each other. He couldn't ignore her forever when she was around every corner. Plan C was working out perfectly and would continue to do so, as long as he was careful. A few controlled encounters, maybe an afternoon coffee date or two, and they'd be just like old friends.

Ransom jabbed the button for the tenth floor and got in, watching the elevator doors slide closed. Really, he was much better at small talk than he ever gave himself credit for. As soon as they got over that awkward moment when he tried to warn her off David Bishop, things went smoothly.

The elevator hummed as it passed floor after floor, and Ransom rocked back on his heels, a warm feeling of contentment lodged somewhere in his chest. Had to be the area, the new surroundings. He hadn't felt this good in years.

The elevator doors opened and he strode down the hall with renewed vigor. Unlocking his office with quick movements, he grinned as he remembered Shelby reaching under his arm that day in class to snag her keys.

He tossed his keys on the desk and stood staring out the window, his gaze wandering across the green expanse of the quad to the little redbrick building on the far edge. His smile faltered as he remembered the heat he felt when he looked into her eyes. Just sparks, nothing more, nothing less. Nothing would come of it. He could never get attached to someone who spent Sunday mornings singing in church.

Lili had been strong in her faith until the end. She'd lost her faith in him, but never God. Even though God was the one who'd started it all.

Ransom shook his head. He was thinking as if God even cared enough to start something, bad or good. He could never convince himself that God didn't exist, but there was no way that an omnipotent being cared about their little lives. If He did, why hadn't He saved his wife? Why had He let their baby die?

Ransom shook off the mounting questions and

shuffled his papers. Circular arguments going nowhere, a waste of time. Shutting down a rising tide of unease, he turned to his desk and did what he always did when he was unnerved. He threw himself into his work.

*More than once did Elizabeth,*
*in her ramble within the park,*
*unexpectedly meet Mr. Darcy.*

*—PRIDE AND PREJUDICE*

# CHAPTER EIGHTEEN

Another Wednesday, another early-morning class. The term was flying by, and Shelby had the uncomfortable feeling that she would wake up tomorrow and it would be June. It felt like spring in the middle of November, and the ice storm seemed as if it had happened in some other year. Shelby grabbed a pale pink linen dress out of her closet. And of course, Rebecca had a pair of shoes to match. In fact, she had five pairs and wanted Shelby to try them all, but Shelby snagged a pair of slingbacks that weren't too hard to walk in, added a simple pair of pearl earrings and called it good.

"Wait, I'm not finished," Rebecca called as Shelby tried to get out the door.

"I'm dressed, leave me be," she said, searching for her keys.

"It's a little chilly." Rebecca emerged from the bedroom with what looked like a small white bunny.

Shelby stared at it in horror, but when it turned out to be possibly the softest cashmere cardigan ever made, she couldn't help grinning. "I feel so . . . fuzzy." She slipped it on, smoothing the amazing fabric over her arms.

"*Now* you're dressed," Rebecca said with satisfaction.

After popping upstairs to the lounge for a Diet Coke, Shelby made her way to the department office. The door was open and the lights were on, of course. There were few days when Shelby could beat Jolee to the office.

Shelby started speaking before she completely entered the office. "Hi, Jolee! I was just wondering if—" She stumbled to a stop when she saw Ransom Fielding standing in front of the mail-boxes, sorting through what looked like a pile of notices. At her words he looked up, pausing with his hand full of papers. Jolee hovered behind him. At little over five feet, she barely reached his chest.

"Shelby, honey! Come on in! I made some marmalade muffins earlier and there's just two left. You have to have one, it's my granny's recipe." Jolee twirled around and grabbed a paper plate, the bottom sticky with orange residue, two small muffins sitting in the center. Deftly stepping around Ransom, she presented the little plate.

"Well, thanks." Shelby shifted her grandfather's

leather satchel to her shoulder and politely took a muffin, the glaze dripping over her fingers. It was surprisingly light with a hint of honey and had the aroma of orange zest. Her eyes drifted closed for a second as she savored the perfect combination of flavors. She chewed slowly. Aunt Junetta would love this recipe, maybe even use it to win a blue ribbon at the Flea Bite Creek Fair.

She looked up and saw Jolee was waiting for a verdict, her blue eyes wide with anticipation. Ransom seemed lost in thought, watching Shelby chew. The last bite was as good as the first, and Shelby tried to surreptitiously lick the glaze from her fingers, wishing for a napkin.

Ransom turned swiftly back to his in-box, the fistful of papers crumpled a little in his hand. Shelby gave him a quick once-over now that his back was turned. He was wearing what seemed to be a nicely tailored suit, a light tan color. And his shoes, undoubtedly handmade Italian leather. Rebecca would know.

"I'll have to get the recipe," she said, and Jolee beamed. Shelby's fingers were turning numb from the chilled Diet Coke in her hand.

"Mr. Fielding wouldn't take one. I think he's afraid I put some poison in them." Jolee winked at Shelby, who glanced up in time to catch a flicker of annoyance cross his face as he turned at the sound of his name. He returned to sorting the slips of paper, faster now.

*Now that's more like it, back to the prickly exterior,* thought Shelby.

"That's a pretty outfit! Are you going with Mr. Fielding and Mr. Finch to that meeting at the Plaza?"

Shelby felt anger stir somewhere in the middle of her chest. Of course she wasn't going. She didn't even know what "meeting" Jolee was talking about.

Without even waiting for a response, Jolee said, "I have something for you. I left it downstairs on the conference table. Just a second."

Shelby stepped aside to let her pass. Jolee gave her a perky smile, closing the door just a little. If she hadn't known better, Shelby would have thought that Jolee was trying to give them private time. That woman was deluded if she thought privacy would do anything other than bring out the worst in both of them. Especially since apparently only one of them was going to an important meeting with the boss.

He glanced at her as the door closed. Shelby refused to meet his gaze, instead focusing out the window. She stared at a different section of the same branch that passed her window, willing Jolee to come back.

Ransom cleared his throat and Shelby reluctantly turned to acknowledge him.

"I was thinking—"

"Today I—"

They started simultaneously and each broke off in an uneasy silence.

"Go ahead, please." Ransom gestured for her to continue.

"I was just going to say they might be able to arrange to have your departmental mail delivered to Agate Hall. There's no reason for you to have to come all the way over here to pick up phone messages." Shelby smiled in what she hoped was a friendly way.

He seemed to consider this for a moment. "They probably could. But I don't mind coming by."

Oh, well, it was worth a shot. "Your turn," she said brightly. She unscrewed the Diet Coke and took a sip, replacing the cap a little crookedly. She clenched her jaw, irritated at the trembling in her fingers. It wasn't really from anger, but she wished it were. She lowered her satchel to a spot by her feet.

"Well, I was wondering—"

The rest of his sentence was lost as the bottle slipped from her hands. Desperately snatching for it, she slapped its side, speeding the downward trajectory. It slammed to the tiny area rug and erupted, sprinkler style. Diet Coke exploded two feet in every direction.

Shelby crouched and tried to grab the bottle while shielding her face from the spray. She clutched at the base but it was slippery and it landed a second time, right between Ransom's feet. He had jumped forward to grab Shelby's leather satchel and held it shoulder high. The bottle let forth a final, voluminous spray before subsiding into a fizzing puddle.

"Oh my . . . I'm so sorry . . . I just . . ." Shelby could hardly look at him. Her hair and face were dripping, the side of her pale pink skirt was soaked and both Rebecca's expensive shoes were splattered with brown drops. She gazed in horror at Ransom's suit. The only real damage was up the inside of both his trouser legs.

Shelby rushed forward with tissues from the box on Jolee's desk. Crouching down, she mopped his shoes, then his cuffs and was working her way up to his knees when she finally heard him, his voice sharp with alarm. "Miss Roswell, stop! Stop!"

He had hold of one of her hands, the other still holding her satchel. She futilely pressed the tissues to his knee with her free hand and looked up.

He was laughing.

Coke dripped onto her cheek from a curl of her hair. Taking a deep breath and rising, she dropped the sodden tissues in the trash.

"I'll pay your dry-cleaning costs . . . if the suit can be saved," she choked out. A new wave of horror swept over her. "The meeting. Do you have time to go home and change?" If Finch found out that Ransom Fielding was going to miss an important function because she'd sprayed him down with Coke, Shelby was sure she'd hear about it.

"It doesn't start for another hour. I can probably run home." He was still grinning.

"I don't know what to say." She couldn't keep the despair from her voice. It wasn't really the cost of the cleaning, or the suit, or ruining his morning that bothered her. It was that, yet again, she had created a minidrama.

"What is there to say? You turned my suit into a catastrophe and the janitor will be really ticked at that carpet stain." His voice warmed with barely suppressed laughter, but Shelby didn't smile.

"Thank you for rescuing my satchel. It would have been difficult to clean."

"You're welcome." Then he seemed to notice it for the first time. "That clasp . . . and the stitching . . ."

"It was my grandfather's, and he inherited it from his father. Some of the best Savannah leatherwork of its time. Built to last. I don't carry it often, just on days when I . . . when I need to feel his presence, some connection to him. He died my freshman year in college. It was my high school graduation present." The words tumbled out.

Ransom gave a low whistle, turning the satchel carefully over in his hands. "It's beautiful. Remarkable. I have a friend who's very interested in textiles and leatherwork. Mostly from the war, but later, also." He passed it back gently. "It must be going on a hundred years now."

"I keep my current research notes in it, sort of a good-luck charm." She stared at the stain soaking into the little area rug that Jolee had brought in to brighten up the office space and sighed. "You remind me of a John Newman quote, that one definition of a gentleman is one who's merciful to the absurd."

"I wouldn't say you're absurd . . . but there is one thing"—he stopped to wipe a drop of Coke from the back of his hand—"you could do for me."

Shelby said nothing, waiting to hear what he had in mind, a strange feeling in the pit of her stomach.

"There's a fund-raiser for the Southern Historical Society, on Saturday, two weeks from now. It's at my aunt's home, Collier House. One of those horrible, mind-numbing affairs where people mingle and chat and generally try to outdo one another. It would make it a little less painful to have someone new with me. I mean, not so jaded. . . . I'm not explaining this well." He made an impatient noise in his throat, ran his hand through his dark hair, then continued, "In all honesty, I was going to ask you anyway, before you ruined my suit, so it's not really related. And I can't promise you that you'll have a great time. But you might find it beneficial."

Shelby wanted to have him repeat the invitation, not at all clear on what he meant. And she desperately wished her heart would stop pounding. "Beneficial?"

"Yes, sort of a way to regain your footing here, because of our . . . trouble."

As he spoke, Shelby's eyebrows raised higher and higher. He was offering her an old-fashioned social arrangement. She would accompany him, and he would make it known how friendly they were.

She thought back to her argument with Jennie Anne. Was this the same? Could it be just a social occasion, with no hurt feelings or misunderstandings?

"You're debating," he said simply. He leaned back against the edge of Jolee's desk, one of his pant legs plastered to his calf with Diet Coke. "Care to share why?"

Shelby paused, wondering why she felt like sharing anything that was going through her head. "In the pro column—"

"Starting off on a positive note," he interrupted, smiling.

"I really haven't been out in a while and I've been hankering for a reason to dress up and hobnob."

Ransom's blue eyes narrowed. "Funny."

Shelby laughed outright. "Okay, seriously. In the pro column, I do feel bad about this"—she waved her hand over the mess—"and I would feel better knowing I'd made it up to you a little."

"No debt. I already said that."

"I know you did. But that's what I feel," Shelby insisted.

"Fine. Debt would be canceled. Any other pros?"

"Well, as you noticed"—here she raised her chin a bit—"you're right that my departmental standing has taken a hit of late. It just might do me good to appear friendly with the great Ransom Fielding."

He grimaced a little at her word choice. "And the cons?"

Now, Shelby decided, she would lie, because the biggest con of all was the way Ransom Fielding affected her. His review should be front and center in her mind, but every time they met, it became less and less relevant. He was like a drug she wanted more and more of, but couldn't get.

"I've never really liked cocktail parties, especially where the crowd might be less than receptive to me," she said.

He straightened up and checked his watch. "And have you decided?"

Shelby noted that he didn't bother to allay her fears. She took a deep breath and threw herself on the side of all women like Jennie Anne. She hoped this wasn't the top of a slippery slope.

"What time?"

"I'll pick you up at six. E-mail me your address. If you're comfortable with that, I suppose we could meet there, but it's a bit of a drive."

Shelby briefly considered. A car ride together? What if they argued? And then she laughed at the thought. They weren't teenagers and he wasn't going to make her walk home if they fought.

"No, that's fine."

The door swung open and Alicia Hines strode in, her reedy frame made leaner still by her all-black ensemble. The manner of the new professor of the Renaissance period made her one of the least popular staff members. She seemed to be in a perpetual hurry; no one was fast enough and nothing was done quickly enough for Alicia's taste.

"Jolee, why are you standing out there? I've got those letters I need to send and you know I can never get the postage machine to work for me. Come on in here!" Alicia barked, motioning urgently.

A sheepish-looking Jolee followed Alicia through the door, refusing to meet Shelby's glare.

"Oh, I couldn't find what I'd left down there, honey. I'll have to put it in your box," Jolee said, then exclaimed, "Heavenly days! What happened to you two?"

Ransom smiled. "I'll let Shelby handle that one." And he left her to explain the state of the office.

*I had hoped that our sentiments coincided in every particular, but I must so far differ from you as to think our two youngest daughters uncommonly foolish.*

—MR. BENNET TO HIS WIFE

# CHAPTER NINETEEN

After a quick trip home to change into navy slacks and a button-up before class, Shelby spent fifty minutes trying to lecture a room of sleepy freshmen, then settled in for her usual Wednesday office hours. She answered the phone on the first ring, her left hand lifting the receiver while her right hand clicked "save" on the document she was working on.

"Shelby, it's Ellie. How are you?"

"What's going on?" Shelby thought she'd better cut to the quick. Ellie never called to chat. It wasn't money she wanted, that was her daddy's area. It wasn't advice, that was their mother's domain. They weren't close enough to share personal details. That was reserved for Jennie Anne.

"Oh, not much. I was just going to tell you a little story, something that happened here, and see what you think."

A bad feeling crept over Shelby, and an image popped into her mind of a little black storm cloud on the horizon of a sunny day. “Go ahead.”

“Well, see, there was this professor we didn’t like—”

“Who’s *we?*” Shelby didn’t feel bad about interrupting. Ellie could talk for ten minutes and Shelby wouldn’t have a glimmer of hope at understanding. Better get specific.

“Lauren, my sorority sister. We’re really close, she knows all my passwords. I let her choose my hairstyle last time when I couldn’t decide between growing my bangs out or just letting them flop over one eye, like everybody else. If I grew them out, then I’d have to use a hair band and I knew I’d look like Tina Turner in all her videos so—”

Too specific. “Lauren is a friend. Okay, and the professor?” Shelby felt a growing sense of dread. Ellie had less respect for her professors than she did for their parents.

“Some old hag teaching the creative writing class. She’s about ninety thousand years old and has crusty, orange clown hair. She’s always going off about plotlines and realistic characters. She even told me that my story, this really awesome description of a Prada store in Manhattan, wasn’t realistic, and I’ve actually been to the store! She doesn’t know what the—”

“So you don’t get along with your professor. What happened?” Shelby rolled her eyes heavenward. Ellie's description probably included a lot of words like *awesome*.

"Well, Lauren and I were passing a note back and forth during class—"

"And she took it from you?" Shelby had seen a lot of note passing in her day. She preferred to ignore it.

"No, we were super-careful. She didn't see a thing."

"Okay, so she never saw it." Unlikely. Students always think teachers are blind and deaf.

"So, I carefully tore the note up into little pieces and dropped them in the trash on the way out—"

"Wait. Why tear up the note?" Shelby sat up straight in her chair.

"Um, well, Lauren's kind of a gossip vulture, and she heard that Mrs. Horowitz had all her fifty cats removed by the Humane Society because she was dressing them up like real babies and so—"

Shelby dropped her head in one hand. Is this what her students were doing in class?

"I thought we'd better get rid of the note. Because there was a little bit of meanage, just some words."

There was a long pause. Shelby tried to speak calmly. "So, let me review. You and Lauren, your BFF, passed a note in class about your professor. The note had rumors in it and some words you probably don't want to specify."

"Yeah, so then we get called in to the dean of

students' office and we're sitting there totally clueless, when he pulls out this envelope that's got CONFIDENTIAL stamped all over it in red ink. He opens it up and there's the little piece of paper, all taped together. It was our note! From the trash!"

"And what did he say?" Shelby's stomach churned. Mama would be so upset if Ellie got suspended.

"He said he was putting a note in our file, like a disciplinary thing. He wouldn't even listen when we told him the note was private and it wasn't meant for anybody else. Can you believe it? Anyway, I was hoping you had some sort of rule or something we can quote to get it out of our files."

"A rule? What, that anything you write in class is protected by the First Amendment?" Shelby couldn't disguise her frustration.

"Exactly! Does that one cover everything written down?" Ellie's voice had risen in triumph.

"I was kidding. There's no universal rule you can use. You go to a completely different university. I don't even know what our dean would say about that, but probably it would follow the same lines. You insulted a teacher, spread lies about her, and used profanity. I would say a written censure is perfectly fair."

"Are you serious? Chad Thurman wrote some nasty junk about his adviser on his Facebook page and everybody just laughed about it. We pass a note and get something in our file? That's totally unfair. What about the fact that we threw it away? She dug it *out of the trash,* Shelby!"

"I understand that, but the trash isn't off-limits. Anything in public can be used against you, especially once you've let go of it. Haven't you ever heard of the police going through the garbage for evidence? You would have been better off just taking it with you."

"That's so not helpful. Obviously, we already *did* throw it away and now we have to figure out a way to get around their scheme. He's clearly her little revenge artist, making us pay so she won't look bad."

"He's just doing his job. Do you even know what's in your Student Code of Conduct? If you read it and there's nothing in there about slandering your professors, then fine, go ahead and contest. But I think you got off lightly. She could probably push for disciplinary probation or even suspension."

"Figures you would take her side. You don't even know this psycho woman and you're defending her. Don't you care what Daddy's going to feel when he gets the letter in the mail?" Ellie whined.

Shelby's head popped up. "Are you saying that your misconduct, and Daddy's disappointment, will be all my fault because I haven't helped you wiggle out of this jam? It's not my responsibility to get you out of trouble."

"You've never really cared about me. You were always so busy with your research and your letters. All those dead people from a hundred years ago matter more to you than your own sister," Ellie accused shrilly.

"That's not true. My family has always come first, Ellie. I know that our age difference has made it hard to be really close sometimes, but I've tried to be present in your life. I'm not going to engage in this sort of dialogue because it makes no sense." Shelby tried to keep her voice from trembling, but her hand was clenched around the receiver.

"Whatever. I guess I'll try to find somebody else to help me. It's a total setup and I'm not going to let them put some stupid letter in my file."

"I wish I could—" The click on the line told her that Ellie had hung up. Shelby slowly replaced the receiver in its cradle.

Digging notes out of the trash and taping them together, what self-respecting person did that? Would she ever stoop that low? Shelby tried to shrug off the whole episode but her focus was gone.

Shelby flipped open her instant-messenger window and sent her housemate a quick note.

Up for a trip to the Grind? I need a sanity break.

Moments later she was locking her office and heading out into the sunshine.

*"I like her appearance," said Elizabeth, struck with other ideas. "She looks sickly and cross. Yes, she will do for him very well. She will make him a very proper wife."*

*—PRIDE AND PREJUDICE*

# CHAPTER TWENTY

Shelby dropped into a chair at their usual table by the front window, the prime spot for watching the people pass by. The noonday sun slanted through, casting shadows behind her. The bitter smell of roasting beans in the coffeehouse was like aroma-therapy, and Shelby stretched the tight muscles in her shoulders.

Ellie's phone call had upset her more than she wanted to admit. Why were her sisters so intent on destroying any chance at respectability? Her mother encouraged their behavior and their father never rebuked them. Something terrible was going to happen, she could feel it.

"Shelby!" Zoe the barista zipped over to the table and plopped herself in the opposite chair. "You have to tell me everything. Who is he? Is he yours?" she demanded in an urgent whisper. Her dark eyes were heavily rimmed with gray liner that matched her shimmery top, and her perfume had a sharp, clove overtone.

"Zoe, I have no idea who you're talking about." That wasn't exactly true but Shelby was on the defensive.

"You know, the hunka-hunka who came here yesterday. I almost passed out with excitement when he said he was here to buy your usual coffee and could I help him please," Zoe squealed, her whisper gone. "Could I ever! I would sell my sweet old auntie for a chance with him. He was amazing, his hair all ruffled like that, and he just oozed the smell of old money . . ."

Shelby let Zoe go on for a bit until she was calm enough to listen. "Actually, I barely know him, and what experiences I *have* had with him were mostly humiliating, except for the ones when I wanted to poke him in the eye. So, don't worry, there's hope for a happy future for you."

"But what was he doing buying you coffee? That's so romantic, so thoughtful. I mean, what better gift than a big mocha? Of course, I'd prefer a triple shot, myself, but he's obviously the whole package." The bangles on Zoe's wrists rattled as she gestured.

"I loaned him some books, that's all." Shelby shrugged and glanced out the window. Rebecca had said she'd be here.

"I have to start reading more. Nerds can be so hot. In fact, I'm going to go over to the library today as soon as we close. It's off the quad, right? What are their hours again?"

Shelby wasn't offended that Zoe assumed she would know the library hours because, frankly, she did. "They're open until eleven every night except Saturday, when they close at nine. Is that a new scarf?" she asked, desperate to redirect the conversation.

"You like?" Zoe twirled the snow-white scarf around her hand and held it up so the fuzzy fibers stuck out all over. "I knitted it last week. It's made of dog hair, totally organic. My sister has a malamute and I asked her if she could save everything he sheds. I think I'll make a pair of matching mittens."

Shelby was momentarily at a loss for words. "I guess that saves on yarn as long as you're not allergic. Some people have terrible—"

She broke off, midsentence. Walking down the sidewalk was Ransom Fielding in a deep blue suit. All signs of the Diet Coke fiasco were gone. Clutching one of his arms was a slim woman with shiny blond hair and high heels. Shelby slouched down, inexplicably filled with the desire to hide.

"What? What is it?" Zoe peered out the window. "Oh my gosh, it's him, and, hey, there's some chick with him. That better be his sister or he's a total rat. You know, you just can't trust anybody, can you? You think you know somebody and the next—"

"Zoe! Please be quiet, I think they're coming in here." Shelby felt her face flushing with embarrassment. *Please walk by, please walk by, please—*

The door swung open and Ransom ushered the willowy woman in. Shelby couldn't resist stealing a quick glance. The young woman was strikingly beautiful, with eyes like enormous blue marbles set over perfect cheekbones. Her deep red shirt dress matched her large ruby drop earrings.

"Quick! Introduce me," Zoe hissed, standing up and tugging down her short black skirt. It seemed made out of some kind of shiny plastic.

"Why? You were just saying that he was a rat," Shelby couldn't help hissing back.

Too late, Zoe was already standing in Ransom's path. "Hello! Remember me? You came here to buy coffee for my friend Shelby? Look, she's here, too! How fun is this?" Zoe bounced on her toes and ignored Shelby's glare.

"Of course I do. You were very helpful." Ransom's eyes flicked over to Shelby, who studiously arranged the sugar packets on the table. Out of the corner of her eye she could see the blond woman facing away, not remotely interested in being introduced.

"You know, I'm a big reader, too. I was going to borrow those same books but you beat me to it. In fact, I was headed to the library this evening. You wouldn't want to join me?" Zoe laid a hand on his arm, the nails painted a deep gray.

Shelby glanced up and almost laughed out loud at Ransom's expression, somewhere between amusement and total confusion. He didn't seem at all uncomfortable with Zoe's asking him for a date, even if it was to the library. He must have loads of practice at turning women away.

Zoe was now positioned between Ransom and the tall blonde. Shelby stole another peek, noting that she was slim and her skin was flawless, if a bit too tan.

"Ah, I see. Well, those diaries are fascinating to read. I'm sure you'll enjoy them. And I'm afraid I'm busy tonight, but thank you."

"Ransom, dear. We need to hurry. The Purple Parasol closes in two hours and I want to have time to really look." The blonde's voice was high and breathy. She didn't spare a look for Zoe. It was as if she didn't exist. The blonde let out a tiny sigh and checked her delicate silver watch.

"Tasha, this is Zoe, the barista." A smile played around the edges of Ransom's lips. "And this is Shelby Roswell, one of my colleagues."

Shelby stood and extended a hand to Tasha. "A pleasure to meet you."

Tasha stared at Shelby's outstretched hand for a moment, as if considering whether to take it. Then she grasped it as if she had been handed a used tissue, dropping it just as quickly.

"Well, my break is over. I've got to get back

behind the counter." Zoe waggled her eyebrows at Shelby and slipped by.

"I'm so sorry I'm late!" Rebecca flew through the door and then stumbled at the sight of the group. She looked from Ransom to Tasha to Shelby. "I just got off the phone with Carlisle Roundtree," Rebecca blurted to no one in particular.

"The editor? Carlisle is a good friend of mine. We were roommates at Georgetown." Ransom's voice was light, friendly and he held out a hand to Rebecca.

"Ransom, this is my roommate, Rebecca. She's an associate in the English Literature department." Shelby tried to communicate several paragraphs of information with one look, but Rebecca glanced from Shelby to Ransom with a curious expression.

"Now it's a party." Tasha smirked, her eyes untouched by the smile on her lips. "And an English teacher! Are you going to correct our grammar?"

Shelby could see Rebecca struggling to choose her words. "I don't correct anyone's grammar unless they're under five."

Tasha just smiled and patted Ransom's shoulder. "Let's get our coffee. Nice to meet you." She waved airily as they turned toward the counter.

Ransom made no move to follow. "Shelby, don't forget to e-mail me your address. It's about a half hour drive from here so we should leave around six on Saturday." His low voice resonated clearly despite the background clatter of the coffee shop. His gaze was intense, as if no one else existed except for her.

Shelby was distracted by the look of outright surprise that flickered on Tasha's face and then settled into guarded curiosity. She gave Shelby a much closer look, from the top of her auburn hair to her sensible navy shoes. Then, as if deciding there wasn't any threat, she turned her back as Ransom joined her at the counter.

"What on earth?" Rebecca whispered as she slid off her suede jacket and laid it across the back of her chair.

"What's the Purple Parasol?" Shelby asked softly.

"It's a bridal boutique out on Tower Road. Why?"

"They're headed over there next so she can look around."

"Sounds like there's gonna be a wedding. Do you think she minds he's a widower?"

Shelby stared at the tabletop with unseeing eyes. Something constricted painfully in her chest. She fought to focus on what Rebecca was saying. "Why would she? My cousin Langston married a widower. It's not a bad thing, certainly."

"No? Think about it." Rebecca peeked at the couple as they ordered. "An ex-wife in the background is a lot better than a dead wife. He'll always see her as a flawless woman, and no one can compete with that."

"I'm sure he remembers some flaws. You don't whitewash someone's memory just because they died." Shelby's stomach clenched, now imagining Ransom's dead wife and hoping she had major flaws.

"It's true, believe me. Some sort of psychological phenomenon, to remember them at their very best. If they'd divorced, it would be a hundred percent better."

"Certainly less tragic." Shelby fiddled with the white-and-pink sugar packets in front of her. "I did feel a little guilty for disliking him so much, after knowing he lost his wife that way."

"See? Exactly what I mean. His dead wife doesn't have anything to do with you and you're already—"

Rebecca broke off as Ransom and Tasha passed by them. She went first, head high, and didn't spare a glance in their direction. Ransom followed, carrying both of their drinks. As he passed, he nodded to them.

Rebecca continued when the door closed behind them, "Those red stilettos are this season's hot item. I saw them in Barneys when I was home. They cost eight hundred dollars."

Shelby tried not to gape. "For shoes? That's insane. The wedding dress she buys will cost the same as a small car, then. But she *is* very stylish . . ." Shelby's voice trailed off as she gazed out the window at their retreating figures. If only she hadn't sprayed Diet Coke on her perfect outfit and perfect shoes first thing this morning.

Rebecca snorted softly. "Oh, and jealousy rears its ugly head."

"I'm not jealous in the slightest. It just seems unfair that I meet his fiancée when I'm wearing old, sensible shoes."

"You've never cared about your shoes before. And what was he talking about that's a half hour away? Are you two going to some meeting?"

Quickly Shelby filled Rebecca in on her agreement to accompany him to the party.

Rebecca frowned down at her hands. "I don't know, Shelby. That just doesn't seem like a good idea. And have you ever had a conversation with him that went well? Those parties are bad enough when you go with people you actually like."

"Hold that thought, I'm going to go order." Shelby slipped out of her chair and went to the counter. She was glad to get a few minutes to collect her thoughts. Could she have imagined the heat that passed between them? Or worse, if it was real, did he expect her not to care that he was engaged?

But maybe it didn't matter. Maybe she didn't have any right to be thinking that way about him anyway, as he'd never mentioned anything about his beliefs. Usually something that important came up in conversation somewhere, sometime. She couldn't go setting her sights on someone who wasn't a believer. That just led to broken hearts all round.

After she collected their drinks, she said, "All right, I'm ready. Lay it on me."

"I'm not going to argue about it. It's your decision, but this seems a sudden reversal from what you said before." Rebecca wrapped her hands around the hot tea Shelby had brought her and took a sip.

"Well, it's not like I'm going into this with my eyes closed. And if I got the cold shoulder for six weeks because we argued, maybe I can raise my standing a little bit by going to one party with him."

"You refused David Bishop for basically the same thing. So, if he had been taller, richer, more handsome, a historian, brought you a mocha, et cetera, it would have been okay?"

"But David assumed that I was going to jump at the chance to go out with him."

"So, it's in the delivery? He hurt your pride so you turned him down?" Rebecca gave her a level gaze.

Shelby made an exasperated noise. "I know where you're going, but . . ."

"Don't get me wrong, David Bishop is a total Mr. Collins."

"The toady cousin who proposes to Elizabeth?" Shelby snorted, remembering the BBC version of *Pride and Prejudice*. "He was repulsive."

"You know, we all know Jane Austen never married, but we're not sure exactly how many offers of marriage she turned down. She must have had her own Mr. Collins. People were more honest about their intentions back then. It was perfectly acceptable to marry for status and money. Now marrying for anything less than love makes you a shallow person," Rebecca mused, gazing out the window.

"People now don't have to decide between marrying someone and starving to death. Back then, if you couldn't inherit money and couldn't have a job, marriage was about the only thing left." Shelby twirled the little red straw in her drink. "But you're the last person to be recommending a return to arranged marriages. Your parents would have you married off to some stockbroker in an instant."

"Well, if I get to thirty-five and haven't found the one, maybe I should let my mom take a turn. My parents have been happy enough. She must know something about it."

"And that's exactly why *my* mother needs to let someone else take over. I don't know what my parents ever had in common." Shelby sighed.

"Not everyone marries for love. Maybe they had their own reasons. You have to understand each other, come from the same perspective. Your parents met at church, right? They already had a lot in common right there. I say I would never marry for anything less than love, but I don't want to be eighty and holding out for someone who doesn't exist."

"But you're the one in love with Darcy! Comparing men to Austen heroes is totally unrealistic."

"No, he's perfect *because* he's so human and flawed. Really, you have to read it again. You'll see what I mean." As Rebecca wagged one finger, she looked for once just like an English professor.

"No thanks, I don't want to be an Austen fanatic like you are. And I don't have time to be searching out the perfect man right now anyway. I have an article to finish."

"Except that you're going out on Saturday . . ." Rebecca let the rest of her sentence hang in the air.

Shelby laughed. "I think I can spare a few hours. And see, Ransom asked me to go so that it wouldn't be as boring for him and it might show everybody we're not really sworn enemies. David Bishop asked me because he thought I needed what he had to offer."

"Still sounds the same, but it's your social life. Hey, did you hear Raymond Masterson has a new girlfriend? She's a flight attendant from Atlanta. They met on a flight to Memphis and he dumped the old one by e-mail before they even landed."

"How do you find out these things?" Shelby was astounded at how easily Rebecca ferreted out the juicy gossip.

"I'm not standing around talking about old battlegrounds, my dear. Anyway, you think showing up to a party with him might really help your standing?" Rebecca looked incredulous.

Shelby watched a passerby on the sidewalk for a moment. A bulldog tugged at his leash, and the owner, deep in conversation with a tall woman, ignored him. Shelby nibbled a nail.

"I'm sick of being blacklisted. It's worth a try. And if he's engaged, then there's no romantic issue." For him, at least. Her stomach gave another lurch as she remembered Tasha's grip on his arm.

Rebecca's clear brown eyes were dark with concern as she shook her head. "I don't think this is a good idea. You can't be blacklisted forever for barging into his class, and that review might eventually fade away. But if you mix up all these social aspects, things could go badly right when you're trying to get tenure. I think it's too much of a risk."

Shelby lifted her chin. "It's just that I've tried for so long my way, maybe I need to try something different. I'm tired of being left out of the loop." She stared out the window for a moment. "I just hope I'm not digging my own grave."

“Well, if you are, I’ll come with flowers on your birthday every year, okay?” Rebecca’s tone was light.

Shelby shrugged off the little worry that crept around her brain. It was just a party, not even a real date, and she was determined to do whatever it took to get her academic reputation back.

*There is a stubbornness about me that can never bear to be frightened by the will of others. My courage always rises at every attempt to intimidate me.*

—ELIZABETH

# CHAPTER TWENTY-ONE

Shelby strode down the sidewalk, inhaling the brisk fall air. Saturday had never been so welcome. No family commitments, no grading, and if it weren't for the constant loop of worry running through her mind, she would be completely content. As it was, her decision to accompany Ransom to that party was looming large, like a storm cloud on the horizon of her life.

The red door to Tansy's art gallery shone bright in the sunlight. Shelby grasped the handle and pulled, her spirit lifting automatically. She loved helping out in the gallery, but even more, she loved the comfort that came from surrounding herself with inspirational art and like-minded artists. She spied her friend struggling with a piece of electrical equipment, her glossy black hair pulled back from her face with a brightly colored scrunchie so that the ends stuck out in a fan behind her head.

"Tansy, I can't believe how successful this place is after two years. You have a real gift," Shelby said. She reached out to steady the spotlight that Tansy was working to aim just right over an enormous metal structure that reminded Shelby of a squatting eagle.

"It helps that interest in modern art has taken off around here." Tansy DiGuardi wiped her forehead and sat on an overturned bucket. "That piece is worth about six million dollars, and the insurance is staggering. Plus, the gallery in Berlin that loaned it to us practically made me promise them my firstborn child if it got damaged."

"Well, it's amazing. Huge, but amazing."

Four hours later, they both plopped into chairs, sweaty and exhausted. The sculptures were set up and arranged by other teams, but the gallery work was just as demanding.

Tansy let out a breath, giving a final survey of the large, industrial space filled with metal figures. "I can't thank you enough. This would have taken me all day. Ron wanted to help, but one of his old friends showed up and I knew he wanted to have the chance to catch up."

"You know I love this place," Shelby said. "And it's good to catch up." With their random schedules, getting together was hit-and-miss.

"True." Tansy paused, as if choosing her words carefully. "But you haven't said much about your new departmental addition."

Shelby stared up at the ceiling, wondering if there was any way to get around this topic. She loved Tansy, but Ransom Fielding belonged in another world, a world of professional and emotional angst, not here in a place where Shelby was so comfortable. “He’s fine.”

“Uh-oh.” Tansy laughed outright, the sound bouncing off the bare walls of the gallery. “Fine is what you say when someone is driving you to the brink of insanity.”

Shelby smiled. “You know me so well. But . . . really, I think everything will be okay. We might even be friends by the end of this year.”

Tansy opened her mouth as if to ask another question, but Shelby stood quickly and stretched. “I should go. You need help tomorrow for the final setup? I can snag Rebecca for an extra pair of hands.”

“That would be great. Ron will be here, too.” Tansy gave her a quick squeeze and unlocked the gallery door.

Shelby walked quickly back toward campus. Her bright red sweater felt much too thin for the sudden gust of wind that blew down the narrow street. A few leaves skittered in front of her. The sky was turning a deep rosy orange, the clouds edged with pink, and Shelby felt her body relax into the rhythm of her stride. She took a deep lungful of air and sent up a quick prayer of thanks for this body, even though she could never eat all the chocolate cake she wanted or risk turning into a doughy lump.

Her gaze dropped down to a group approaching on the sidewalk. One man was half turned around, looking up at the sky behind them. Shelby smiled, knowing that the man was appreciating the same blue sky she was. Then he turned, and she recog-nized the familiar dark hair and severe expression. Her eyes flashed to his companions. A tall, laughing man walked near the wall, and a blond woman teetered on high heels, one arm looped with Ransom's.

Shelby ducked her head and watched the sidewalk squares pass. Soon she could hear Tasha's lilting, breathy voice.

"Carl, I promise, you won't have to look at a single invitation sample or hear about the weight of the paper."

Shelby's stomach clenched. The wedding again. Did Tasha ever talk about anything else? Shelby heard the easy laugh of their companion—they were just a few feet away. She moved to step off the sidewalk.

"Hello, Shelby." A deep voice stopped her in her tracks, one foot on the sidewalk and one in the gutter. Shelby raised her face and forced a smile.

"Carl, this is my colleague from the history department. Shelby, this is my cousin Carl Bradford, visiting from Natchez," Ransom said.

Carl stretched out a hand, grinning. He must

have gotten all the warm-personality genes. But those bright blue eyes—definitely related. "Finally. I was beginning to think you were purely Ransom's imagination." Carl's face was open and pleasant. He shook her hand warmly, putting his other hand over hers.

Shelby glanced at Ransom, a question on her lips, but he was already speaking. "And you remember Tasha, I'm sure."

"Nice to see you again," Shelby said, wondering if she would get the same limp handshake.

Tasha looked as if she wished there were a polite way to keep walking without any response. Instead, she nodded and wiggled her fingers in Shelby's direction, a bright smile fixed on her face, albeit so briefly it seemed to convey the opposite of a smile. Close up, Shelby could see that her smooth skin was too tan, bordering on orange. Her teeth were blinding white and the approximate size of Chiclets. The bright pink sundress she wore, with ruffles along the hem and spaghetti straps, was more suited to the middle of summer.

*I can't even get dressed for a party without Rebecca. And Tasha's hair is perfect. I wonder if she had it professionally blown out.* Shelby was suddenly brought out of her reverie by Ransom's voice.

"—won't you?" He looked to Carl, who nodded enthusiastically.

"Excellent idea. I'd love to talk to you about your research on Aaron Schumacher. Ransom gave that article to me last weekend and I was blown away."

"Excuse me?" Shelby stuttered out.

"I'm sure she has somewhere to go. You can't just pull people off the street, Ransom." Tasha laughed lightly but her eyes had narrowed.

"I'm sorry, won't I what?" Shelby's face flushed.

Ransom motioned to the restaurant entrance just a few feet away. "We were going to dinner. Would you like to join us?" His eyes were intense, speaking volumes.

Shelby shook her head, flustered. "Oh, I couldn't. First of all, I'm not dressed for it at all." She waved at her comfortable black slacks, her cardigan. She was glad she'd put up her hair in a ponytail before she'd left the art gallery, at least it wasn't blowing around her face in a curly mess.

"See, she doesn't want to come. Now let's get inside before I freeze to death." Tasha tugged on Ransom's arm, but he wouldn't be budged. She slipped her hand free and went to the door. Carl opened it for her, smiling warmly over his shoulder at Shelby. She couldn't help smiling back and then started, as Ransom stepped close and bent down to whisper into her ear.

One word, softly spoken: "Please."

Stepping back, he stood waiting, his eyes locked on hers. Shelby half raised a hand to her ear, where it seemed to echo with Ransom's voice. His warm breath had tickled the fine hair at her temple, and now the breeze moved those same strands. She felt heat rise into her cheeks and willed herself to look cool and collected.

"I suppose there's no harm in it," Shelby said mildly, as if she accepted dinner invitations on the spur of the moment every day.

A slow smile spread over Ransom's face and he motioned her to the door, where Carl stood waiting. As she passed, out of the corner of her eye she saw Ransom flash a quick thumbs-up. Carl must be tired of being third wheel to the happy couple.

The host, in artfully faded jeans and a black cashmere sweater, materialized in front of them. He checked their reservations while Shelby glanced around. Bright yellow and black squares bordered the entryway, and the bass thump of modern techno music set an underlying pulse. The air was filled with the scent of lemongrass and ginger. The host gestured for them to follow him and led them to a table in the corner.

"I asked for a good table." Tasha had an orange fist planted on one bony hip, her lips pursed in irritation. "Is this the best you have?"

Their host ducked his head and hurried away. The group stood awkwardly in the far corner of the restaurant.

"Tasha, if you take this chair by the wall, you

can still see most of the place," Carl said reasonably, but she turned her face away from him and refused to sit. Ransom said nothing, instead he gazed off into the distance. Shelby couldn't believe a grown woman would be such a pain in the rear.

"He sat us right by the kitchen," Tasha hissed angrily, flipping her stick-straight blond hair over one shoulder. "I'm not going to eat next to the kitchen, with all the smells and clanging pots and yelling."

"You don't really eat anyway." Ransom's voice wound lazily through the group, like a bee at a picnic. It came to rest with a sting, on Tasha.

She gasped. "That's not true. I eat, and when I do, I like to have a quiet table away from the kitchen, where I can see the other guests. Is that so much to ask?" Her face had gone from that of a haughty woman to petulant child's in an instant. Her lower lip, glossy and plump, stuck out a bit, and her eyes misted with tears. "Why are you so mean, Ransom?"

Shelby shifted uncomfortably. Did she really want to be the fill-in blind date with a bickering couple?

As if Ransom had read Shelby's mind, he put his hand on Tasha's shoulder. "Don't mind me, I'm just hungry."

"You know how cranky he is when he doesn't get fed on time. Oh, here he comes," Carl said with relief as the maître d' waved them to a new table. This one passed Tasha's inspection, being squarely in the center of the room.

"I hope we're not in the direct path. I don't want people brushing past me all evening," she said fretfully, as Ransom held out her chair.

All evening? This had better not take more than an hour or so. Shelby smiled at Carl as he held her chair, and she tried to settle her bottom into the odd wicker shape. Now that she was closer to Tasha, she could see the lightest sprinkle of freckles over the bridge of her nose.

"I'm going to the ladies' room." Tasha folded her menu and stood, her gaze already canvassing the room. Ransom drummed his fingers on the tablecloth as he read through the dinner options. Carl met Shelby's eyes over his menu and grinned.

Shelby watched Tasha stride away, her long legs toned and perfectly smooth under the short sundress, heels clicking on the polished floor. Shelby wondered how old she was. Older than Jennie Anne, for sure. It was hard to tell with all that makeup.

"Very pretty, really," Shelby spoke half to herself, still watching Tasha's retreating figure.

"And astronomically expensive, I'm sure," Carl said.

Shelby paused in confusion. "Not the dress, I meant Tasha."

Ransom snorted. "Her, too."

Carl chuckled appreciatively and flipped through the menu. “I don’t know what to get. Maybe the chicken with black-bean sauce and garlic noodles.”

Shelby’s stomach gave an audible rumble and she hoped the ordering wouldn’t take too long.

Ransom grinned at the sound and said, “Good thing we grabbed you off the street. You might have starved before you made it home. Jolee said the pork chops with tonkotsu broth was good. Maybe the grilled tuna with snow peas and feta. Or maybe the prawns in lemongrass beer. Except that I don’t know what lemongrass beer *is*.”

“Rebecca and I came in with some friends,” Shelby said. “I got the ginger garlic peppered beef. It was very tasty. It had key-lime juice in it. I think she had the bourbon chicken; it’s a kind of a stir-fry with bourbon whiskey and soy sauce.”

She remembered the evening well. The two engineers they were with downed several pints of dark beer each and Shelby had to drive them home.

“That’s it. I’m having the bourbon dish.” Carl clapped his menu closed decisively.

Ransom saw Tasha approaching and leaned over to say quietly, “Thank you for coming. You’ve saved me from a night of endless wedding chatter.”

“I don’t know how I can stop that from happening, but you’re welcome all the same.”

Bridezilla must be making his life painful right now. It was a satisfactory thought.

Tasha swept back to their table and seated herself with a flounce. Shelby noticed the freckles had disappeared underneath a fresh layer of makeup. Those were sweet; Tasha should have left them alone. Still, Shelby felt like the poor cousin at the family reunion and self-consciously ran a hand over her ponytail, hoping the curls weren't too wild.

Tasha hadn't missed the gesture. "You have naturally curly hair? I know a wonderful stylist in Oxford that could straighten it for you. It's quite a long process, but I think you'd be really happy with the results." Tasha carefully adjusted the large diamond ring on her right hand. Shelby tried not to ogle as it flashed brilliantly in the low lights.

"I don't know why everyone feels the need to look like someone they're not." Ransom also spoke from behind his menu, but his voice was tense.

Oh, great. Now they were going to argue about her hair. Shelby rushed to defuse the situation. "Thank you both. And I would appreciate any help I can get, Tasha. I don't think men can understand what a trial it is." Shelby laughed lightly and took a sip of ice water.

"I've always been partial to curly hair, myself," Carl joined in, winking at Shelby. With any other man, it might have seemed smarmy, but with his good-natured smile it was simply casual flattery.

"People who advocate the 'all-natural' look are usually those who are effortlessly beautiful. But then, of course, there are things about ourselves we try to change when we shouldn't," Shelby said thoughtfully.

"I say whatever we want to change, we should. Why live with an ugly nose?" Tasha shrugged one flawless, tanned shoulder.

"My friend Tansy is an art collector. A few years ago she told me about wabi-sabi, the Japanese aesthetic. It's the beauty of the imperfect and incomplete, of what comes with age and asymmetry," Shelby said.

"I've heard of that," Carl said. "The pottery is worth more because it's handmade, even if it does have slight flaws. The machine-made pieces are soulless, have no character. I guess with people, you could say the lines on a person's face show their beauty through how much they've laughed or cried." The laugh lines around his own brilliantly blue eyes were evidence of his happy nature.

Without his aquiline nose, Ransom would be physically perfect, every feature symmetrical. But that nose gave him something else. His eyebrows were still too low, he seemed brooding, severe. He might not actually be, but that was the impression. And those deep lines around his mouth, as if he laughed a lot . . . or used to.

"Miss Roswell, you're staring at me," Ransom said, never taking his gaze off the menu.

Shelby flushed and turned away, catching Carl's eye. He was grinning.

"Wrinkles are worse than being poor." Tasha rolled her eyes.

Trying not to grimace, Shelby said, "There are other natural imperfections that are beautiful. Freckles, for instance, only add to the charm of a pretty face." She spoke offhandedly, but she took a chance, hoping Tasha would accept the compliment. *I'm not your competition, so just relax already.*

Tasha stared. Shelby could see the gears turning in her head. Friend or foe? Then Tasha made her choice and Shelby saw her eyes narrow.

"Yes, some of us are thankful that freckles are the worst of our worries." Again the flicker of a smile that never reached her eyes. Shelby sighed inwardly. This was going to be a long dinner.

*Your cousin will give you a very pretty notion of me and teach you not to believe a word I say.*

—ELIZABETH

# CHAPTER TWENTY-TWO

The waiter appeared and Tasha ordered a plate of fresh baby spinach, no dressing, with dried cranberries on the side.

Maybe she had allergies. Or maybe she didn't want to drip any sauce on her dress. Shelby shoved the mean-spirited part of herself aside and tried to think positively. Suddenly her phone trilled with an incoming message, the sound clearly audible. She twisted around to get her purse, digging through the contents. Somewhere in the bottom. "I'm sorry. Just let me . . ." She shrugged apologetically and peeked at the text.

Where are you? Want to get Thai takeout or make spaghetti? Your choice.

How to answer? Should she go all the way to the foyer to text Rebecca a message? As she sat there undecided, Ransom spoke, not raising his eyes from the menu.

"Have to run?" His voice was slow, unconcerned.

"No, it's just Rebecca. She doesn't know where I am and is wondering what we're doing for dinner. Do you mind?"

Carl slapped his hand on the table. "I'm a urologist, and last week a patient of mine was texting during an exam. Unbelievable! Go ahead and text her back. Really, we're not going to be offended."

Shelby responded as quickly as possible and tried not to grin as she imagined Rebecca's reading the message.

At Chinois with Ransom and Tasha. Will explain later.

"Is that the woman from the coffee shop? You seem very close," Tasha said, leaning forward. Her slow, careful movement reminded Shelby of the way Sirocco stalked birds in the backyard.

Refusing to take the bait, Shelby said, "We are. We've been friends since we met in graduate school."

"I have plenty of old friends, but nobody I'd like to live with," Tasha said pointedly. "What about you, Carl? Is there anyone you'd like to live with?"

"Male or female?" Carl cocked an eyebrow.

"Oh, you! I understand about men and their space. You don't find many men living together as roommates past their twenties. And you are past your twenties, right, Shelby?"

Something in her tone made Shelby wish to be twenty-one again. "Not quite yet. And Rebecca has been a real blessing. There's just something about coming home to a sympathetic ear. Plus, she has a much better wardrobe than I do. And she's hard to offend, makes the world's best brownies, loves to shop for groceries, does dishes . . . You get the picture."

"No man can compete with that," Carl said glumly.

"And you haven't met anyone that you wanted to marry?" Tasha's face was creased with concern, her heavily made-up eyes wide.

*She's worse than my mother. Sorry, Ransom, I'm going to have to throw you under the bus.*

"Well, no, but every time I hear someone planning their wedding, it gives me a little thrill." Shelby ducked her head and pretended to examine the silverware. Ransom made a sound that could have been a squawk of protest, but she wasn't brave enough to look.

That was all the encouragement Tasha needed. She started with the season's colors and had moved into engagement rings before they were interrupted by the waiter's refilling their water glasses. Shelby hoped there weren't many more refills before the actual food arrived or she was going to have to eat her napkin.

"Now did you say six months' salary for the ring? I thought it was two." Shelby could feel Ransom's eyes boring into her but flatly refused to acknowledge him.

"The engagement ring is so much more important now. It's an investment. Do you prefer square cut or original five point? Or perhaps teardrop?"

"I haven't really thought about it," admitted Shelby slowly. "But I don't think it would be a diamond."

"You mean, you'd like a large sapphire, like Princess Diana's. After William's wedding, it's been the hot new ring." Tasha nodded knowingly. "It has excellent resale value. And you'll know by the size of the ring what kind of equity he has. You never want to attach yourself to anyone with less than fifty thousand in savings. I just read that in an article."

Shelby gritted her teeth and suppressed the urge to ask exactly where Tasha had read that bit of financial information. Probably *Cosmo*.

"Actually, I don't agree with the way most diamonds are mined. The working conditions, the wars they've funded, the child-labor issues, environmental disasters . . ." Shelby's voice trailed away as Tasha looked incredulous.

Shelby reached for a slice of bread. She hoped no one else wanted any because she was going to eat the whole basket if they didn't bring their plates soon.

"But surely, if your fiancé presented you with a three-carat, radiant-cut white diamond set in platinum, you would be happy?" Tasha nervously stroked the band on her own finger.

"I would hope that my fiancé would know better than that." Shelby buttered the slice of bread and took a bite, chewing thoughtfully. "Usually those things come up in conversation."

"The kind of ring you would prefer will pop up in conversation?" asked Ransom, his hand hesitating over his glass.

"No, the injustices of the world." She glanced around. "Don't they? When you know someone long enough you find out what they would change in the world if they could, what keeps them awake at night."

"Too true. And that's how we know that Tasha can't sleep when there are really awful flower arrangements in the world," Carl teased. He flashed her a grin.

Shelby couldn't help answering with her own, as if he were magic. Tasha let out a trilling laugh, but her eyes remained cold.

"Why is resale value so important?" Shelby asked. "Don't most people pass rings down to their children?"

"Well, we don't like to talk about it, but if it doesn't work out, you can always sell it." A slight grimace and a shrug were all the apology Tasha gave for this absurdity.

Shelby felt heat rise in her face as embarrassment for Ransom flooded over her. He never lifted his gaze. She couldn't even tell if he was even listening.

Tasha continued, "So, emerald or sapphire then, not that you've given it much thought. You're probably consumed with your work, no social life allowed." She giggled, the same breathy laugh that had first caught Shelby's attention.

At that moment their food arrived, artfully arranged on white plates and smelling wonderful. The waiter deftly set the dishes down, and Shelby wondered if she had ever been so happy to see a pork chop. She glanced at Ransom from under her lashes as she took a bite. He and Tasha were so different, not even a hint of affection between them. But maybe Tasha complimented him, made him feel powerful.

"Ransom, I don't see how you can eat feta. It smells like old socks and it's so nineties." Tasha waved a hand, her pretty face wrinkled in horror.

Or maybe not. Shelby grinned into her napkin.

Her plate untouched, Tasha held her fork poised over the small pile of baby spinach. "So?" She leaned in, eyes glimmering. "Tell us about your perfect ring."

Groaning inwardly for ever mentioning blood diamonds, Shelby took a breath and focused her eyes on Carl. His kind face, framed by blond hair just long enough to curl over his collar, and easy smile were the encouragement she needed.

"Well, I was looking for war letters and diaries a while back. An old woman called and offered me her family's history. When I went to see her, I noticed her ring. It was a thin gold band, with several different stones set in a line. I asked her if it was a family heirloom. She was ninety-four and her fiancé had given it to her before he'd gone to Italy during World War Two. The first letter of each stone spelled out a word. Her ring was hematite, opal, peridot and emerald."

There was a silence at the table.

"*Hope?* And what happened?" Tasha asked, perplexed.

"He didn't survive. She never married and was an only child. She was going to be buried with the ring." Shelby thought the end wasn't the point, but shared it anyway.

"Oh, how depressing! That's a terrible story!" Tasha gasped. The strap on her pink sundress slipped lower on one shoulder.

"Is it any worse than discussing the resale of a love token?" Ransom's voice cut drily through the theatrics.

Shelby looked to Carl, but he was completely unconcerned. Maybe they fought like this all the time.

"It's incredibly romantic. I've always thought so." Carl beamed around the table. "My great-grandmother on my father's side was given a ring that had"—here he stopped to tick them off on his fingers—"fire opal, opal, ruby, emerald, variscite, emerald and ruby. *Forever.* Ransom inherited it. It's a treasure, right, Tasha?" Carl again playing the peacemaker.

"Yes, it's wonderful." Her tone said it was much less than wonderful. "And I know I should wear it more often. But it's so hard to match with anything. A diamond is the perfect stone for everyday wear." She wiggled her hand once more, in case Shelby had missed the big rock the first time.

Shelby felt her eyes widen. Tasha had been given a ring, just like the one Shelby had described, passed down from generation to generation, carrying the blessings and love of countless moments in time . . . and she preferred a generic diamond set? Shelby slid a look to Ransom and realized how very much he must love Tasha. His face was impassive, except for a slight frown that furrowed his brows. Of course, the ring wasn't the most important part of the marriage. It was, after all, just a ring. But the idea of a family heirloom being tucked in a drawer for not matching was ludicrous. It just showed how powerful love was. Any logical person would see the family ring was miles above something mined half a world away, by people not paid enough to care for their families.

"I'm not an expert on jewelry, but I think the

ring can be symbolic of the entire relationship. I proposed to Lili with a ring that she designed." Ransom's words dropped into the conversation like a stone into a placid pond. The ripples radiated out, touching each person at the table again and again.

Shelby couldn't help glancing at Tasha, trying to gauge her response. Is this something they discussed? Tasha's pinkie finger was rubbing furiously against her band. Her lips were a thin line and she blinked several times.

Was he going to tell them exactly how he proposed? In front of his current fiancée? Shelby felt the question pulse in her head and waited, trapped in her chair. Carl looked unsure for the first time and shifted uneasily.

"She was a talented metalworker, and she said one day, when we were looking at her art, that this one ring reminded her of everything that was good about the world," Ransom said.

Shelby stared at him, trying to imagine it.

"She was beautiful, very beautiful. I remember when you first brought her home from college," Carl said quickly into the silence at the table.

"No, she wasn't," Ransom said. "Every woman in this room is more beautiful than Lili was. She had a space between her front teeth, her eyes were too close together and her hair always frizzed up in the humidity. She carried about fifteen extra pounds for her height, and for that matter she preferred to eat food so sweet it could choke a horse."

He went on, "But she was beautiful to me. Funny, too. She mocked me to my face and I couldn't help but laugh. Her impressions of our friends and family were dead-on. She saw through all the lies and stories we spin around ourselves."

Tasha cleared her throat as if to speak, but Ransom continued, "But she wasn't cruel. When she recognized your weakness, she would do anything she could to ease your way, to protect you. You felt you could be yourself around her. She had this faith . . ." He paused for a moment, then continued as if he'd changed what he'd been going to say. "When she had faith in you, it made you feel like you could do anything."

Shelby let out a quiet breath and blinked back unexpected tears. She stared down at her dinner growing cold, pork chop congealing in its pale sauce.

"You know, it's not just the stone, but where the ring comes from, that makes a difference. No one wants a plain black box. It has to be from Tiffany's, or I wouldn't even open it." With that insipid proclamation, Tasha reclaimed the conversation.

As she rattled on, Ransom stabbed another bite of tuna. His movements were quick and decisive, as if he had already finished his meal and were walking away from the conversation.

Shelby's mind whirled, and she felt as if the room was too loud, too warm.

"Shelby, I don't know how you can stand to live in this place year-round. Memphis is a little too big, and Atlanta is just a nightmare, but this city has hardly any restaurants." Tasha fiddled with the cranberries, dropping just a few into a pile of spinach leaves.

"Shelby comes from a truly tiny town," Ransom said, and winked ever so slightly at her.

Shelby's face grew warm and she took a sip of water, hoping to cover her confusion.

"Oh, so is this a 'big city' for you, then?" Carl smiled.

"She probably feels like she escaped a slow death," Tasha snorted. She turned to Shelby. "I think it's wonderful you have Rebecca as your roommate. And the college is right to hire her. I think we should help those people out whenever possible." Tasha took a tiny bite of raw spinach.

A tableful of forks stopped in midair. Shock kicked Shelby back in her chair. She stared at Tasha, trying to make sense of what she'd just heard.

"Did you just say you think Rebecca was hired because she's African-American?" Shelby asked, a bubble of fury rising in her throat.

"Well, it's true that they have to hire a certain number of women and minorities. What?" Tasha stared around the table. "It's a fact. My sister told me all about how they have to do the hiring in her firm. In your department there probably aren't that many women. But they have to hire a few, don't you see?"

"Oh, now *I'm* the mercy hire? So, if the department were full of women, then I could feel a bit safer?" Shelby's voice had risen and she leaned toward Tasha. Skinny, orange and ignorant, too!

"Now, I don't know if that's exactly what she was meaning to say. It might have gotten out before she realized quite how it sounded." Carl laid a soothing hand on Tasha's arm. "Let's just relax."

"I think she meant it exactly the way she said it," Ransom said. He lazily pushed his plate away. Shelby could have sworn she saw a smile playing around his lips, but she was too angry to wonder why.

It wasn't so unusual for Shelby to encounter bigotry at the dinner table. She had a flash of her uncle Warren, who moved to Oregon after his boss retired and he didn't want to work under the new, African-American boss. He chose Oregon because he'd heard it was a relatively white state. But for someone so young, educated and, worst of all, someone who would be marrying Ransom, who was representing the South to the rest of the nation, it was more than Shelby could stomach. She took a calming breath and tried to inject a note of common sense into the conversation.

"So, if you're a woman or a person of color, how do you know you've been hired for your skills?"

"I suppose you can't ever really know, can you? But see why marriage is so beautiful? You're chosen for who you are, not because some hiring guy says he needs three of this and two of that," Tasha said, flipping her hair over her shoulder and smirking at Shelby.

"Oh, now I hate to say this, but maybe marriage is the very last place you're chosen for who you are. You yourself just said that you shouldn't marry anyone with less than fifty thousand in savings."

"She has a point. When do we know we've been chosen, by our employers, or friends or spouses, for who we are?" Ransom leaned forward, attention fixed on Shelby.

"You and your philosophical conversations. I was only trying to say that I think everyone should be given a chance. That's all," Tasha said.

"Except for anyone without fifty thousand in the bank? And maybe we don't need your chances. Maybe we can do just fine without any extra help." Shelby was shaking her head in disbelief. She could see Ransom laughing at her and glared back. "It's not funny. This is why women and people of color have so much trouble getting ahead. Sure, departments need to make sure that it's not an entirely male arena, but there are plenty of qualified candidates to choose from. They're not scraping the barrel, pulling people off the street."

"So, you don't think about a man's profession or how wealthy he is before you go out with him?" Tasha fired back. "Or, how about his education? Have you ever dated a guy who never graduated from college?"

"Only when I was still in college myself, but when would I ever meet someone who didn't have a college degree? I'm a professor. All my time is spent in academia. And how would I find out, ask them? It's sort of a personal question."

Tasha shrugged, unconvinced.

Shelby continued, "Anyway, it's true that what a person chooses as a profession might say something about their ambition, but it might not. Some days I wish I had chosen that path instead. I could spend my days painting in a sunny room, instead of trolling through dead ends. But I wouldn't have a steady income."

"I think it's more acceptable for a woman to choose a profession that doesn't provide much salary," Carl said.

"Really? If a man is committed to building up his financial situation, wouldn't he be careful of attaching himself to a woman who doesn't have much earning potential?" Shelby asked.

Ransom made some sort of sound into his hand—it could have been a chuckle or a grumble.

"No. Because women are much more likely to

stay home when the kids come along, I don't think they receive the same scrutiny men do." Carl held his hands out, palms up. "I'm just saying. Don't bite my head off."

Shelby took a breath. "All right, so men don't give as much weight to a woman's career because she might stay home at some point in their family life. Now, don't you think that this is one of the reasons women have a hard time getting ahead in the workplace? If you dismissed her career ambitions so easily, what do you think her bosses are doing?"

Carl looked around, appealing for help from the others, but Tasha wore a blank expression, as if she were watching a tennis match from too far down the court.

Ransom cleared his throat. "So, back to marriage. Maybe women's bank statements should be held to the same scrutiny that men's are? We should institute a new rule, that women must also buy a man some object, to prove her worth. Of course it would be marketed as a token of love, just like the engagement ring." Ransom's face was solemn, but his drawl was heavy with irony. His mouth twitched up at one corner.

"Fine idea! I vote for a flat-screen television. Or maybe season tickets to the guy's favorite football team." Carl chuckled and slapped his leg.

"That wasn't my point, but it's not a bad idea.

What I was trying to say was that to constantly carry the burden of proof, to prepare to defend your *existence* in your field, to know that people see you as a temporary worker who will leave the moment the babies start arriving—that's incredibly detrimental to a woman's ability to achieve any sort of scholarship, let alone be admitted to the top-tier universities for research."

Tasha tutted and poked at her spinach, spearing a cranberry on one tine of her fork and examining it. "I think if women stopped complaining so much about inequality and just dug in, it would be a lot better for everybody."

Feeling as if her eyes were going to pop from frustration, Shelby gritted her teeth and stared into her plate. Ransom was shaking with laughter. Slapping your dinner partner is bad manners, isn't it? She struggled to organize her scattered thoughts but fury simmered inside.

"Is that why you never had children, Shelby? Were you worried about having a career and kids, too?" asked Tasha.

Shelby laid her fork on her plate and stared; the bass beat of the techno music matched the angry pulse in her head. "Why I never had children? I'm not dead. I'm not even past thirty."

"Well, there's no need to be so angry about it," Tasha sniffed, rearranging her spinach leaves. "There are plenty of other options for people in your situation. Like adoption. I have a very good friend who adopted the sweetest little girl. She's got blond hair and everything."

Shelby felt like dropping her head on the table in despair. It didn't help that Ransom seemed to find the conversation highly amusing. "I never said . . ."

"But why do you think having a baby is so bad? What if you get married and your husband wants one and you don't?" Tasha looked down her pert nose, gleefully triumphant.

Shelby shook her head in defeat. Carl nervously tried to pass her the bread, but she waved the basket away. "First of all, I love babies. Because I don't have one doesn't mean I don't like them. Second, I know there are babies out there to adopt. My cousin Langston adopted a beautiful baby last year. And third, the conversation about whether or not to have children would certainly come up somewhere in the dating process. It would be ludicrous to be married and suddenly realize you'd never talked about it."

"Well, sure, people talk about it, but they may not really mean it. You know, dating is when you don't want to look high maintenance." Tasha watched a middle-aged woman totter by their table, a tiny handbag on her arm.

"High maintenance? Is that what you call being honest? And will you stop laughing!" Shelby said furiously, whirling on Ransom.

He held up his hands in surrender, his face

creased in mirth. He took deep breaths, his shoulders shaking. “Sorry. Don’t mind me. I’m just enjoying the free exchange of ideas.”

“Yes, please let’s stop arguing. It’s giving me a headache,” Tasha said, rubbing her temples and pouting.

Shelby had the irrational urge to keep arguing until Tasha agreed with her. But that was futile and she knew it. “Absolutely right. Let’s get back to weddings. You said something about wedding portraits being more intimate, less formal?” Shelby studiously avoided Ransom’s eyes and reached for her glass. If she could get out of this restaurant without causing Tasha any physical harm, she’d be proud of herself. She wasn’t perfect, and she needed to let Tasha be who she was, too. Shelby took several calming breaths and then a sip of ice-cold water. She said a quick prayer for patience and tried to focus on what Tasha was saying.

“. . . and then just a few weeks ago a good friend of mine surprised her husband with a small album of wedding photos that were a bit risqué. You know the usual bridal photos they take before the wedding, where the bride is wandering in a pretty field or by a pond at sunset? Well, these were just like that, but the dress was slipped down, not really showing anything, but only because her hands were placed here and here.” Tasha demonstrated, hands placed on her chest.

Shelby inhaled the next sip of ice water in surprise and started to cough. Ransom reached over, patting her on the back several times between the shoulder blades. His hands were warm and steady. Her heart pounded, not completely from inhaling water, and she quickly waved him away, still struggling to breathe.

"They—they were nude bridal shots?" she choked out.

"Of course not! That would be sleazy. These were very classy, very nicely done. I especially liked the one where she was looking over her shoulder, with a well-placed—"

"You *saw* the photos?" Carl's eyebrows had risen to his hairline.

"She shared them with me because she thought I might like to incorporate them into my own plans," Tasha said defensively. "As I said, they're very classy."

Shelby burst out laughing at Ransom's expression. He looked faintly scornful, but not as horrified as a man should be when he finds out his fiancée is planning to pose without her wedding dress. Who were these crazy people and why was she having dinner with them? She was at such a loss, she was having trouble finding words.

"Maybe . . . maybe that would turn out really nice. But you may want to make sure the negatives are part of the package. Or the digital equivalent. I could see some crazy photographer storing piles of naked-bride photos for his own collection," Carl said.

"Oh, what would they want with someone else's pictures? No, I think it's a wonderful idea, and such a sweet gift for her husband. I haven't heard how he liked them yet." Tasha flipped her hair over her shoulder again and smiled.

Shelby was so relieved to see their waiter approaching that she quickly laid her silverware across her plate.

The waiter asked if they would like to see the dessert menu, but they shook their heads.

"I guess not. It seems as if we're ready to return to the real world, sadly." With that Ransom looked directly at Shelby and smiled, a slow, warm smile. The noise of the restaurant seemed to recede and Shelby fought to stay focused. He looked completely different when he was not scowling. His eyes seemed so much bluer, with specks of gold in the centers.

The waiter returned quickly with Ransom's card and the receipt.

Carl said, "Well, shall we go?" He scooted Tasha's chair back as she struggled out from under the tablecloth. Shelby followed silently behind them, aware of Ransom's quiet presence at the end of their strange little troupe.

Outside the restaurant Shelby breathed in the cool air, closing her eyes for just a second.

"I smell spring, almost," Carl said.

“I smell rain.” Shelby scanned the dark sky, but the streetlights made it impossible to tell if there were any clouds.

“We’ll give you a ride home. Come on.” Ransom started, Tasha beside him, in the direction of the parking lot.

“No, no thank you. I don’t live that far away. Just a few blocks.” Shelby pointed in the other direction, behind her.

“You can’t walk home in the dark. It’s late, it’s not safe,” Ransom called.

Shelby stood stubbornly on the sidewalk. Her Southern genes were refusing to let her turn around and walk in the other direction. As if to seal her fate, large drops began to fall, spattering the sidewalk.

Ransom glanced over his shoulder and waved her on, smiling. Carl was politely waiting, unwilling to leave her alone in front of the restaurant. Shelby sighed, shrugged and fell into step next to him as they trudged after Ransom and Tasha.

A cream-colored SUV beeped and flashed its lights as they drew nearer to the parking lot. Shelby felt a flash of heat spread over her face as she remembered the night of the ice storm. And the woman calling his cell at midnight must have been Tasha.

*Elizabeth had never been more at a loss to make her feelings appear what they were not.*

*—PRIDE AND PREJUDICE*

# CHAPTER TWENTY-THREE

"You'd better sit up front. Tasha and I are headed over to Angeline's to meet some friends for drinks. Ransom's gonna be a good boy and head home," Carl said, deftly maneuvering himself between the two women and effectively herding Tasha to the backseat. Shelby was certain she saw a flash of resentment on the young woman's pretty features and groaned inwardly.

Sliding into the leather seat, Shelby was thankful for the darkness. She was painfully aware of how close Ransom was in the driver's seat. He remained as silent as a prisoner of war while Tasha rattled on in the back, unwilling to be both out of sight and out of mind.

As they pulled up outside Angeline's, Carl slid out, saying, "It was real nice to meet you, Shelby. I'm sure I'll be seeing you again. Later, Ransom." Tasha was already halfway to the open door, the live music spilling out onto the sidewalk.

Ransom turned back into traffic. “You’ll have to give me directions.”

“You’ll want to turn right on McClellan Avenue. It’s about five blocks down. Winter Street.” Shelby felt the hum of the engine through the seat and wondered what kind of music he had on his stereo. As if he’d read her mind, he switched on the radio, and hip-hop music blared from the speakers. Shelby felt as if her eyes were going to bug out of her head as the heavy bass filled the confined space.

“Sorry, let me just—jeez.” Ransom struggled to get the stereo under control and focus on the red light coming up.

Shelby reached over and lowered the volume until the windows stopped vibrating. “That’s a nice stereo system.” Even if he did listen to junk.

“Sorry again. Carl borrowed my car earlier and he must have been exploring the music options.” Ransom shook his head and chose another station. A simple melody wound softly from the speakers near their feet.

“I wondered.” Shelby laughed. “You didn’t seem quite the type to get jiggy with it.”

Ransom grunted, checking the rearview mirror before changing lanes. “No, definitely not real jiggy, as you say.”

A group of students wandered through the crosswalk in front of their car. She could hear their excited voices even though the windows were up. She stared out the window as if looking for answers in the darkness. "I'm sorry if I made Carl uncomfortable at dinner. It's difficult for me to let go of an argument."

"Please don't apologize. It was the best dinner conversation I've had in a month." A warm chuckle filled the space between them. "It sure beats wedding chatter any day."

"I'm sure it gets old, but a lot of women become obsessed with wedding details." Shelby tried to empathize, but she wanted to grab him by the front of his shirt and shake him. Why would he marry a woman like that? And why did she even care? Like a pendulum, she swung between irritation at him and frustration with herself.

"*Obsess* is an understatement," Ransom said drily. He turned right on McClellan and Shelby said, "There, it's the little white house on the left, picket fence, magnolia tree, cat in the window." The porch light was on, and as usual a furry shape was sitting in the front window, waiting for her return. Shelby hoped that Rebecca had made some chamomile tea in the special pot she'd brought back from England. A hot cup of tea would be the perfect end to the weird little evening.

"Is that the attack cat?" he asked, nodding at Sirocco's dark form.

"No, that's Rebecca. I'm real progressive, you know."

Ransom snorted. "Tasha's not the first, and she won't be the last, to say that type of thing."

So Tasha's bigotry wasn't new. Shelby was mystified that Ransom could stand listening to it, attaching himself to her, looking toward a future of living with it. She said nothing, hating her own cowardice and the feelings that rioted inside her.

"What's the kitty's name again?"

"Sirocco."

"Isn't that a sort of warm ocean breeze?" Ransom glanced at Shelby quizzically as he turned off the engine.

"Well, my friends gave her to me when they moved away, and her name comes from . . . See, she had a slight intestinal problem in her kitten-hood."

He let out a bark of laughter.

"It's all fixed," Shelby said reassuringly. "She needs special food, but there's no reason to fear her now."

"Good to know." He grinned and hopped out.

She grabbed her purse and opened her door to find him waiting on the other side, helping her out of the high vehicle. They'd hardly reached the front door before it swung open. "Come on in, you two. How was dinner? Where's Tasha?" Rebecca peered behind Ransom, as if the rail-thin woman could be hiding behind the porch post.

"Tasha and Carl—that's his cousin—went on

somewhere for drinks. Ransom was just bringing me home." Shelby turned to him and said quickly, "Thanks again for the dinner and—"

"Come on in, I just made some tea," Rebecca interrupted, waving Ransom through the door. Shelby stood, stunned, as he accepted warmly. He settled into their couch and Sirocco came to inspect him, bushy tail swishing curiously. Rebecca bustled around, handing out tea mugs and making small talk. Shelby tried to catch her eye, but her roommate was clearly refusing to look at her.

Shelby excused herself, slouched into the bathroom and stared at her reflection in the old built-in medicine-cabinet mirror. Wild curls escaped her ponytail and framed her face. A delicate necklace of gold glinted in the light, and she touched the small cross at the base of her throat. Feelings rioted around in her, so many feelings she was having trouble even identifying them all. She squeezed her eyes shut and tried to calm her nerves. She splashed cold water on her flushed cheeks and wished she could go to her room and hide. What was Rebecca doing? Shelby patted her face dry and then froze, remembering what Ransom had said when she'd introduced them at the Daily Grind. Rebecca had run in, late from a phone call with Carlisle Roundtree. He was the editor of a big comparative-literature journal and Ransom's old roommate. Rebecca always knew how to play her cards right. Clever, clever girl.

They were already conversationally midstream when Shelby returned. Curling up in the armchair across the living room from Ransom with a hot mug of tea, she listened to the easy flow of small talk between them. Sirocco claimed her rightful place on her lap, and Shelby ran her fingers through her soft fur, feeling the vibrations of the cat's rib cage as she purred.

"And thank you for rescuing my roomie. I would have had to learn to cook if she'd frozen to death on the side of the road," Rebecca said.

"There was no danger of that—" Shelby started.

"She really wasn't in any—" Ransom broke off as they both spoke at once.

"—happening. My car was fine, I was just waiting it out." Sirocco purred and stretched her claws. Shelby chewed her lip for a moment. She sounded so ungrateful. "But she's right. Thank you, again."

"You're welcome," he said simply. "You're both up for tenure?" he asked, turning to Rebecca.

"Right, and both nervous wrecks about getting some new articles published," she said in an off-hand tone.

"The year I was tenured was probably one of the most stressful periods in my life," he said, nodding.

"Well, Shelby isn't going to have any problem,

just as soon as she solves her little mystery. That paper she's working on is going to blow their socks off." Rebecca winked at her over her mug.

"Aha, nothing better than a little mystery." His eyes darkened with interest.

Shelby felt her cheeks grow warm under his gaze. "I want to find out the identity of someone. Susanna Caldwell uses initials for her schools' benefactor. I'm sure you noticed that in the papers I loaned you."

"I did, actually. I think naming that benefactor would make a great paper. And I understand the appeal of a mystery. You think that clue is going to be in the next letter, the next stack of records? But a lot was lost, forever. Do you have any ideas at all who it might be?"

"Not really. A man, wealthy, white. That's about it. None of her correspondents mention him, and she names him only in her diary and four letters. None of her friends have those initials, and none of the big givers of the time that we know of would match. It's just really odd." Shelby lapsed into troubled silence. She wondered if Susanna Caldwell had ever written the name down at all. Maybe she took the secret to her grave more than a hundred years before.

"You could probably publish the paper without the name," Ransom said.

"It would be such a better paper with the name,

that's all. I hate to give up." Shelby shrugged, running her hands through Sirocco's fur.

"Obstinate, headstrong girl." Ransom chuckled. "Just finish it and submit it. The tenure—" He stopped midsentence as Rebecca gasped, eyes wide.

"Did you—Was that a quote from *Pride and Prejudice*?"

He blinked. "Sure, the heart of the book is the scene with Lady Catherine, when she's attempting to bully Elizabeth into refusing Darcy's offer of marriage. What?" He cocked his head and regarded Rebecca in amusement. "Men like Austen, too."

Tears were leaking from Rebecca's eyes as she rocked with laughter. "No, no, men do not like Austen!"

"Well, I'm here to tell you that we do. Don't be sexist." His bright blue eyes crinkled with laughter.

Rebecca was struggling to control her giggles. Every time she glanced at Shelby, she started again, and there was no way she could explain why Fielding's quoting Austen was quite so funny.

"I think what she's laughing about is how you dropped it into the conversation, so naturally," Shelby hastened to explain, while inside she was cringing.

"Well, now that I've given her the giggles, I should get home." Ransom smiled, bemused, and crossed the room to Shelby. "Thank you for coming to dinner."

Shelby started to stand up but he waved her back down. "Don't dislodge the cat, she's happy there. See you at work."

Rebecca had recovered enough from her giggles to open the door. "Have a good night!" she said, waving merrily.

"You're awful," Shelby hissed, the moment they heard his car engine start up.

"I couldn't help it! Nobody could have. Our Darcy quoted *Pride and Prejudice* to you! What are the odds of that?"

Shelby sulked for a moment, then let out an exasperated breath. "He must have thought you were having a mental breakdown."

"Well, I couldn't exactly explain, could I?" Rebecca giggled a little and gathered up their mugs. "You have to tell me everything that happened at dinner before I go to bed or I won't be able to sleep from curiosity."

"Pure insanity. His fiancée is a bridezilla, and the only time she stopped insulting me about my age and unmarried status was when she was giving me tips on how to adopt a nice white baby and how to pick an engagement ring, not that I'd ever be lucky enough to get one." As they washed and dried the mugs, Shelby gave a condensed version, highlighting Tasha's wedding mania, including how she refused to wear Ransom's family heirloom ring because it didn't match, and noting Carl's pleasant nature, but skipping over the comments on Rebecca herself. No sense spreading the meanness around.

Rebecca yawned and stood up from their little kitchen table. "How did you get roped into that anyway?"

Shelby thought back to Ransom's whispered plea and felt herself start to blush. "He was desperate for some distraction from wedding chatter, I guess," she said quickly. She nudged Sirocco out of her path and stretched. "I better get to bed or I'll be a wreck in the morning. Thanks for the tea, even if you did invite him in without asking." She playfully punched Rebecca's shoulder.

"Ow, housemate abuse! I couldn't resist. If he has any pull with Carlisle, then I need to be as friendly as possible."

"And who cares about me, right?"

"Exactly. It's tenure, baby. All's fair in love and war . . . and academic pursuits of a professional nature." Rebecca draped an arm over Shelby's shoulders. "It wasn't so bad, was it? I'm sorry I didn't ask first, but you'd just had dinner with him. What's wrong with a little tea and small talk?"

Shelby sighed and smiled. "Nothing, you're right. And he didn't stay long at all."

Later that night, as she slipped down into sleep

like falling underwater, Shelby struggled to banish visions of Ransom seated on their maroon couch, mercurial emotions playing over his features, eyes dark and thoughtful.

Ransom wandered down the flagstone path to the home he was renting from the college, his gaze unfocused. Tonight was the most fun he'd had in a long time. An image flashed in his mind's eye of Shelby's furious expression, words clever and sharp. A shiver of unease went up his spine. He thought of the years he'd spent dating nice, safe women. Women who said one thing but did another. The kind who never argued and were happiest when shopping.

He jammed his key in the old lock of the heavy oak front door. He would never let another woman into his heart as he had Lili. It was better that way. And he was determined to remember that.

*I understood there were some very strong objections against the lady.*

—COLONEL FITZWILLIAM

# CHAPTER TWENTY-FOUR

"Katie, you promise you'll have the first draft in by the end of the month?" Shelby dropped her head onto her hand and closed her eyes. She hated these types of calls. Not that she'd ever had to make them before. Nagging her graduate student to actually turn in the work she needed for her degree wasn't something she'd ever experienced before this year.

"Sure, right." Katie sounded distracted, distant. "I'm just polishing it up. I want it to be as clean as possible when you read it over the first time."

"Can you give me some sort of outline? Then I can start making notes while you're polishing." Shelby had a bad feeling that Katie wasn't polishing anything but was frantically writing a first draft.

"No, no. My draft is just a jumble of notes. I mean, I can read it, but it wouldn't make any sense to you." Her voice held a note of panic. "Anyway, I have to go. But I'll see you in a little bit."

"By the end of the month. You promise? We're months overdue here. I'll have to notify the head of the department if we don't make some progress." Shelby said it as gently as possible, but there was no getting around the reality.

"Sure. I'll write it down and sign it. It can be like a contract." Katie sounded a bit sarcastic. "I'll drop it off in the office."

"Okay." A signed note wasn't going to help much if she never turned in any work. "And, Katie, if you ever need help, with anything, even if it's outside of class, I'm here for you. Even just to talk. I'd be glad to."

"I've got to go." Katie disconnected and nothing but silence was left at the other end.

Shelby placed the receiver down and stared at her papers. Something bad was happening to one of her best graduate students, but if she wouldn't confide in Shelby, she could do nothing. She said a small prayer for Katie, then tried to put it all out of her mind.

"I want to wear something I'm comfortable in, otherwise I'll spend the whole evening tugging at my neckline and checking my hem." The week had progressed steadily until Shelby could no longer deny that she needed to prepare for Margaret Greathouse's fund-raising party. Waiting until a few hours before should have kept her mind off the task, but somehow she felt more nervous than ever.

"All right, but at least let me pick the shoes. You really have the most boring collection of footwear on the planet," Rebecca said.

"You don't even want me to go, so why the big deal over what I wear?"

"Call it a matter of honor. You can't expect me to let you walk into a room full of vipers while wearing ugly shoes."

Shelby snorted. "Vipers. Really that's very dramatic. They're going to be old and stuffy and probably a little snobbish, but nothing I haven't seen before. Remember, I've been toted around to these parties since I was fifteen."

"Maybe you know what you're doing, but I'm still picking the shoes." Rebecca closed the discussion by pulling boxes from her large closet. Her room was immaculately clean, the polar opposite of Shelby's chaos. The soft gray silk bedspread was wrinkle-free, and throw pillows were artfully arranged across the head. Her research papers were organized in white folders, and reference books were shelved alphabetically on custom-made, floor-to-ceiling bookcases. A black-lacquered corner desk waited, the top clear of bric-a-brac and dust. A bright red Mac laptop was the only focal point. As much as Rebecca loved color in her wardrobe, her work area was nearly monochromatic.

"Don't you want to know what I'm wearing?" Shelby asked, nervously peering over Rebecca's shoulder.

"Oh, well, I assumed that old navy one . . . again." Rebecca's head was buried in the back of the closet and her voice came out muffled. "I have some great peep-toe pumps in here somewhere."

"I was thinking about that green dress Ellie gave me."

Rebecca pulled her head out of the closet and stared at her for a moment.

"You know, that one with the sequined crisscross right here." Shelby drew a line from between her breasts to her hips on either side.

"Well, this is a switch. You told me there was never going to be any place you could wear that dress, it was just too . . . 'flashy' I think was the word you used."

Shelby felt herself blush a little and raised her chin. "Better late than never, right? And if I'm going to make an impression, I better look the part."

Rebecca grinned. "I definitely have the shoes to go with that dress. Hang on a second." Her head disappeared again and she finally emerged with a box. She opened it and folded back the tissue to reveal emerald-green sandals with a perfect kitten heel. A row of glass jewels shaped like strands of ivy shone at the toes.

"Wow," breathed Shelby. "Those are works of

art." She gingerly removed one shoe and put it on. The shoe sparkled even in the overhead light. "I would never have the courage to wear this outfit for a date. It's so obvious."

"Now, as your friend, I have to say this." Rebecca sat on the edge of her bed, holding the shoe box. Her face was set and grim.

Shelby paused in the examination of her foot, a delicate strap crossing one slim ankle. "What now? You know something I don't? What new gossip have you heard?"

"No, nothing like that. And it's totally your business, but you've already admitted, well, that you think he's pretty cute. . . ."

Shelby straightened up. "Spit it out."

Rebecca took a deep breath. "I just don't want you to get hurt. Not academically . . . but romantically. I'm afraid you might fall in love with him." She shrugged apologetically and waited for the explosion.

Sitting down next to Rebecca, Shelby carefully unfastened the strap on the sandal. She let her hair fall across her face, hiding her churning emotions. When she straightened up, she said, "Thank you. Only a good friend would care enough to say that. I'm not very experienced, and the right man, or the wrong man, might break my heart into pieces." She handed the sandal to Rebecca to put in the box with its mate. "But I wouldn't go to this party if I didn't think I could handle it . . . or him."

She studied the floor. "I feel perfectly comfortable admitting this, since he's engaged and therefore totally off-limits . . . but when I see him across a room, I do think, 'There's a handsome man,' like everybody else does. But when he's *near* me . . ."

Rebecca's eyebrows were raised, a grin slowly spreading over her face.

"Stop that. As I was saying, when he's near enough to smell, I feel the strangest sensation, like electricity. My fingers tingle. It's really odd . . . and annoying. The more I try to keep myself from reacting, the worse it gets. I feel the heat spread out from my chest, down my arms." Shelby stared down at her bare toes.

"So, you get a hot flash and your hands go numb? Sometimes I get that feeling when I open my credit card bill."

"Be serious. I'm trying to be objective about this," Shelby said, glaring.

"Fine, you get all hot and tingly? Hm." Rebecca pretended to contemplate Shelby's revelation, with one finger pressed to her chin.

"You make it sound so improper. I'm sure dear Jane has a better phrase or two," Shelby retorted.

"No, Austen didn't describe much of that. That was for the reader to infer." Rebecca nodded, eyes wary. "Anyway, I get it. I have to say, I knew somebody would float your boat eventually. I just didn't think it would be Ransom Fielding."

"Not a big deal. Just pheromones, remember?"

"Right. But in the back of my mind I always wondered if you preferred books to people."

Shelby rolled her eyes. "Pot, meet kettle."

"No, I do love books, it's true! But next to a real live person, I'd probably choose the person." Rebecca replaced the last shoe box in the closet. "Actually, now that Mr. Miami finally called me, that's probably a definite."

"It's going that well, huh?" Shelby grinned over at her roommate, noticing once again how happy she looked.

"He's funny and faithful and smart, too. Not just geek-squad smart, either." Rebecca chuckled to herself. "He wrote a poem about me and set it to 'The Raven' by Poe. I couldn't stop laughing while he was reading it."

Shelby blinked. "That crazy poem with the bird that repeats the same word over and over?" Somehow, Poe just didn't fit her definition of romantic *or* humorous.

Rebecca laughed, shaking her head. "You'd have to hear it, really. I was dying." She gave Shelby a quick squeeze around the shoulders. "Anyway, we've still got work to do. And now for your hair . . ."

Two hours later, Shelby stood in their living room. Her normally curly hair had been smoothed back into a fancy chignon, kept in place with several delicate pins, a few tendrils loose about her face. A large, simply set moonstone pendant on a silver chain rested against her throat. Smoky-gray eyeliner made her eyes look even larger, and the green dress brought out their flecks of gold. She'd managed to get a lot of the paint from under her nails, and with a fresh coat of polish, her hands didn't at all look as if she'd spent the morning painting. Her arms felt uncomfortably bare and she nervously checked the straps over her shoulders one more time.

"Don't fidget, it ruins the effect," Rebecca reminded her. "You have to wear it with confidence."

"I'd feel a lot more confident if I didn't feel so naked." Shelby smoothed her hands down the skirt. The silky material gave more than a hint of the curves they covered.

"You have beautiful legs. And those perfect ankles were made to wear sandals like these every day. I don't know why you always want to wear pants." Rebecca tilted her head and assessed Shelby's lower half.

"Because I have to walk around in front of a class full of students and I don't want to worry about my skirt being tucked into my underwear, that's why," Shelby retorted.

"A totally unreasonable fear, if you ask me." Rebecca picked a piece of lint off the skirt and sniffed the air. "You smell incredible. What is that?"

"You know Mama is always giving me perfume. I thought I would crack open one for the occasion." Actually, Shelby had opened about ten bottles of expensive perfume her mother had given her over the past few years and selected the one she thought was the least intrusive. They had to ride together in the car, so nothing too heavy or sweet.

Rebecca inspected Shelby's hair one more time. "If these jeweled bobby pins start to come loose, don't try to put them back in. You'll ruin the shape of the bun. Just try to slide them out and tuck them in your purse."

"Are you saying I have to worry about the hair, too?"

"I'm just saying 'in case,' that's all. No stress!" Rebecca backed up with her hands out, a big grin on her face. "I have to say, this is probably my best work yet, by far."

"Jane Austen would be so proud. Another girl trussed up for a fancy party."

"On the contrary, she'd be horrified. All that skin. You'd need about another five yards of material."

At that moment the doorbell sounded. Shelby grabbed Rebecca's hand, a panicked look in her eyes.

"I've changed my mind," she hissed. "Tell him I'm sick!"

"Not a chance." Rebecca gently led Shelby to the door. "It's going to be amazing. You're going to meet tons of important people and get an editor interested in your paper and whirl around looking gorgeous and everyone will know your name by the time the evening's over."

Shelby took a deep breath. "And if you're wrong?"

"Then we'll cry about it over ice cream afterward," Rebecca whispered, and stepped back as Shelby opened the door.

Ransom stood with his hand raised, as if he were just about to ring the bell again. His eyes opened wide in surprise, taking it all in, from the perfect tendrils falling about her face to the dress that hugged her figure to her matching sandals that revealed perfectly manicured toes.

"Um, Shelby, I hope I'm—Hi, Rebecca. It's—am I late?"

It was such an odd statement that for a moment Shelby stared, speechless.

He cleared his throat and frowned.

"Would you like to come in?" Shelby said politely. He looked about the same as the last time she'd seen him, and that was stunningly handsome. The party was formal wear only, but his tuxedo was several steps above what Shelby considered the usual tux. It was fine black wool, clearly cut to measure. The gray, pin-striped vest covered most of his white shirt and matched the style of his black jacket, cut long. It wasn't modern or retro. It was timeless.

For just a moment, Shelby saw Darcy.

Then as if he felt uncomfortable under her scrutiny, Ransom adjusted his cuffs. She blinked, and Darcy had disappeared.

"Thank you," he said, and she stepped aside. Suddenly it seemed the living room was half the size it had been before. He stood awkwardly near their old red velvet couch, and Shelby waved him to a seat. He sat at one end, his eyes following her as she walked to the love seat.

"Can I get you a drink, Ransom? We have iced tea, water, soda, some juice," Rebecca offered. Shelby smiled at Rebecca's effortless hospitality. She could put anyone at ease.

"No, no." Ransom abruptly stood. "Thank you, but we should be going."

"Sure. Let me get my purse." Shelby grabbed it off the table as Ransom headed for the door. Rebecca gave her a questioning stare and Shelby shrugged in response. Maybe he liked to be on time.

To her relief, the SUV had been replaced by a sleek black Saab. She hadn't thought of trying to hop into the higher vehicle until that moment and sent a thankful prayer skyward. Crossing the porch, she caught the toe of her sandal on the step and Ransom's hand shot out to steady her.

"I'm not used to these, I guess." She peered down at her sandal. "I don't think it hurt anything." His hand still gripped hers and she felt electricity pass through her. Breathlessly, she tried to focus on where she was walking while gently removing her hand.

"You're worried about the shoe? You could have broken your leg." He glanced down and Shelby swore she could feel the path of his gaze.

"They're Rebecca's. She has so many that she probably wouldn't cry if I brought it back with a strap broken, but I don't want her to regret loaning me the pair."

"And the dress?" he asked lightly, glancing over as he opened the car door.

Shelby's face turned pink. "It's mine, actually." No reason to be embarrassed. It was a little shorter than she was used to, and the bodice was very fitted, but it covered everything well enough. She lifted her chin and tried to remember Rebecca's advice about not fidgeting.

Sliding into the black leather seat, she adjusted the dress fabric carefully, making sure her skirt stayed close to her legs. He settled in behind the wheel and smoothly pulled away from the curb.

"It's very nice," he said simply. Silence descended heavily into the small space.

*Oh, please, don't let us ride there in awkward silence,* Shelby thought desperately. *I'd rather argue the whole way.*

*He was struggling for the appearance of composure, and would not open his lips till he believed himself to have attained it.*

*—PRIDE AND PREJUDICE*

# CHAPTER TWENTY-FIVE

"Thank you for coming. This night should be a lot more fun than it usually is." Ransom smiled and she was suddenly aware of how close they were in the cockpit of the car.

"Well, don't thank me yet. I could turn out to be a total bore. Maybe I can rustle up some long story about my last dental appointment." She kept her voice light and tried not to look directly at him. She could smell what she was beginning to think of as "his" scent and was tempted to inhale deeply.

"I don't think you could be boring if you tried." He sounded serious and Shelby longed to peek at his face to see if he was teasing her. She pretended to examine her nails for rough edges and wondered why Tasha wasn't able to go.

"I've seen pictures of Collier House. It has a fascinating history. I think General Ewell stayed there after he lost a leg at Second Manassas." When in doubt, talk about history. She felt herself relaxing a little.

“He did. Old Baldy was wounded eight times and came to recuperate at Collier House twice. I’ve never found the place that soothing, personally.” Ransom’s mouth quirked up on one side.

“Perhaps you need to lose a limb first.” She couldn’t imagine wanting to spend much time around Margaret Greathouse. Especially as an invalid. “Since your aunt lives there, she probably doesn’t keep it open to the public year-round, right?”

“A few times a year my aunt lets tours go through, mostly in the main house and the preserved outbuildings. Being on the Historical Register helps keep the developers at bay, but there are still a few that try to convince her to sell.”

David Bishop’s beach houses flashed through her mind. “I’ve met someone like that. He asks them to name a price and hints that it will be refurbished and they’ll fight to get it on the register. Once the deal is done, then they do what they want, usually by replacing all of the original fixtures and gutting the inside. At the worst they just tear it down and build something else on the site.”

“Disgusting. But Aunt Margaret is more than a match for them. I witnessed some poor guy after he’d spent ten minutes on the receiving end of her wrath. He could hardly talk straight.”

Shelby shifted uncomfortably. If it was anything

close to what her nephew could do with a book review, she knew exactly how that man had felt. She turned her head and watched their neighborhood slide away.

"Greek Revival architecture would be difficult to work with, those pillars and long windows. I don't know why they would bother," Shelby said.

"Probably just making offers for some Wall Street type who wants a vacation home. Federal style has become really popular lately in subdivisions. Up in New Haven they have whole neighborhoods that look like groups of tiny plantation homes, without the land, of course, or any kind of yard."

"Growing up celebrating Christmas at a place like Collier House must influence your tastes. It's hard to have enjoyed a stay in a real historic home and appreciate any kind of imitation."

Ransom glanced at her in surprise. "I didn't visit until I was an adult. My aunt and my mother never got along. I was raised at Bellepointe, in Natchez, at my father's family's estate."

Shelby's mouth fell open, and she struggled to cover her surprise. Bellepointe was one of the most beautiful plantation homes to survive the war.

Shelby frantically searched her memory for any tidbits that Rebecca had passed on—and remembered nothing. She cursed her own failure to research his family. *Five minutes on Google and you wouldn't seem quite so out of the loop,* she chided herself.

"My mother had a falling out with her family sometime after she married my father. When my parents divorced, she decided that the South was the worst place to raise a child when you're trying to live in the modern world. I'd have to agree with her."

Shelby almost choked. She clenched her teeth until the urge to start a fight had passed. So what if the man didn't want to raise children in the South? Tasha looked as if she would be more than happy up in Connecticut.

"Do you visit Bellepointe very often?" Shelby had an idea of it as an impressive, pale stone structure with a sloping roof. The original property had tens of thousands of acres but was a quarter the size now.

Ransom was quiet for a moment. "He sold the place when I was an undergraduate. I approached the owners a few years ago, hoping they would be interested in selling, but they're happy with it." His eyes were tight and his lips were a grim line. "They've made a very successful business there. It's a top-rated inn with a five-star restaurant. The weddings are booked a year in advance. They put in an Olympic-sized pool at the back and exercise gym in the basement." He sighed. "At least they preserved the old greenhouse. My grandfather and I spent hours there every day in the spring and fall. He had an award-winning African-violet collection. It will always be home to me, even if I can't go back."

Shelby dared a glance at him. The shadow of pain that flickered behind his eyes made her heart twist in her chest. "I'm sorry. My own family home was built around the turn of the century and it gives me comfort to know that three generations of Roswells have raised their children there."

"Do you have older siblings? Who will it pass to?" He checked the rearview mirror and switched lanes. As they passed a classic forties red Ford, Shelby returned the smile of a thin, elderly man in a cowboy hat.

"I'm the oldest by eight years. We haven't discussed it much, but it seems my two younger sisters aren't nearly as interested in the old place as I am. One of them has said she'd just sell it to the highest bidder, and the other admits that she detests all the old wallpaper and fixtures and would renovate it into something unrecognizable. I know it's been hard for my parents to keep up with it lately. You have to be a gardener, plumber, carpenter, reupholsterer and refinisher all in one."

Ransom chuckled and Shelby warmed to the sound. Rebecca would be so proud. They weren't arguing one bit.

"I've been trying my hand at carpentry, and it

can be a test of wills. You accidentally split a prime piece of oak while putting on the last touches and you can't fix that. It's taught me some patience, for sure. Some things can't be hurried."

"My aunt Junetta is always trying out new hobbies. She took a class on woodworking and loved it."

"The same aunt you were visiting before the ice storm?" He glanced over, his lips touched by a smile.

"Right. We spend a lot of time together, when we can. She's the most like me, or maybe I'm the most like her." Shelby laughed, thinking of her aunt's opinionated ways. "We like to cook . . . cook and talk."

"Ah, cooking and gossiping, that's a lethal combination."

"No, she doesn't believe in gossip, it's against her faith. We do talk, but mostly about our plans, things we could do, or change, if we could. I've had bigger brainstorms in her kitchen, kneading pie dough, than anywhere near Midlands." Shelby paused, considering. "And when I think of home, I think of her."

"She sounds like a wonderful woman," he said, his voice soft.

Shelby jumped when her purse vibrated on her lap. Frowning, she opened the green silk clutch and peeked at her phone. "Excuse me," Shelby muttered, and flipped it open.

Hope everything goes well! Remember, no arguing!

Shelby flushed and typed back:

Go away, we're conversing.

She couldn't believe Rebecca's nerve, but had to smile. She snapped the phone closed and returned it to her purse.

"Sorry about that. I think it's horrible manners when people text during a conversation."

"But you just did." He raised his eyebrows. "At least you have it set on stun."

"It was just Rebecca reminding me not to argue with you." Shelby felt obligated to share the contents of the text so that he wouldn't think they were discussing him. Well, they were, but not in a bad way.

He laughed, so long and so loudly that Shelby started to protest.

"It's not that funny," she said, frowning.

"Oh, yes, it is. One, your roommate knows you so well that she's giving you advice by text while you're on your date. Two, then you shared that advice with me, your date." He glanced over his shoulder and then quickly passed a slower vehicle.

"I can certainly feel free to share it with you since you're not really my date."

"I'm not?" He turned to look at her now, brows

knitted together. "I thought that was the definition of a date, when two people attend a social function together. They arrive together, spend a majority of the time at the function together, and leave together. Unless you're planning on disappearing once we arrive and going home with someone else?"

His tone was still light but Shelby blushed deeply. "No, I wasn't. But you can't say we're on a date, can you? That implies something else entirely."

"How so?"

He looked her in the eyes and Shelby felt as if the logic had fallen out of the conversation. How to explain that they weren't on a date because that implied romance? He was engaged and she was just along to make some social connections.

"I thought we agreed . . . I thought you understood that I was coming along because . . ."

"You agreed to come because you think it will raise your social standing. I understand. And I understood when you accepted." Shelby saw an emotion flicker in his eyes, and then it was gone. "I will do my utmost best to introduce you to anyone and everyone that could further your career." He bowed his head briefly in mock gentility. "I must add that I think you have done very well for yourself without any pandering. There may not be any benefit from this outing at all."

Shelby chewed on one nail and considered that

for a moment. "Rebecca doesn't approve. She thinks this could backfire and I could be in a worse position than I am now."

He glanced at her sharply. "In what way?"

"Well, I do have a habit of speaking my mind, and if I manage to offend someone influential"—*more influential than you,* she thought—"someone who might have helped me get published, then I'll be in a deeper hole. Deeper than if I had just stayed home and submitted my papers the traditional way."

"So, your outspokenness is in private as well as public? At a small party as well as, say, in front of hundreds of people?" He wasn't smiling, but Shelby felt laughter lurking under the surface of his words.

"You know," she sighed, "I've been meaning to say—"

"Oh, don't take it back, please. It is truly one of the few moments that I will never forget. More than ten years of teaching and they all start to blend together."

"I wasn't going to take it back. I think you showed sloppy research. Unless you have someone else do your research, and in that case you probably should fire them immediately."

"Excuse me?" He looked as if he'd been slapped. "I do all my own research, thank you. And Beverly spent time in Oxford in his twenties, so I wasn't so far off."

"Now you're making excuses. Time there in his twenties equals a hometown?"

His gaze stayed on the road ahead but his eyes narrowed. Shelby noticed the speedometer creeping higher.

"I see your point. I admit I was wrong on the exact town, but it was a tiny detail."

She gasped. "A tiny detail? Forget that Flea Bite Creek is my hometown, just for a moment. As historians, can we say anything is just a 'tiny detail'? It *all* matters. Otherwise we should just throw up our hands and start writing fiction."

He sighed deeply. "Fine, I agree. But maybe next time you can avoid barging into my class to correct me." He seemed to consider the road ahead of them for a bit. His face was emotionless and he calmly flicked the setting on the air-conditioning to high. "Attempting to undermine my authority was a petty way to get revenge for that review."

Shelby opened her mouth, shut it again. Revenge? "That's not what I was doing. Look, I don't how it is at Yale, but we're a little more relaxed here. We don't draw and quarter the kids for bad classroom etiquette." She clenched her hands in her lap, wondering if this was the moment when they started yelling at each other and she had to walk home.

He turned and held her gaze for a few powerfully charged seconds. Then he seemed to come to a decision. “I’m sorry. That’s not who you are, is it? Someone who plots her revenge, I mean. And as for the kid, I may have overreacted,” he said simply.

All the words she had been preparing to say slipped away. “Oh. Well, we all make mistakes. I suppose I could have had a word with you after class.”

He glanced at her, his expression inscrutable. “I’ve heard through the grapevine that some of the students think we planned it, sort of an opening-day skit.”

She started to laugh. “Excellent. One of those times that truth is stranger than fiction? Who would think two professors would dislike each other enough to air their grievances in front of a whole class?”

“Yes, exactly. Let’s just hope it was a onetime performance.” He turned to her, laughing. That perfect combination of dark brows and blue eyes, the thick hair that curled just slightly over his collar, the strong jaw and the shadow where he shaved—it broke over her with a force that made her breath catch. Her heart was beating so fast that she thought he might be able to hear it. Shelby realized she had forgotten her resolution to avoid looking directly into his face. She swallowed and quickly turned her head, pretending to look out the window at the scenery speeding by. He was engaged, that was what mattered.

"Speaking of differences between the universities, why are you at Midlands?"

"Is there something wrong with my school?" Her tone was a warning he seemed to miss, or to ignore.

"You know Finch doesn't like you. You said you went to grad school here and so he was probably your adviser?" She didn't answer and he continued, "Sort of like in the Bible where it says a prophet doesn't get any respect in his own lands, I think grad students should move on when they get their degrees. You'll always be subpar to him."

Her heart continued to beat a staccato rhythm, but now it wasn't from Ransom's good looks. Shelby was so angry she felt tears prick her eyes. "And you would suggest I aim *higher?* Say, Yale?"

He made a sound in his throat. "You know that's not what I meant. But change might be good for you, for your career."

Shelby gritted her teeth and reminded herself that they were only beginning the evening.

The wail of an ambulance siren cut into her thoughts. Ransom swiftly maneuvered the car to the side of the road and the ambulance sped by.

Shelby whispered a silent prayer for the poor people in need of emergency help. At the end, she raised her head and saw him glance at her.

"What did you do there?" he asked, slowly turning back onto the highway.

"What?"

"Just now, when you were very quiet."

"Oh." She felt her face warm. "My second-grade teacher taught us to say a prayer when an ambulance passes."

"And you think it helps?" His words were even but his mouth was a tight line.

"I wouldn't do it if I didn't."

There was an awkward silence. With a sinking heart, Shelby realized she had the answer to her unspoken question about faith. She felt a momentary gratefulness for Rebecca. They lived so easily together. They didn't have to explain or defend.

"My mother taught me the same thing. . . . But it's been years since I did it."

She nodded. It wasn't so unusual to lose your childhood faith. Terribly sad, but not unusual.

He continued, "I wonder if anyone said a prayer when my wife was hit by a half-ton pickup truck."

She opened her mouth, but no words could express what she felt as she watched pain flow over his features.

He ran a hand through his dark hair and let out a breath. "Sorry, I don't know why I said that."

"No, it's all right. It's a natural thing to wonder." She bit her lip, wishing she knew how much was too much, what words would bring him pain and which would comfort.

"It's been a long time since I wondered about it, really. Maybe it's being back in the South, or being near my hometown, but I've thought about her more in the past few months than I have in a long time."

"Places do bring back strong memories." Shelby paused, considering whether asking a question was wise. "Was she from around here?"

"Oxford. She sure was proud of her hometown. Fifth generation, and we thought there would be a sixth." He stared out at the roadway, face impassive.

Those words, so simply stated, cut through Shelby like a knife. How it must have felt for her parents to bury the child they thought would carry on their family's history.

"I'm sorry," she said, wishing there were something more, something real, she could offer.

He shrugged and turned with a look that seemed to say it didn't matter, that it was all in the past. But whatever he had been planning to say, he decided against it. His eyes were dark with an old sadness. "Thank you," he said, turning back to the road.

She thought of how she noticed all the subtle changes in his face, and she thought about what it might mean, and worry wrapped around her heart. She shivered, and he reached out to switch off the air conditioner.

The sign for Collier House appeared on the

side of the road. She'd been so sure she was supposed to approach this whole night with bold confi-dence, but now she wondered for just a moment if it wasn't too late to call the whole thing off.

*And this is all the reply which*
*I am to have the honor of expecting?*

—MR. DARCY

# CHAPTER TWENTY-SIX

The road to the plantation home had been paved several years ago, a simple blacktop with no painted lines. A long line of oaks sheltered travelers along nearly a mile of winding driveway, curving up around a perfectly maintained lawn of several acres.

Shelby couldn't suppress a gasp as the house came into view, situated high on a rise. The proportions alone of the enormous structure were a statement of great wealth. Wide porches wrapped around the entire first and second stories, with the third story placed squarely in the center of the building like a topping on a wedding cake. The symmetry of so many pillars, each rising from foundation to the top of the second floor, was overwhelming. Without the soft green grass of the hill and a row of mature maple trees behind the house that marked the edge of woods, the arrogance of the architecture would have been intolerable. But the gentle surroundings were the perfect complement to the stately mansion. After giving the travelers their first glimpse of Collier House, the driveway continued to curve away around the east side of the hill.

"I'll skip the valet service, if you don't mind, and park out here by the old dairy barn." Ransom turned off the main drive, and soon they were in front of a redbrick structure that looked nothing like a dairy barn at all. Graceful lines and a gabled roof made the centuries-old building seem like a transplant from the English countryside.

"Did they actually keep cows in there?"

He chuckled as he helped her step out of the low car. She carefully smoothed her bell-shaped skirt. The light breeze felt good against her flushed skin, and she hoped her hair hadn't started to make its way loose from Rebecca's creation. She glanced up and shivered. The sky had turned ominously dark.

"It was where they brought the milk and made cheeses. Now it's been refurbished as a small guesthouse."

Shelby gazed up at the main house, and from her present vantage point it seemed like a giant with its back turned. A dark thundercloud was building steadily over the house as if it were a made-to-order backdrop. A sudden niggle of nervousness went through her, and her hand touched the pins in her hair, smoothing errant strands.

"If you'd like, we can stop in the back entrance at one of the restrooms," he said.

She wondered how many times Tasha checked her outfit before their big entrances. "No, I'm fine. Just a bit nervous." She started up the path that led around to the front of Collier House. *Aunt Junetta would love his manners,* she thought. So thoughtful to offer a chance to check her makeup and hair. But there wouldn't be much she could do, other than call Rebecca to the rescue.

The row of large maple trees they had glimpsed from the driveway formed a natural break between the outbuildings and the main house. They walked beneath them in silence.

" 'I entered on the deep and woody way,' " he said softly.

"Dante's *Inferno*. Though I think the famous 'abandon all hope, ye who enter here' might be more appropriate," she said drily. A fat drop of rain landed on her bare shoulder.

"That's not very positive thinking, is it?" Ransom chuckled, thrusting his hands deep in his pockets.

"Maybe not, but it's realistic, and I'm nothing if not a realist." She wondered if her hair was going to survive until they reached the house.

"You don't strike me as a realist at all. The way you speak out when you think there's been an injustice. Those are the actions of an idealist."

He stopped for a moment and gazed up into the branches of a towering tree. "Now, who was he with? Beatrice? So, I'll be Dante and you be

Beatrice." The rain came more quickly, pattering loudly on the canopy of branches above.

"Not to be contentious, but he was with his learned guide, Virgil." Shelby suppressed a snort as an image of herself with a long white beard popped into her head. The staccato sound of the rainfall grew louder. The smell of wet rock and the thick Kentucky grass filled the air. Somewhere over the hill was a creek, and she could hear the rush of water.

"Not that I don't consider you highly educated, but you bear a greater resemblance to the angelic Beatrice at this moment." He didn't seem to notice the heavy drops landing on his shoulders and hair as he smiled down at her.

A flush of heat spread up her neck. He was standing near, and she tilted her head back as her gaze searched his face. She barely registered the rain that dripped off the branches above them. An impulse raced through her to raise her hand and trace the deep dimple that marked one of his cheeks. She struggled to focus.

"Poor Beatrice was impervious to the rain but I am not, so we'd better—" She looked up then toward the house and marveled anew. From her new perspective, the spotlights at the base of each pillar changed the house into an illuminated palace. The front door stood open, and an immaculately dressed butler stood ready to receive them.

Turning back, she was about to comment on the difference between night and day, between reality and fairy tales, when she saw his expression. His eyes seemed almost black in the dim light and the lines around his mouth deepened. A feeling of intense anticipation pulsed through her as their eyes met.

It didn't matter what he'd written about her. She didn't care if he got every fact about her hometown wrong. All the departmental drama in the world couldn't come between them. Nothing mattered except the two of them. It seemed so perfect, so right, to be standing here with him under the trees.

But it wasn't right. Tasha should be standing here, watching him lower his head, eyes locked on hers.

Shelby took an instinctive step back, feeling as if she had stepped out of the warm sun into a frigid shadow. The charged atmosphere was broken by her movement, replaced by a dull throb of energy.

Ransom shook his head as if to clear it, then offered his arm. "It's tapering off. Shall we make a run for the door?"

"Please, before my hair decides to return to its true form." She placed her hand on his arm.

He turned back to the house and the gravel crunched under their feet as they hurried to the green double doors. The pretty sandals slowed her progress and she stopped twice to remove a small stone.

The butler led them through the entryway, and a straight-backed young man appeared to take any coats or purses to the cloakroom. She wished she had brought a wrap. After the storm passed, the cool air would settle on them like a damp towel, although for the moment her skin was flushed with heat.

The highly polished granite floor echoed with each step as they entered the great room, and the enormous chandeliers sparkled with light. The windows were festooned with deep green garlands and bunches of tiny white berries, and the heady smell of jasmine mixed with the sounds of people busy in conversation.

She had never enjoyed large groups of people, and to see so many unfamiliar but exquisitely dressed people sent a thrill of panic through her. Shelby had a crazy urge to break out in laughter and she forced herself to remain calm. Ransom's arm felt tense under her hand but his face was utterly bland.

"Ransom, dear, there you are." His aunt swept through the guests as if they were sheets hung on a backyard laundry line. Margaret Greathouse wore a long, gray silk column gown with a silver-fur wrap, her hands encased in matching gloves to the elbows. Her large rings flashed in the light, and several elaborate jeweled cuffs adorned her wrists.

“Aunt Margaret.” Ransom leaned down and pecked the unnaturally smooth cheek.

Her small, dark eyes never wavered from Shelby’s face. Margaret smiled, her tiny white teeth bearing traces of coral lipstick. It reminded Shelby of a shark after a feeding frenzy. “And the girl from Flea Bite Creek, if I’m not mistaken.”

“Shelby Roswell. It’s a pleasure to finally meet you,” Shelby said, her throat almost closing around the words.

His aunt made no response. Her expression was icy.

“Ransom, you must find Arlene Tower. She’s been very anxious to clarify some points you made in that last paper. She seems to be under the impression that you believe the Southern constitution has distinct similarities to the present Republican Party line.”

“And I do. I’ll be sure to find her sometime this evening. First, we’re going to find the drinks, if you don’t mind,” he said, his expression mild.

“As you wish.” Margaret turned back to Shelby and cocked her head to one side. Her stunning silver hair looked like a cresting wave. “What an interesting choice of a dress. Are you sure you won’t be cold?” Then she smiled languidly and turned to greet another guest who had been hovering a few feet away.

Shelby resisted the sudden urge to chuck her beaded clutch at the back of Margaret’s head.

Ransom turned Shelby toward the far side of the room, where a full bar stood. "Well, that didn't go too badly," she said, sarcasm coloring her words.

"I hope you're not thinking we should leave. First of all, I've already seen two editors you might be interested in meeting. Second, we've already attracted too much attention to slip out unnoticed. You don't strike me as a woman who runs away from conflict."

He lowered his voice and whispered close to her ear, "Sorry about the Flea Bite Creek comment. Not many people can hold on to their dignity when my aunt starts in on them." His breath was cool and tickled her neck.

"You just *think* I was holding on to my dignity. Truthfully, I didn't know what to say," she whispered back. She didn't mind the reference to her hometown at all. As they passed, a young woman flicked her eyes down Shelby's outfit and turned quickly to her friend, whispering. Shelby wished with every passing second that she were wearing something more sensible, such as her trusty navy dress, which was much bigger than this slip of fabric.

"So, you can rebut criticism in front of hundreds but get tongue-tied by my aunt?"

"I wasn't expecting her to be . . ." Shelby paused, checking her words. With money, the family name and the mansion, apparently good manners are optional.

“I was caught off guard,” she said simply.

He chuckled, the sound cutting into her. “You should have spent more time preparing to defend yourself.”

Shelby straightened her shoulders, wondering if he was enjoying this. Maybe needling the aunt was the real purpose of their date. A movement caught her eye and she turned in time to see David Bishop walking away from the drinks table. She was sure he had seen her, had, in fact, been approaching them, but had turned the other way.

Good. She had enough on her plate without adding some crazy to it.

“What would you like? White wine? Champagne? A mixed drink?”

“Actually, some lemon-lime soda is fine.” She needed her wits about her tonight. Frowning, she wondered if he would have anything. Probably one drink wouldn’t be a problem, but he was driving.

“All right. Two lemon-lime sodas.” He turned back in time to see her expression of relief. “I’m just not much of a drinker,” he said almost apologetically. “But my dad spent a lot of time on my wine education.” He took a sip of his soda, pursed his lips. “A bright, lively beverage with a fine balance of citrus aromas; especially pleasing is its brilliance in the light.”

She regarded her own glass. The ice tinkled in the crystal tumbler. “My friend Erica is a real oenophile. She joined a group that visits different wineries on a tour, several times a year. Makes her happy to have people to talk to who appreciate wine." Shelby took a sip. "Let me try. . . . Definitely fruit forward, off dry, bit too flabby but with a vivid finish."

"Very well done. That's the poet in you. My father also tried to build my appreciation for Southern whiskey, but it doesn't agree with me at all. I'm afraid he considered it a statement on my manhood." Ransom's eyes were crinkled in laughter. "He was quite the character. I think he would have liked you."

"Was? I didn't realize your father had passed away. I'm sorry." Shelby kicked herself mentally for the second time.

"About five years ago now. He had some health issues and just finally wore out. We always think doctors can fix everything, but when your kidneys decide to quit, life gets a lot more complicated." Ransom's tone was matter-of-fact but she noticed he didn't meet her eyes.

"Are you ready to meet and greet?" He nodded toward a group of older gentlemen. "That's Arthur Cavendish over there. He's the editor of the *Southern States Historical Journal*."

"Really? I submitted a paper there last quarter and it was rejected, but he wrote a very nice note. He said he was interested in what else I had." Shelby appreciated the time he'd taken to write a personal letter. She wasn't one of those writers who grieved over every rejection, but she realized how busy editors are. If one took the time to write some encouraging words, it meant a lot.

"Well, he's talking to Elliott Pace, the newly appointed editor of the Association of Southern History journal."

"I can't believe it! This is better than a history conference." She started to laugh. A warm feeling of belonging and contentment suffused her. Rebecca was wrong. It was all going to go so well. As long as they kept away from Ransom's evil aunt.

"Right. Let's go make casual conversation." Ransom's mouth quirked in a lopsided grin. Shelby turned away, shaking off the little spark that zipped its way toward her heart.

*But disguise of every sort is my abhorrence.*

—MR. DARCY

# CHAPTER TWENTY-SEVEN

A few moments later they stood next to a motley crew of senior editors. Elliott Pace was youthful looking for a man in his sixties, his receding hair cut military short. He turned and seemed to assess Shelby like a vulture from its perch.

"Just a moment, Ben," he said to a lanky gentleman in a wrinkled tan suit who was in the middle of a rapid-fire monologue. "We have visitors. Nice to see you, Ransom." Elliott's mouth turned up at the edges but his eyes were coldly appraising.

"Hello, Elliott. This is Shelby Roswell, from Midlands College."

Shelby held out her hand, willing herself to relax. This was what she was here for, to make social connections. They wouldn't be asking any hard questions.

Elliott enclosed her hand in a surprisingly firm grip. "Yes, I was just talking to Margaret about you. Seems you made quite an impression when she visited Ransom's class."

Shelby's cheeks turned pink but she held

Elliott's gaze, letting out a little laugh. "A difference of opinion. We sorted it out."

"Actually, she was right." Ransom's deep drawl wound its way through the tense atmosphere. "It was a bit heavy-handed. And I need to be more careful with my research." The small circle seemed to contract and expand with his words. A gray-haired woman in a flowing purple dress tilted her head and made a noise, somewhere between a snort and a grunt.

Elliott's eyebrows went higher. "Oh, I'm sure your research is perfectly adequate. Any of us could have made a similar error." His gaze was trained on Shelby with a malevolent intensity.

"Arthur, I heard the next issue is going to be on constitutional debate in the years before the Civil War." Ransom quickly turned the topic, and Shelby felt a wave of gratitude sweep over her. Whether he'd brought her to vex his aunt or not, she appreciated the diversion.

"As usual, Ransom, you have all the inside information. I don't have to ask where you heard it," Arthur said. His thick glasses made his eyes seem unnaturally large, and this combined with his bald, pink head reminded Shelby of an overgrown baby.

"There are some advantages to being the nephew of your oldest friend." Ransom chuckled. "My uncle Cephus gives me a heads-up now and then. He considers it his duty to advance my career." Ransom said this in a stage whisper to Shelby, and Arthur chuckled approvingly.

"You're going to have her up to speed in no time." Arthur turned his magnified gaze to Shelby and smoothed his tie. "It's a pleasure to meet you. I'm quite intrigued. We all tread lightly around Ransom, but you don't seem to be afraid of him at all."

"That's absolutely untrue, don't believe a word he says," Ransom protested quickly.

Shelby ignored him. "He rescued me when I was stranded on the side of the road, in the middle of the night, during an ice storm. But if I were a student, I would be shaking in my shoes."

Arthur laughed. "He takes pride in weeding out the least dedicated. I've heard that some drop out of college entirely after taking one of his ill-fated courses."

"There now, I can't regret setting the bar higher than most. With low expectations the students will produce only as much as is required."

"Yes, I agree. But you forget what a rocky start you had yourself." Arthur turned to Shelby. "I was his adviser once upon a time and there were moments when I'd given him up for lost."

Shelby glanced at Ransom in surprise. His cheekbones seemed a bit pink and he opened his mouth to speak.

"Shelby! I didn't know you were coming." Ron DiGuardi came toward her, reaching out a hand.

He was wearing a button-up shirt in a pale yellow, like fresh-churned butter. The other hand was being held by his wife, Tansy. Her jet-black hair was in a sleek bob, as always, and a red patterned wrap dress displayed her petite frame to great advantage. She gave Shelby a quick peck on the cheek, her dark eyes sparkling with curiosity.

"A last-minute decision. Hi, Tansy." Shelby hugged her, loving how the lithe woman radiated energy.

The circle that had once seemed so hostile now subtly shifted and Shelby found herself comfortably flanked by Ransom and Tansy. While Ransom answered Ron's questions about the new class, Tansy whispered to Shelby, "Making friends, are we?"

"Rebecca already reminded me to play nice. I guess I'll have to give up my plan of causing some social spectacle." Shelby barely moved her lips as she spoke.

"What a disappointment! Please reconsider. But I understand completely if you won't." Tansy looked pointedly at Ransom and gave the barest of winks.

"Now, don't start. He's already taken and I have no urge to steal him away." It was not exactly true; maybe one or two small urges. Nothing she couldn't handle.

Tansy's eyes widened. "Really? I hadn't heard. What—"

“Dear, did you say that the Huntsville Museum of Art had agreed to send some of their exhibit up here?” Ron broke into their whispered conversation.

Tansy nodded. “The Red Clay Survey was last month, and there was a photographer I was interested in contacting, but he never answered his phone.” Shelby recognized the name of the annual art symposium that brought the newest and best talents to the forefront, focusing on contemporary Southern artists. “I thought it would be great to have a show of his. So, really, just one artist, not the collection,” Tansy patiently clarified in a soft voice. Shelby loved being near the couple. Their conversation seemed free of the minor irritations that bedeviled a long-term relationship.

“Oh, that’s right.” Ron smiled and turned back to Ransom.

“I hadn’t heard that he was seeing someone. Are you sure?” Tansy dropped her voice again, eager to hear the details.

“Pretty sure. She’s not from around here, but definitely serious. They were going bridal-gown shopping the day I first met her. Then after I helped you set up the gallery last week, I got roped into this strange dinner at Chinois and she talked weddings the entire time.” Shelby sipped her soda and peeked at Ransom’s profile. He was deep in conversation with Ron.

"Hm." Tansy frowned. "Who goes gown shopping with her fiancé?"

"Apparently she does!" Shelby giggled.

"But you think he would have mentioned it before. He was over for dinner on Tuesday and didn't say a thing about getting married."

"Who knows. Maybe he's the private type." Shelby felt an irrational jealousy. Ron and Tansy were her friends and she knew them first. Now Fielding was butting in.

"He and Ron sure got on a roll, telling stories from their graduate-school days. I finally had to leave them to it, I was exhausted." Tansy smoothed her glossy bob and peeked around Shelby. "I was thinking you two would make a good match, even after the rough start. But now that you say he's getting married, no sense in that."

"It would never have worked anyway. We hardly agree on a thing." Shelby shrugged, but deep down she knew that wasn't quite true. She wished she could change the topic. Discussing what kind of couple she and Ransom would have made if Tasha didn't exist was making her inexplicably irritable.

"I was over by the bar and I heard David Bishop say you two were dating." Tansy let the sentence drop into the conversation with an innocent tone.

Shelby whirled, mouth open. "What? He said that?"

Tansy grinned. "I knew that wasn't true. What a nasty little man he is."

"Who was he talking to?" Fury rose in Shelby at the thought of being linked to David's wheeling and dealing.

"Some older couple. He was assuring them their mansion would be properly treated if they let him handle some transaction, I don't know what. He said that his girlfriend was a renowned Civil War historian at Midlands and she helped get houses on the Historical Register."

"Did you say anything?" Rage made the words come out in a squeak. Who over the age of fifteen used the word *girlfriend* anyway?

"I felt like a masked avenger." Tansy laughed out loud, clearly enjoying herself. "I inserted myself in the conversation and asked if he was talking about Shelby Roswell. He looked like the proverbial deer in the headlights. He stuttered around for a bit, then I said never mind, he couldn't mean you, because you thought he was a scam artist."

Shelby's eyes opened wide. "Did you, really? Oh, Tansy, you're the best!" She laughed out loud.

"That poor old couple sure made a quick escape. I didn't wait to see what David was going to say. That guy is slicker than a greased pig."

"Miss Roswell again!" A hearty voice came from behind her, and Shelby turned to see Jacob Stroud.

"Dr. Stroud, how are you?" She struggled to shift gears, noticing that Ransom had moved next to her again.

"And Ransom Fielding, I believe." Dr. Stroud was shaking Ransom's hand, smiling hugely. "Last time I saw you in uniform, it was at dawn near Pittsburg Landing and I never got to ask whether you survived the siege."

Shelby turned to Ransom with a muffled gasp. Was he a "bloater"? Jennie Anne's story of the brass buttons flashed through her mind and her eyes opened wide.

"That I did. I was taken prisoner with my commander. An inglorious end, but preferable to taking a shot to the femur and undergoing an amputation." Ransom held his hand near his heart, reciting the words in a passable imitation of a stage actor.

"And how I would have loved to assist you in your time of need." Dr. Stroud turned to Shelby. "Will we be seeing you out in the field, living the history perhaps as a nurse, Miss Roswell?"

Shelby blinked. The thought of herself in a Civil War reenactment was ludicrous. It was a hobby for obsessed men who had copious amounts of time on their hands.

"I doubt she's interested. It's dirty, smelly and usually starts before daybreak." Ransom grinned down at her, his blue eyes teasing.

"Ransom is right. I'll stick to reading the letters

that the soldiers wrote home. But it's an interesting hobby." She silently congratulated herself on her diplomacy.

"Hobby? Did you hear that, Ransom? You'll have to work on this girl. Get her out into the field where she can feel the rush. She'll see it's more than that."

Where she could feel the chiggers, more like it. "Excuse me, the word *hobby* implies a certain triviality. It doesn't do justice to an act that preserves sacred history." Shelby fixed Dr. Stroud with her best professorial expression.

He regarded her for a moment, then burst into laughter. "Oh, she's a keeper, to be sure! I tell you, every marriage where the husband is spending his weekends in a ditch, the wife has to join him on the field, or at least see the beauty of the history."

"Oh, we're not . . . I'm just . . ." Shelby's face flamed and she looked to Ransom for help.

He was nodding in agreement, oblivious of Stroud's gaffe. "Penn's last girlfriend refused to even look at his gear. She didn't last more than a few months. You know how proud he is of that uniform. He sewed it himself after dying the wool with an authentic recipe."

"I think Shelby's going to be a great new addition. Have you talked about what you would wear on the next outing?" Dr. Stroud was giving her the once-over, visibly calculating the chances of getting Shelby into a scratchy wool nurse's uniform.

"No, no. I'm positive about that. I doubt that there's anything I would enjoy out in the field at dawn. I admire the dedication, but no. Not for me." Shelby shook her head emphatically. The time for diplomacy was gone and the moment to avoid playing dress-up in the mud had arrived.

"Oh, don't be a Smedley. We'll show you that it will deepen the admiration you have for those soldiers. Now, Ransom, there's someone I'd like you to meet, if you don't mind. He's had a good turnout over in Tennessee and we were thinking of some kind of collaboration." Dr. Stroud stroked his white beard.

"Of course. Shelby?" Ransom turned to her, and Shelby wasn't sure what he was going to say, but she had no interest in tagging along.

"Go ahead. Tansy and I can chat for a bit." Shelby waved him away with a smile. As he made his way through the elegantly attired partyers, she noticed how heads turned as he passed. What a charmed life he led.

"Smedley? What was that about?" Tansy watched as the tall, white-haired doctor walked away, chattering excitedly to Ransom.

"I think he meant Smedley Butler. After Stonewall Jackson's arm was amputated, it was buried at Ellwood Cemetery in Virginia. Then it was dug up and buried again by Union soldiers a year later. During some maneuvers on the site in 1921, Smedley Butler said he didn't believe that Stonewall's arm was under the marker, so *he* dug it up."

"Whew. Poor arm."

"Poor Stonewall Jackson. He didn't live long without it, though. Anyway, I think he was calling me a doubter." Shelby laughed and shrugged. "There's no way you'll find me out there in a ditch, though."

"Never say never," Tansy warned. "But tell me more about this fiancée."

"Fiancée? What fiancée?" Ron interrupted with interest.

"Shelby says that Ransom is engaged. Did he mention it to you?"

"No, nothing. Are you sure?" His round cheeks were slightly pink, and his glass of wine was almost empty.

"Pretty sure. I went to dinner with them. They've been bridal-gown shopping and he gave her his family's heirloom ring." Shelby didn't add that it wasn't good enough for the bridezilla. Shelby felt a twinge of guilt. Maybe she shouldn't have said anything, maybe Ransom wanted to announce it himself.

Tansy looked to her husband for his opinion. "You know him best, dear. You've always said he's reserved."

"I suppose. But to not mention that he's getting

married . . ." Ron shook his head and drained his glass.

Shelby glanced at Ransom, now in a far corner of the room. He was taller than most of the other guests, and she had no trouble finding him. He was facing her, laughing at the animated conversation of a robust-looking man with wildly curly hair. Dr. Stroud stood to one side, smiling. Ransom looked up at that moment and met her gaze. Shelby felt her fingers tingle. A familiar warmth spread through her body and she hoped that she wasn't blushing.

Odd, he must be thirty feet away. It still felt as if someone were running his fingers down her spine. Can't be pheromones from this distance. Shelby was completely absorbed by this development and missed Tansy's next question.

"Who are you looking at?" Tansy turned to scan the crowd. Ransom lifted his glass and smiled.

"Oh, I see. You're forgiven." She cut her eyes at Ron.

Shelby hastened to make some comment, about anything. "Ron," she said a bit breathlessly, "how's the seminar on medieval Japan coming along?"

"Fine. But we'll be short one speaker next month. Dr. Morine is having visa issues. It's quite a disappointment since she's the expert in feudal societies and the rise of Buddhism among the common people. I'm hoping we can find a replacement."

Relief flooded through Shelby as the conversation veered. She felt one of the pins in her hair slip sideways and tried to pat it back into place.

"Do you want me to fix that?" Tansy asked.

"No, I just . . ." Shelby struggled with the tiny rhinestone-encrusted pin and sighed. "I'm going to head to the ladies' room. I'll be right back."

Ransom lifted his head as she moved away from the little group. She pointed toward the exit, lifting one finger, and he nodded. She would just be a minute. Passing the large, paned windows, she could see the wind had risen and heavy drops thudded against the glass.

As she neared the large French doors that led to the hallway, Shelby saw David Bishop slip through. Everything about his posture seemed wrong, almost fierce. She followed a few steps behind him and saw a young woman in a maid's uniform try to grab his arm. He angrily brushed her off, his face contorted.

". . . just deal with it. There's nothing you can do anyway." His words were flung at the pretty blond girl as if they were stones. Then he was out the front door.

Shelby watched as the maid stood at the door, hands clenched, watching him leave. The maid spoke to herself, her words soft, but dripping with bitterness. "Left right quick, didn't you? Too bad Stevie couldn't get down here fast enough. He'd sure like to have a word with you. Just you wait, we're gonna make sure you pay." Her tone was pure venom, her eyes bright with hatred.

*My dear Jane, Mr. Collins is a conceited, pompous, narrow-minded, silly man; you know he is, as well as I do.*

—ELIZABETH

# CHAPTER TWENTY-EIGHT

Shelby cleared her throat.

The young woman whirled around, her hand on her heart. "Mercy! You scared the daylights out of me."

"I'm sorry. I was just trying to find the restroom. But that man sure didn't seem like he wanted to talk," Shelby said, adopting an innocent expression.

"No, no, he didn't." The maid's face was a mixture of fear and mistrust. "And I'm sorry about what you just heard. Please don't tell my boss. I really need this job," she said, voice trembling.

"Don't worry. I understand venting a bit of frustration. But"—here Shelby decided to take a chance—"why are you so angry?"

The maid's eyes narrowed, as if judging whether Shelby could be trusted. "My brother had to sell his house to cover that loan, and we still didn't get all the repairs finished."

"What loan? I thought David worked in real estate."

The pretty maid could not possibly look any more furious. She was so angry she was having trouble forming words. "I don't know what he really does, but he told us he would lobby to get it on the national register of historical buildings. We signed all sorts of papers." Her hands were shaking as she pushed her blond hair back from her brow.

A bad feeling settled in the pit of Shelby's stomach. "Go on."

"So, we got it appraised. My grandpa was so worried about fixing the upper floors, and he just didn't have the money to make those kinds of repairs. He trusted David. We all did. Grandpa signed everything he told him to sign. It was going to be the best thing ever." The maid lowered her voice. "Well, then David said the money came through and gave my grandpa twenty thousand dollars. He spent it right away, making the repairs he needed to the top floor so it was safe. We were thrilled. It's been in our family for a hundred and fifty years." Her voice trailed off. Her blue eyes were unfocused, gazing out the hall window into the stormy darkness.

Shelby held her breath and waited for her to continue.

"Then, we started to get papers from the bank. It was so confusing. At first we just thought it was a mistake. But when he wouldn't answer his phone, we knew that David hadn't told us the whole truth. We just had no idea how bad it was going to be." Her eyes began to fill with tears. She didn't even seem to know Shelby was there. "My grandpa went straight to the bank, to ask about the papers they were sending. It wasn't grant money we got. It was a loan. For seventy thousand dollars. He had signed all those papers, there was no way to get out of it."

Shelby felt faint. "So, the loan had to be repaid?" she whispered.

The young woman nodded, tears spilling out from under her lashes. "We had to pay it off directly, or they'd charge interest. My grandpa didn't have that kind of money. So, my brother Steve, he sold his house. He and his wife and their three kids moved into the top floor. I had a college account that was going to get me through my last year. I drained that. Between us we got most of it paid off, enough to get the payments down. But I had to drop out and get a full-time job. Maybe in a year or so I can finish my degree."

"I'm so sorry this happened." Shelby reached out, putting a hand on the maid's arm, hoping that her expression said what she felt.

"You're probably thinking we're idiots for doing everything he told us to, without even checking. But we trusted him!" The young woman suddenly grabbed Shelby's hand. "He was so convincing. He knew all about the history of the house and we really thought . . ." She shook her head, words finally failing her.

Shelby stood still, her mind struggling to accept the story. All of David's lies loomed hard in front of her. It sounded impossible, yet the truth of it grew heavy in her heart.

"I wish there was a way to make sure he never did this to anyone else. When we went to the police, they said there wasn't enough evidence. All we had were the papers with Grandpa's signature on them."

Shelby squeezed the maid's hand back. "There must be something that can be done. Don't give up."

A few minutes later Shelby had found the women's room, a note tucked into her clutch. On the slip of paper was the contact information of Marissa LeJeune, victim of David Bishop's realty scam. Shelby knew just the lawyer she would call when morning came.

Ransom appeared at Shelby's shoulder as she reentered the ballroom. He glanced at her hair and tucked an errant curl behind her ear. Shelby shivered at the warm touch of his hand and struggled to focus on what he was saying.

"I think my aunt is about to speak. Let's move farther to the front of the room so you can see." He smiled down at her.

"Of course."

Shelby allowed herself to be led to the front of

the room. Margaret, carrying a tidy stack of note cards, stood apart from the crowd. Soon, a young man asked for their attention in a loud, clear voice. Margaret glided forward and the crowd hushed immediately. Shelby was surprised that she did not use a microphone, but the room's acoustics seemed good enough for her voice to carry naturally.

"When Albert Hardy asked me if I would have a fund-raiser at Collier House, I couldn't contain my enthusiasm. My dear friend has always known when the time is right to bring our community together. As we explored the idea during dinner at Alice LaRoche's mansion that night . . ."

Shelby could feel her eyes losing focus and wondered how many names would be dropped in the speech. She glanced at Ransom, wondering if he was listening. He seemed to be absorbed in the tale of how they had all come to be in this room.

". . . and I told Mark Lutie that if there was anything I could possibly contribute to the preservation of our society, then I was at his service. The next day Angeline Frankel, who runs the planning business La Petite Fête, called from Charleston with some wonderful ideas. I was struck by . . ."

Really, how many people in this room wanted to know who organized the caterer and the music? But that short man over there was nodding his head off. He was going to lose his glasses if he didn't take it down a notch. And the wolfish-looking lady in the black sequined dress seemed completely captivated.

"As a Southerner, a woman whose great-great-great-grandfather returned to a ruined city, I feel a kinship with the refugees of the world. Ten percent of the proceeds from tonight's fund-raiser will be donated to the Red Cross."

Shelby's eyes widened. Oh, Margaret was not all bad then. Feeling guilty now . . .

". . . hope we will be able to exceed Mariah Parker's foundation."

Back to the bull-pucky. Shelby noticed Finch, tie knotted tight and gray hair slicked down, near the long table of food. He hadn't said he was coming to this. But then, she wasn't exactly on his short list of confidants.

". . . so that the battlefield of Samfer Hill will be protected against corporate exploitation and development."

So many battlefields were under threat of being paved over, and one could almost lose track of all the places lost to parking lots and strip malls. But the battlefield at Samfer Hill had been granted protection from development six months ago. An article had appeared about it in the *Flea Bite Creek Gazette*. Shelby's friend Alan Norton, the editor, had called her for a quote. Shelby frowned and looked across the room at Ron. His brows were drawn down as he peered into his wineglass. Shelby couldn't tell if he was listening or just wishing for another refill. She turned to Ransom, a questioning look on her face.

He leaned down and whispered, "What is it?"

"Isn't Samfer already on the list of protected sites?" Shelby leaned into his shoulder, using her hand to shield her mouth.

"Is it? But I think she would know if it were," he said, leaning down.

His breath tickled her ear, and as she turned to tell him that it most certainly was, his aunt's voice boomed out over the crowd, venomous and haughty. "Is there something important we need to know, Ransom?"

Shelby's mouth dropped open in shock. Like a third-grader caught cheating, she froze, her breath caught in her throat. Ransom straightened, his broad shoulders now turned away from her. She wasn't sure what he was going to say, but it was her fault his aunt had stopped her speech.

Shelby quickly stepped forward and said coolly, "We were just discussing the fact that Samfer has already been added to the list of protected sites. Perhaps there's another battlefield that could benefit from your generosity."

A flicker of fury flashed across Margaret's face.

*"But it is not merely this affair," she continued, "on which my dislike is founded. Long before it had taken place, my opinion of you was decided."*

—ELIZABETH

# CHAPTER TWENTY-NINE

Margaret Greathouse recovered quickly. Her look of fury was quickly covered with a mask of amusement, her lips curled in a tiny smile. "Still lobbying for that backwater Flea Bite Creek? Our little friend, always the center of attention. I'm almost done, my dear. Then you may have your turn."

It seemed as if all the air had been drawn from the room in one great whoosh. Shelby had a vague impression of dozens of shocked faces, heads shaking back and forth. Murmurs arose in the silence, one that went on and on as Ransom's aunt stared down the great empty space at Shelby. With that, Margaret swiveled slowly on the spot, redirecting the end of her speech to the other side of the room.

The ground was dropping away under Shelby's feet. Had Margaret Greathouse really just called her a liar? Her eyes searched for Ron. There he was, across the room, eyes wide, a pained expression on his face. Tansy stood beside him, one hand pressed to her mouth and the other clutching his arm. They couldn't have looked more shocked if they had witnessed a terrible roadside accident.

Polite applause spattered around the room as the speech was concluded. Shelby numbly turned to go, not sure where, but somewhere other than this room.

"Why did you say anything? I was going to handle it," Ransom said, voice low and urgent, one broad hand on her shoulder. It was soothing and electric at the same time and she repressed a shiver.

She shook her head dumbly. The words she wanted to say stuck in her throat, causing a lump that was making it hard to breathe.

"Jeez, Shelby." Ransom's expression was a mixture of disbelief and amusement. He raked his fingers through his hair and let out a short bark of laughter. "You just can't do that sort of thing, correcting people in public."

Something in the way he said that, the words *that sort of thing,* rang a bell deep inside her. She hated the idea that she should always be coy and use flattery, that she should nod and smile while dishonest people trampled over the weaker ones.

She whirled on him and shook off his hand.

"I'm not the kind of person who smiles at a lie, who flirts with power and hopes some bone gets thrown my way. You should know that, Ransom. I don't know why you invited me, but if it was because you wanted a show, you got it." Somewhere in the back of her mind, the voice of reason shouted a warning, but she was too angry to listen. "Maybe you already knew that field was protected and that she was still raising funds for it. Maybe you knew I'd open my big mouth. How was it? Did I live up to your expectations?" Her cheeks were flushed, her eyes flashing.

He took a deep breath and seemed to be counting in his head. Some of the guests moved closer as quickly as they could to get to the conversation between the fiery woman in the green dress and the famous Ransom Fielding.

"How was I supposed to know you would interrupt her speech?" His eyes were so clear, so blue, she had trouble focusing on them. She yearned for them to look as they had for that moment under the tree, his eyes deep with possibilities. The sudden memory, side by side with the present moment when everything had gone horribly wrong, made her throat squeeze shut. She turned away and lifted trembling fingers to whisk traitor tears away from the corners of her eyes.

"Maybe you two planned it," Shelby said, her back turned. She knew it was crazy as soon as she said it, but she couldn't fight the pain that was welling up in her chest.

Ransom turned her around, one hand gripping her bare shoulder once more. His eyes widened, then narrowed to slits. "Really? That's what you think of me? That I would drive you all the way up here so my aunt could commit a bit of public humiliation? Revenge, I suppose. But that's an awful lot of effort for some silly antics in front of my class. How important do you think you are?"

She gasped as if he had slapped her. Wordlessly, she turned and walked toward the foyer. Out of the corner of her eye, just as she turned, she saw him shake his head and reach out for her.

"Shelby!" Tansy was there, grabbing Shelby's hand and pulling her to the side. "Are you okay? What was that about?"

"I just—I don't know. I can't tell you any more than what you saw. Are you guys going home now?" Shelby stuttered. Ron was there, a reassuring presence. His somber expression mirrored Tansy's.

"We will if you want . . . if you need a ride." Tansy glanced behind them at Ransom.

Shelby knew he was there, feet behind her. She refused to look at him, his angry words ringing in her ears.

"Please, I'll take her home." His voice was low, subdued.

"No, the party just started. You should stay.

Thank you for inviting me." Shelby's Southern manners rallied for a moment and she managed a wobbly smile. She could feel tears on her lashes and hoped he couldn't notice. She didn't meet his eyes but looked somewhere over his broad shoulders.

"Shelby, please. That came out wrong. I'd be glad to take you home. I'm sorry for what—"

"We're leaving anyway, Ransom. See you Monday." Ron gave him a look, something between a brotherly smile and a warning nod.

Ransom fell silent and stepped aside.

Tansy slipped Shelby's arm through hers and they made their way out to the foyer, then to the car. Numbly, Shelby settled into the backseat and stared out the window as they drove the same road she had just traveled a short time before. The bright bubble of happiness she had felt so briefly had gone without a trace. All her hopes for the evening, all her plans, ruined. Her friends loyally argued that Margaret was a tyrant, a bully. But Shelby shook her head and said nothing; her face felt heavy with unshed tears. The drive seemed to last forever.

As the door to her house closed behind her, she finally let hot tears slip down her cheeks. The house was dark, Rebecca already asleep. She clutched the satiny fabric of her dress between her fingers as the dam of emotion broke over her. After what seemed like hours, she stooped to loosen her sandals and stared unseeing at the fanciful decorations.

She felt like such a fool. She should never have accepted his invitation. Shucking the dress from her body, she stepped into the shower, where her tears mixed with the scalding-hot water.

Lying awake, staring at the ceiling, Shelby resolved to straighten it all out. If she got the chance.

*We must not be so ready to fancy ourselves intentionally injured.*

—ELIZABETH

# CHAPTER THIRTY

After the rough night, Shelby felt as if she had an emotional hangover on Sunday. Rebecca listened to her moan and groan, then told her to get back to work. Worse had happened, she was sure, although Rebecca admitted she couldn't think of anything at the moment. Monday arrived with a vengeance, and Shelby wished she could curl up in her closet for the rest of the semester. Instead, she struggled to ignore the dull throbbing near her temple and got ready to face the day.

The phone rang just as Shelby tucked her lecture papers into her satchel, coffee mug balanced in one hand. Sirocco wound around her ankles, tripping her as she turned to grab the receiver.

"How are you getting along, honey? The beginning of the term runs pretty smooth, if I remember correctly." Her aunt Junetta's warm voice was like a sedative to Shelby's frayed nerves.

"Good so far." She tried to inject some enthusiasm into her voice and hoped it didn't sound as flat as it did in her own ears.

Aunt Junetta chuckled. "Now that's a whopper if I ever heard one."

Shelby grinned in spite of herself. "I never could lie to you."

"You never could lie to anyone, honey. So, is it something you want to talk about?"

Shelby perched on the edge of the sofa for a moment and squeezed her eyes closed. Where could she possibly begin?

"Is that historian giving you a hard time again? The one from the magazine?"

She sighed. "Sort of. I mean, yes, that's who it is. But he's not really giving me a hard time. I made a mistake. I don't even want to tell you what it was, but then everybody was giving me the cold shoulder, and he said that maybe we could pretend to be friends and things would settle down. . . ." She trailed off as she realized how little sense she was making.

There was a long pause on the other end. "You know you can tell me anything. I've done some plain stupid things in my time, don't you think I haven't. But it sounds like you were getting it figured out, the two of you." Her words held a question.

Shelby felt her head throb with the beat of her heart. "First, I corrected him in front of a lot of people, and not in a nice way."

"Ohhh."

Shelby grimaced, knowing that tone. "And then

we went to a party together and his aunt said something that wasn't right, so I corrected her."

"Ahhh."

Shelby dropped her head in one hand. "And then I got mad at him when he said I shouldn't have corrected her and I said some mean things that weren't true."

"Hmmm."

Shelby snorted. "I know what you're thinking."

"Really?" her aunt asked innocently.

"You're thinking I must have misplaced my brains somewhere."

"Actually, honey, I was wondering when I get to meet him."

Shelby's jaw dropped. "What?"

"I've never seen you care what anybody thought. Sure, you like to pick a fight"—Shelby made a sound not unlike that of an angry goose—"but this man must be different. Where's he from again?"

"Not that it matters in the slightest, because you're wrong, but he's from Natchez, originally, although he teaches up North."

"Oh, up in Jackson?"

"No, I mean, North as in Connecticut. He was raised at Bellepointe. His parents sold it after they divorced."

"That gorgeous old place? I'll never forget your cousin Isla's wedding there a few years ago. You were stuck over on the West Coast at that conference. The tin type ceiling sparkled like a new penny and the marble entryway seemed to go on for miles. Just lovely, every bit of it."

Shelby sighed, wondering how they'd ended up talking about Bellepointe, when they were supposed to be talking about her. Then something Ransom mentioned on the drive came back to her.

"Did you see a greenhouse in the back? He said that his grandfather raised violets as a hobby."

"Can't say I remember a greenhouse. But it's a huge place, it could have been tucked away on the grounds somewhere. Maybe you could go visit and look around. Your friend might give you a tour, do you think?"

"I don't think that will be happening. I'd be surprised if he speaks to me at all now."

"I bet you're wrong," Shelby's aunt proclaimed, a note of mischief in her voice.

Another pulsing throb reminded Shelby she needed to get going or give up and go back to bed. "We'll see. But I need to get to class."

"Shelby, I'm always praying for you. And let me know when to make some pecan pie for his visit." Her aunt chuckled and the line went dead. She was from a whole other era, when men and women treated each other with respect. Not like the free-for-all Shelby lived in. She knew her aunt abhorred bad manners, and Shelby seemed to be the queen of gauche lately.

• • •

"Daddy, I know you're retired, but I need some help." Shelby flattened the wrinkled piece of paper onto the desk. Marissa's story had touched her in a way that was hard to shake. She'd lain awake, staring at the ceiling, hearing the echoes of Marissa's tale, over and over. The image of her young face streaked with tears was as clear as the moment they'd talked at that awful party.

"Anything for you." Her daddy paused, a chuckle sounding from the other end of the phone. "Well, almost anything. There are certain things, like extended shopping trips, that no man can endure."

She snorted. "And sometimes no woman, either." She took a deep breath. "It's a complicated story, but I just can't let this go. These poor people need our help." In the next half hour, she explained as well as she could how Marissa's family had been robbed, of money and their home. Her father asked detailed, numerous questions, and then they outlined a plan. When she hung up, Shelby felt a weight lift from her shoulders. It might not be enough, but it was more than sitting around and doing nothing.

Shelby sat for a moment with her hand on the receiver until a sharp knock at the door interrupted her thoughts.

"Hey, Shelby." Katie Young stuck her head in and looked around. "I'm not ready to turn in my draft yet. Gonna need a few more weeks." She gazed at some point over Shelby's head.

"Katie, please come in." Shelby came around the desk and gently tried to usher Katie into a chair. The young woman's brown hair looked lank and dull. "How are you feeling? Are you still sick?"

"Sick? What are you—Oh, yeah. I'm feeling a lot better, thanks." Her blue eyes looked unfocused and she tapped her fingers against jeans that carried several layers of grime. A bright green snake with ruby eyes wrapped itself around her wrist, the skin around it red and swollen, as if the tattoo was recently done. "I just need some time. You know?"

Shelby folded her arms over her chest and leaned back against her desk.

"Katie, you have to get that draft in this week. It's already months overdue. Professor Finch recommended that you be dropped from the course, but I promised him, like you promised me, that it would be in as soon as possible."

"What? He can't! What an idiot. He never does anything and his classes are totally worthless," Katie hissed.

Shelby shook her head. "That's not fair, Katie. You said once that you liked his Revolutionary War class, I remember."

"Well, duh! I was just saying that because he's the department head. I mean, come on, you don't think he does anything around here, either." Katie sneered and waited for Shelby to agree.

"This isn't a domestic situation where one of us is doing all the chores. This is an academic department, and administration does take a lot of time." And a lot of golf and lunch dates. But that was an argument for another time.

"Whatever. But I'm not going to let some old dude who wrote one book forty years ago decide my future."

Shelby sighed and rubbed her temples. "What's happening here? You're in your third year. I know everything seems harder now. Do you need to take a break, maybe a semester off? Stress can be really difficult to deal with at times. I completely understand the pressure you're under to produce a graduate thesis on a schedule."

Katie let out a laugh that got louder as the seconds passed. "A break? Why would I do that? I just need a few more weeks without anybody getting on my back about it."

Shelby hated to do it, but she was left no choice. "You have until Friday to turn in a rough draft, which means a detailed outline and a list of at least twenty original sources."

There was a short silence. Katie seemed to be thinking, then said, "Uh, no. I said a few weeks. And there's really nothing you can do about it."

Shelby crossed to the filing cabinet. She removed a sheet of paper and handed it to Katie.

"I'm sorry you feel that way. Here's a copy of the paper you signed two months ago when I notified you that your thesis work was behind. You agreed to this deadline." She watched Katie glance at the paper and then start to laugh.

Her pupils were dilated to dime size and her hand trembled slightly as she brushed her hair from her damp forehead. "Whatever. That doesn't mean anything. I know the process to kick me out of this program takes six months. So why not give me a couple of weeks and save us all the trouble?"

"I'm sorry. I really am. I wish this could go differently. Of course, I will still accept the rough draft by Friday, if you change your mind."

The young woman's eyes widened and then she blinked repeatedly. "You'll be sorry. Really, really sorry." Her words were flat; it was the calmest she'd sounded since she had entered the room.

"I think you should leave." Shelby motioned toward the door and a terrible sadness squeezed her as she realized the bright young girl she'd known was gone. A stranger stood in her place, her future uncertain and dim.

Snatching the paper from Shelby's hand, Katie tore it in two.

After the door slammed shut behind her, Shelby sank into her office chair. Her stomach was in knots, her shoulders ached with tension. She replayed the scene over and over in her mind.

Maybe she hadn't spent enough time talking with Katie, getting to know her as a person. She felt as if she had failed as an adviser, as Katie's mentor. But all those times she had called and e-mailed, reminded her that outlines were due, must count for something.

She heaved a sigh. There was nothing to do but take the matter to Finch and recommend Katie be dropped from the program. But the mystery of the young girl's downfall bothered her like a deep and painful sliver.

*Happiness in marriage*
*is entirely a matter of chance.*
—CHARLOTTE LUCAS

# CHAPTER THIRTY-ONE

"Jolee, I'm headed down to the Grind. Would you like a muffin or some tea?" Shelby desperately needed some coffee. The meeting with Finch had not gone well. He had implied that Katie's academic failure was somehow Shelby's fault, even though she had given Katie twice as much time and guidance as the other students.

"Oh, I'd love a little tea, thanks so much." Jolee paused in her typing for a moment and reached under her desk for her purse. "I dread Mondays. When I die, I'm going to ask God what he was thinking."

"I'll buy. I really appreciated your help with that fax this morning. I must have tried it ten times and it wouldn't go through." Shelby prided herself on being tech savvy but that fax had gotten the best of her.

"Anytime. It just takes the right touch, I guess. You're sure you don't want me to—"

"Absolutely not. I'll be back in five."

The morning had turned sunny and clear, with

little wisps of cloud moving briskly across the pale sky. Shelby dodged a skateboarder and glanced across the street, wondering if she should cross. A young woman trudged along the opposite sidewalk, a sleeping baby in her arms and a large green bag dangling off one shoulder. Her bright red hair fell past her shoulders and she paused to wipe her forehead with one sleeve.

"Langston?" Shelby called out tentatively.

"Hi, cousin!" Langston called back, round face breaking into a huge smile, her voice pitched a bit lower, probably so she didn't wake the dark-haired baby.

Shelby jogged across the street and gave her a squeeze. "Is this Nathaniel? He's grown so much."

"Thirteen months old, and he weighs a ton. I'm sorry I haven't called since the adoption party. I've just been so busy organizing the summer projects for the city youth. I just ran over to check out an activity site on my day off." Langston talked quickly and shifted the boy in her arms.

"It's not really a day off if you have to check on work-related projects," Shelby said, teasing. She loved Langston's passion for her job, her passion for life.

"You're right, but I thought it would be a fun outing for both of us. I parked across Ankeny Field. I didn't take the stroller because it was just a block, but while I was checking out the area where we would put in the activity tents, Nat fell asleep on my shoulder. Then when I tried to get back across the field, I found a raging Ultimate Frisbee game on. I almost lost my head, so I thought I better walk around." Langston's face shone with sweat.

"Here, sit down on this bench for a second. You look exhausted." Shelby waved her over to a wooden bench, temporarily occupied by a bright-eyed squirrel. He chittered at them, then scampered up the trunk of an oak nearby.

Langston gratefully collapsed, stretching out one cramped arm, then the next. The diaper bag dropped to the ground at her feet. Nattie's head lolled to one side as she stretched, his silky black hair feathered over his ears.

"Oh, man, I can't feel my fingers." She laughed a little and blew her bangs off her forehead.

Shelby grinned, peeking at the little boy. "How have things been? Are you guys settling in okay?"

"Tom is the best dad on the planet. They went fishing together last Saturday. Barely walking and already holding a pole! Nat sleeps all night but wakes up a little cranky. He's not a morning person, just like his mommy." Langston's pride was obvious in every syllable.

"I didn't really get to talk to you at the Putneys' wedding reception. How was the trip? I think you said the flight to China takes sixteen hours?"

"Yup. It was exhausting. The first two days he

screamed and screamed. They have people who are supposed to help us get used to each other, but there's not a whole lot they can do. He wasn't a newborn. He knew . . ." Langston's voice trailed off and she stroked the creamy skin of his soft arm. "You know, there was this girl, a caretaker there at the orphanage. When we left, they all came out and waved us off, giving him hugs and kisses. But this girl, she was crying. Laughing and kissing him but she was crying. I think she loved him." Her voice cracked at the end of the sentence.

"I bet she did," Shelby said softly.

"They're not supposed to get attached because the whole idea is to care for them until they can find a family. But how do you do that? How do you raise a baby just to give it to someone else? Someone you've never even seen before, someone who could be a total monster?" Langston's eyes were pleading, her voice full of disbelief.

Shelby's heart ached for her cousin. She reached out and touched her arm. "Langston, no one could look at you and think that you were anything other than a mother. Someone who was going to love him with all your heart."

"He won't even remember her." Her red hair fell forward, screening her face, but her voice remained clogged with tears.

Shelby was silent a moment. "Probably not. But thank God for her. She loved him when there wasn't anyone else. I think . . . I think love changes us." The sidewalk bustled with students on their way to class, the sounds of conversation and laughter surrounded them. Shelby watched them, unseeing. "It changes who we are. He won't remember her but his life is different because she loved him. A thousand little gestures showed him he was valuable."

Langston laughed shakily and brushed her hair back. "How did you get so wise? You don't even have kids and you—Oh, that's not what I meant. I'm sorry."

"Don't worry, I'm not offended." Shelby patted Langston's hand. "Mothers are some of the wisest beings on the planet."

"I don't feel real wise. Like right now. I'm so new at this, I'm sure a seasoned mom would have thought about the stroller in the trunk before she walked halfway across campus," Langston said ruefully.

Shelby glanced around. "Listen, where are you parked?"

"I'm right around the corner on Thirteenth, across from the bookstore. Not too far, but it's going to feel like miles."

Shelby turned, thinking hard. "Do you think he'll wake up if you hand him to me? I can sit here while you go get the car. Then you can honk at the corner and I'll bring him over. That will save your arms."

"Would you really? Weren't you on your way somewhere? I can manage, I'll just take a quick rest." Langston was sincere, but her face shone with the hope of some relief.

"Just over to the Grind for coffee. Hand him over, I promise not to run away with your beautiful baby." Shelby laughed and held out her arms.

Langston carefully transferred him over. His head lolled about and she giggled a little as he let out a deep sigh.

"I can't believe he can sleep with all this noise," Shelby said.

"I know, maybe I should record the cars, bikes and people to play at naptime. He certainly sleeps lightly enough then." Langston brushed Nat's hair from his forehead. She gave him a quick kiss. "You're saving my back, you know that."

"That's what cousins are for, right?" Shelby made herself as comfortable as she could on the wooden bench. "We'll be right here."

"Be back in a sec." Langston jumped up and headed through the Business Building toward Thirteenth Street.

The tree overhead offered some shade from the midmorning sun. Shelby stretched out her legs and settled back. The baby's hair was as fine as silk from Indian corn and an impossible blue-black. A light breeze made a few strands of hair move across his forehead. She brushed them back, pausing to run a finger down one round cheek. His skin was slightly flushed from the sun. Turning him gingerly to one side, she admired his ear. A perfect pink shell, a little wisp of his hair curled near the miniature lobe.

Suddenly his dark eyes opened wide and Shelby's entire body tensed. What would the baby do when he realized his mother was gone and a complete stranger was holding him? She tried to smile reassuringly, and to her immense relief his eyes remained unfocused. Gradually the lids slipped to half-mast and then closed altogether. She let out a breath.

"Hello, there." A deep, pleasant voice caught her by surprise. Before she raised her eyes, Shelby knew who it was.

She squinted into the sun, her heart picking up its tempo against her will. So much for avoiding him at all cost. Ransom Fielding was standing on the sidewalk, a curious expression on his face.

"Found a new part-time job?"

Shelby laughed, despite the deep awkwardness she felt. "No, no. A very temporary gig, I'm afraid." She quickly explained about the cousin, the stroller, the Ultimate Frisbee game and a car parked blocks away.

To her surprise, he sat down on the bench beside them. She stole a glance. He looked as if he hadn't slept well. Dark circles were under his eyes and stubble covered his jaw. A clean, faintly woodsy smell drifted to her. The sun felt suddenly hot on her cheeks.

"Look at that." He gently took Nathaniel's foot in his hands, gently measuring the few inches between his thumb and forefinger.

"I was noticing his eyes. See the tiny veins on the lids? And those lashes, at least half an inch. Rebecca would be so jealous." Shelby knew she was babbling but couldn't help herself. Their evening had ended with anger and accusations. She cleared her throat and wished she had prepared something to say, just in case she got the chance.

He spoke first. "I'm glad you're here. Well, not on this bench, but I'm glad we ran into each other." He stopped and looked up at the sky for a moment. "I was going to drop by your office."

Shelby said nothing. Her heart was beating as if she had run a mile. *Help me,* she sent up a desperate prayer. *Help me see him as you do, not as I want him to be.*

He took a deep breath. "I'm sorry how things ended. I didn't mean for any of that to happen. You have to understand that I would never have set you up. How could I have known . . ." His voice trailed off.

"That I would interrupt your aunt's big speech by implying that she was stealing donations for a historic battlefield?" Shelby said drily, a fresh wave of humiliation washing over her.

He laughed, a wonderful sound that made a shiver run down the middle of her back, even though the sun beat down. "Yes, exactly."

"I know that." Her voice was soft. "I'm sorry I said what I did." She didn't know what else to add. How she wished it had all gone differently. But it was better this way. Without that disaster of an evening, she wouldn't have faced her own dishonesty, how she had been practically scheming to steal him away.

He leaned over her and brushed Nat's hair back. The baby's breathing was deep and even, and his chest rose and fell in a quiet rhythm. The conversations and traffic noises seemed to fade away. She was painfully aware of where his shoulder touched hers, how close he was. She tried to shift, casually giving him more room on the bench.

The baby raised an arm and dropped it again. Shelby smiled, wondering what babies dreamed of. He raised his arm again and snuggled one hand into the V of her button-up blouse. Shelby gasped and gently plucked it out. She heard a snort of quiet laughter.

Then the hand came back up and Nat murmured something more insistently in his sleep. As his little fist nestled back into the space between her breasts, she tried to ignore Ransom's deep chuckles.

"Horribly bad manners. His mother should speak to him about that," he whispered.

Shelby's face was flaming. She carefully tugged on Nat's hand, but his eyes opened halfway, and he made an unhappy sound in his throat and squirmed. Shelby sighed and decided to leave the hand where it was.

"She should be back any moment now." Shelby turned her bright red face away from him, trying to spot Langston's car.

"My wife and I lost a baby." His voice was calm and even, but the words dropped like a bomb into the sunny day.

*The letter, perhaps, began in bitterness but it did not end so.*

—MR. DARCY

# CHAPTER THIRTY-TWO

"A baby? You and . . . your wife?" Shelby was so startled she repeated his words.

"About a year before the accident. She was only a few months along, but we'd already made plans and picked names. All gone in a day. Strange, it seemed like we'd lost a whole lifetime with that child." He absentmindedly rubbed his thumb along Nat's small sandal.

"I'm sorry." Shelby's voice came out in a whisper. Nat turned his head toward her elbow.

"I don't think anything had ever gone really wrong for either of us. We weren't prepared. When the pregnancy ended, it broke her heart. No, that's not true." His tone grew fierce. "She was very, very sad, but her heart wasn't broken until I disappeared into my work. I didn't know how to grieve with her. It was overwhelming."

Shelby raised her eyes to his, still unable to think clearly. His voice was even but his face was full of raw pain. At least six years later and the wounds still ached.

"She told me she wanted to separate a few days before the crash." He stared resolutely at the baby's little foot, his eyes narrowed with pain. "Every person who offered me sympathy was like an accusation. If I had been there for her, maybe she wouldn't have been so distracted, maybe she wouldn't have turned in front of that truck."

"Why are you telling me this?" Shelby said, her voice hardly more than breath. She didn't want to know him like this, to see the pain he hid from everyone else. It was so much easier to believe he was arrogant and heartless.

"I don't really know." His tone was both surprised and defensive. "You seem like a good listener. I never feel . . ." His gaze turned to the branches above them. "I feel like I can be honest with you, that I can trust you."

*Honest*. The word pierced her. Shelby looked out at the people passing by on the sidewalk, but saw nothing. She should tell him to go away, to go call Tasha.

"You think your wife died because you were too self-absorbed to help her grieve?"

"I'm almost sure of it." His voice was choked with pain.

"And you carry that around with you, every day." Shelby shook her head and rocked Nat gently.

"Don't give me any sympathy. That's what I'm

trying to avoid by being honest," Ransom said roughly, anger shading every word.

"Oh, I'm not. I think it's a horrible way to live, carrying that guilt around. I'm sorry for the burden." She glanced at him and saw his eyes widen, then his brows draw together. Even confused and angry, his features were heart-stopping. She dropped her gaze, wishing she hadn't looked into his face.

"And how do you suggest that I drop this 'burden'? Because it's been six years and it's only gotten heavier and . . ." A quick intake of air against his teeth spoke volumes. Shelby resisted the impulse to grasp his hand. His pain was so palpable she could almost feel it pressing against her heart.

"You don't believe in asking for forgiveness?" she asked softly.

There was a long pause. Shelby kept her gaze on the baby. It was so much easier to talk when she wasn't distracted by his face. She rocked Nat and waited for Ransom to answer.

"She's gone. There's no point."

"I guess I don't believe that," Shelby said simply.

"I've said I'm sorry a thousand times and never felt a bit better, so—"

"No, I said to ask for forgiveness. That's a different thing altogether. Of course you're sorry."

A light breeze passed over them and Nat sighed

deeply. Shelby watched him, the picture of perfect peace. It was the sleep of the innocent, before we know how to inflict mortal wounds on each other.

"I don't know . . . if it would make any difference." Ransom's voice was hesitant, fearful.

She watched the people pass before them on the sidewalk. "My grandfather had a special painting," she said slowly. "It was of his uncle's farm where he spent summers when he was young. The painting hung over his desk and I loved to look at it when I visited. It wasn't anything valuable, painted by a neighbor, just cotton fields and red-clay earth." It had been a long time since she'd thought about the painting. "One day when he was out, I stood on his chair to get a book from the top shelf. It was an old, wooden swivel chair and I lost my balance. I put out a hand to keep from falling and knocked the painting off the wall. It crashed into the desk and a hole was punched right through its center. It was ruined."

She heard him draw a breath to speak but Shelby rushed on. "I know it's not the same. But I carried that for a long time. I hated it when anyone brought it up. My grandfather never spoke of it after that day, but it gnawed at me. Even after he died I thought about that painting. A few years ago I sat down and wrote him a letter, asking him to forgive me, and asking God to forgive me." She paused, struggling to find the words. "It changed things. He had already forgiven me, but I hadn't been ready to accept it."

"So you want me to write her a letter? And what, send it to the North Pole with my Christmas list?" Ransom's words dripped bitterness.

"She's already forgiven you. Don't you think it's time to accept it?" Shelby had no idea where the conviction came from, but his dismissive words gave her courage. She wouldn't be cowed by sarcasm.

"How do you know that? You say that like you've got a direct line to . . ."

Shelby turned and looked at him fully. She struggled to ignore his bright blue eyes, the striking features. No matter how blessed Ransom Fielding was on the outside, he had been cursed with a tragedy and years of guilt.

"If you could talk to her right now, what do you think she'd say?"

He dropped his gaze, stared at Nat's toes. "She would tell me . . ." He swallowed visibly and took a shaky breath. "She would tell me it was time to let it go. She wouldn't want me to think of her the way she was that last year, the way we both were."

"You knew her. I'm sure you're right."

He reached out and put his hand on her arm. "Shelby, what do you—"

A car horn sounded, loud and insistent. She turned and saw Langston at the corner, desperately waving as traffic stalled behind her.

"Oh, there she is!" Shelby shifted the baby to her shoulder and stood up. "I'll be right back."

She walked as quickly as she could to the corner. Her cousin reached out for the sleeping toddler, a huge smile on her face.

"I really can't thank you enough! You saved me a trip to the chiropractor's, for sure. Can I take you to coffee later this week sometime?"

"Anytime. It was my pleasure." Shelby waved her on into the backseat, where she struggled to buckle the sleeping baby into his car seat. Langston dashed back out and gave Shelby a quick hug.

"Take care," Langston called, red hair whipping behind her as she ran to slide into the driver's seat.

As the car moved away from the corner, Shelby slowly turned back to the bench, her heart in her throat. It was empty. Ransom was walking away, listening to a tall man in jeans and a red T-shirt who waved one hand as he spoke. As she stood watching, Ransom glanced back. His expression was inscrutable, his eyes dark. Shelby raised her hand briefly and he nodded.

On her way back to Chapman Hall, mocha and herbal tea in hand, she tried to take deep breaths of the fresh air. That conversation wasn't the answer she had been looking for. If Tasha had told her a tragic story, it would have been much better, easier. She took a sip of the scalding-hot coffee and wished she could burn away the emotions that rioted inside her heart.

Ransom locked his office door and threw himself in the nearest chair. Taking a long walk hadn't helped at all.

He dropped his head in his hands and groaned. What was he thinking? All the words he'd planned to say, the apology so carefully created, all gone when he'd seen her cradling that baby. What came out was fumbling, awkward. And then he'd confessed his darkest moment as a man.

As the scene came rushing back, he raised his head, eyes seeking answers on the ceiling. Why had he said anything? Maybe the way the sun was playing over her hair, the way she rocked the little boy. Or the tender expression on her beautiful face as she looked at him.

He let out a cry of frustration and jumped up, pacing the office with quick strides.

There was something in her that he couldn't name, some attribute that if he could place it, then maybe her hold on him would fade away. Fine, he would go at it logically. What was she *not?* A flood of words appeared to him—silly, petty, shallow, grasping, thoughtless.

He sat heavily in his chair, his head resting in his hands once more. There was a way about her, as if she came from a time when kindness and loyalty mattered more.

Loyal . . . now she sounded like a dog. His forehead thumped the desk, eyes squeezed shut. Impossible. That's what she was.

Her words echoed crazily in his ears. Ask forgiveness? It wasn't that easy. A painting and a life? Not even close. And he hadn't talked to God in years. Starting now wouldn't make any difference.

Still, he raised his head and his hand crept to a stack of paper. And then found a pen. His chest felt as if it were wrapped with steel bands. Only a few words made it on the paper before his vision blurred with hot tears.

Dear Lili,

Please forgive me . . .

Later, as Sirocco lay next to her in bed, Shelby covered her face with her hands and laid her heart bare. She couldn't erase his words, his expressions, from her mind. He was with her every second, and she had no right to him.

She hadn't gone to that party to make connections. Sure, that's what she had pretended and told Rebecca. But it was all because of him, because of Ransom, that she had dressed up and tried to be someone she wasn't. The pain she felt at admitting that fact was worse than anything related to that evening's humiliation.

Bile rose in her throat as she thought of Tasha, planning her wedding while Shelby secretly wished Ransom would call it off. The wrongness of it, of pretending to be the kind of woman who defends the truth no matter the cost, but deep inside is a traitor, was too awful. She was one of those people who honored with their lips but had a heart far from God.

After what felt like buckets of tears, the weight slowly lifted. If only she could go back a month or two, to before they had ever met. She resolved to make it better, somehow.

"That will be the last we see of each other," Shelby whispered into the darkness, fingers threading through Sirocco's soft fur.

Hours later, staring up at the ceiling, Shelby admitted defeat and rolled out of bed. Wrapping a light blanket around her like a shawl, she quietly unlocked the front door and padded out onto the porch. The breeze carried the scent of rich earth and growing things. The streetlight on the corner shed a little light but most of the neighborhood was left deep in darkness. She moved under the magnolia tree, putting out a hand to feel its trunk, the grass cool and slightly damp under her feet. The air was calm but for a whisper of air every few moments, as if the yard itself were breathing.

Peace wrapped itself around her as she raised her face to the night sky. Raising one finger, she traced Orion's Belt and smiled. Whatever happens, we are not alone here. God is constant.

Crawling under her grandmother's quilt into bed, she reminded herself that something good could come of all of this. She just hoped that her heart didn't have to be broken to find it. "God is faithful and he will not let you be tempted beyond your ability," she murmured. The fierce attraction she felt was stronger than anything she'd ever known before, but now that she'd faced her own dark desires, Shelby knew God would give her the strength to do what was right. Minutes later she sank down into sleep like falling underwater, her trails of tears almost dry on her cheeks.

*The tumult of her mind,*
*was now painfully great.*
*—PRIDE AND PREJUDICE*

# CHAPTER THIRTY-THREE

"Wow." Rebecca shook her head and stared into her half-full mug of black coffee. "Wow."

"I know." Shelby grimaced. The kitchen was flooded with early-morning light and her head ached from snatching only a few hours of sleep. The whole story had taken a while to tell. But she felt lighter, cleaner.

"You know, you're a really good person."

"What?" Shelby burst out laughing, incredulous. "I just confessed just about the worst thing one woman can do to another and I'm a good person? What planet are you on?"

"Listen, you admitted a whole lot of feelings. And that you'd been deluding yourself about why you went to that party. I didn't hear you trying to lure him away with your feminine wiles." Rebecca brushed her bangs from her face, eyes thoughtful. "Temptation is not a sin. That's what the nuns taught us in school."

"Well, stupidity should be. I don't know what I was thinking." Shelby picked at the threads of the place mat. She wrapped her hands around her mug, watching the steam curl up in wisps. "The worst part is that you warned me, and I brushed you off."

Rebecca reached out and squeezed Shelby's hand. "Don't be so hard on yourself. You developed feelings for him, would love for him to dump the tanorexic gold digger, but in the end, you got your act together. No harm, no foul."

"I guess I'm just disappointed. I thought I was a better person than that."

It was Rebecca's turn to chuckle. "I'm glad to see you're as human as the rest of us schmucks."

"Thank you." Shelby paused, wondering how to thank her for being the kind of friend who listens to a confession and helps build you up, rather than tear you down. Shelby blinked back tears. "For being here, and for not losing faith in me."

"Oh, honey." Her roommate left her seat and came round the tiny kitchen table, grabbing Shelby in an enormous bear hug. "We're all a work in progress, and we all fall short." Rebecca leaned back and, eyes wide and solemn, looked Shelby full in the face. "How many times have you kept me from doing something I'd regret? About a million. So lean on me for a bit."

Shelby's throat was choked with tears, but her heart was light. She didn't have to go through the day afraid she would run into Ransom. Whenever they met, she would treat him like any other friend, she was resolved.

The week flew by with not a glimpse of Ransom. And then another. She saw him once, walking down the sidewalk outside Chapman Hall, and she changed direction so they wouldn't meet. Spending quiet weekends at Aunt Junetta's helped calm her nerves even further. Her aunt seemed to guess something was troubling her, but didn't pry, and Shelby was thankful.

After a month, Shelby had almost convinced herself that the worst was over.

In her office by eight one Monday morning, Shelby grabbed her mail from the slot and strode toward her door. Finch's office was dark and silent. He had found her class reviews, finally. But he hadn't mentioned Katie or any actions he had taken. Shelby brushed away a twinge of worry. Surely he would back her up.

Her high-ceilinged office was bright with reflected morning sunlight. Shelby tugged open the window behind her desk and inhaled the heavy scent of winter, the last of the tree's leaves rippling inches from her hand.

She had hardly sat down in her office chair when the phone trilled.

"I just wanted to thank you again, for all your help." Marissa's shy voice carried through the wires.

"It's so great to hear from you!" Shelby trapped the phone between her chin and shoulder, setting her satchel under her desk. "Has your grandfather made any progress with the bank?"

"Well, that's the best part! Early this morning, my brother and I took the papers back to the bank. With your father as our lawyer, they seemed a lot more eager to look them over. We haven't heard for sure what can be done, but they're willing to talk to us."

"That's great news, really." Shelby closed her eyes in thankfulness. "I know they're getting information gathered up in the state attorney general's office, trying to charge him with fraud. It won't make you feel any better, but you're not the only ones."

"I know you won't be needing anything from someone like me, but I wish there was something I could do to show you . . ." Her voice trailed off.

"Marissa, I'm privileged to know you, and I will certainly tell you if I ever need anything." Shelby's voice broke along with her heart. She wished she could raise this girl's self-esteem out of the pit where David had shoved it.

"I'll let you go. But thanks again. For everything."

A knock on the door yielded Katie, hair stringy and limp, shadows under her eyes so large they almost touched her sharp cheekbones. An old backpack hung from one shoulder.

"Come in, Katie." Shelby stood, warily regarding the thin young woman. Her shorts were ragged and her legs bore purple and yellow bruises. Her tank top revealed tattoos of barbed wire circling both biceps.

"I was wondering if you could get the paper we signed, about the schedule for turning in my thesis work. I need to see the original." Her voice was soft, not as belligerent.

Shelby blinked. "You mean the one you tore up?"

"Right. I'm not going to do anything with it, I just need another copy, for Finch."

Frowning, Shelby regarded her for a moment. Why wouldn't Finch have told *her* that? But then again, he hardly ever told her anything.

"It's in the office. We can go get it now, if you like."

Katie sighed and dropped into the armchair by the door. She rested her head in her hands and moaned. "I'm so tired. I just want to go to bed." She lifted her eyes and asked beseechingly, "Could you go? I'll stay right here."

Shelby nodded, sympathy welling up in her for the young woman. "Sure. But, Katie, don't you think you should go to the doctor? You really don't look well."

"I'm fine," she snapped, eyes narrowing to slits. Then she sighed again and said, voice much softer, "Sorry, I'm just . . . tired, like I said."

Shelby slipped out the door and walked down the quiet hallway toward the office. Katie looked as if she was near a mental and physical breakdown. But Shelby couldn't force her to go to the doctor. If she wouldn't confide in her, Shelby couldn't help with whatever was the problem, either. She retrieved the original schedule for Katie's graduate thesis work with a heavy heart. She made another copy, for her files, just in case, and one for Katie.

As she neared her office door, she saw the young woman drop back into the armchair, glancing into the hallway.

"Here you are, and here's another copy. I really wish things had worked out better. You were doing some excellent research—"

"Thanks, that's what I needed." Katie stood up, snatching the paper from Shelby's hand, eyes already on the door. She shouldered her back-pack and strode out. Shelby watched her leave, grimacing at the sight of the large dragon tattoo around her calf. That girl hadn't had a mark on her when they had first met, three years ago. Now she looked as if she should work at the circus. Shelby tried to shrug off the disturbing encounter, but part of her wondered where Katie was going to end up. *Lord, please watch over Katie,* she whispered to herself. *Keep her safe from harm and help her to know Your presence in her life.* Shelby knew there wasn't much else she could do but pray.

Settling back into her office chair, she sorted her few pieces of campus mail into piles, turning a manila envelope over in her hands. The name of the sender jumped out at her—*Ransom Fielding, Agate Hall.* Her heart thudded in her chest and her breath quickened. She hated herself for reacting like that at the sight of his name. She shook her head and ran her fingers around the edges that jutted out against the envelope, wondering.

She gently unsealed the tape that held the envelope closed, and a small leather diary fell into her hand. Dark with age, a few water spots visible on the calfskin cover, the little book looked like a hundred others she'd seen from the Civil War era. The inside page marked it as the property of one Mrs. Marie Joliver. A slip of paper fluttered to her desk when she turned the page. Small, spiky script in a familiar hand confirmed the sender.

I found this in Roanoke on the weekend.
Thought you might want to see it.—RF

She shoved away an image of Ransom and Tasha on a romantic weekend trip. A page was marked near the middle with a yellow Post-it. Her hands trembled, while her common sense screamed at her that it couldn't be, that she should not hope. She scanned the spidery text, barely able to breathe. There, near the middle, were the words she sought. Twice, three times, she read the paragraph, then set the little book down on her desk.

Two years she had searched for the mysterious benefactor's name. Countless tiny libraries, antique shops, historical sections and museums. She'd read so many dull accounts of everyday lives she felt as if she were near three hundred years old instead of thirty. And here it was, in the campus mail, from *him*.

Shelby read the paragraph again and started to laugh. It proved this Marie was whom she'd been looking for, beyond a doubt. She would never have guessed.

> Susanna Caldwell is persistent in her petitions for funding. I suggested that my providing for two schools in the Thorny Hollow region should exempt me from further requests. She demanded to know, quite rudely, if I had run out of money. I assured her that I had no such worries, to which she responded that I must not "be a miser."
>
> She is quite my favorite person. She continues to assure me that no one will know who is donating the funds. My son would have me declared incompetent at once. I know I have the chance to distribute money as I wish only while dear Jeremiah is alive. He does not recognize me at all now, which pierces my heart, but I know he would have approved.

Shelby closed the small volume and held it against her chest. A woman, almost a widow, racing the moment her fortune would be turned over to her male child. Shelby shook her head, trying to wrap her mind around this new version of the "mysterious MJ." And that Ransom had solved the mystery for her. Shelby jumped from her seat and flew out the door.

*Her heart did whisper*
*that he had done it for her.*
*—PRIDE AND PREJUDICE*

# CHAPTER THIRTY-FOUR

Her tentative knock was answered with a brisk "Come in." As Shelby pushed the door open, Ransom's expression flickered, then melted into a huge smile. His white shirtsleeves were rolled up to the elbows, tie loosened. A mug sat near his laptop, papers stacked neatly to the side.

"Did you get the diary? Do you think that's who you were looking for?" He rose from his chair and crossed the room, expression hopeful.

She knew it had been a mistake the moment he came close. A thrill went through her entire body, and she wanted nothing more than to meet him as he walked toward her. Shelby clenched the book in one hand, and her other made a fist so tightly her fingernails made half-moons on her palm.

"Without a doubt. And I wanted to thank you, in person. You must know, you have to understand what this means to me." To her horror, tears appeared in her eyes and her throat closed around the words. She took a shuddering breath. It wasn't just the book or the thoughtfulness. There were so many emotions, they seemed to cancel themselves out inside her.

"Please, sit down." He tried to steer her toward a seat, but she stood resolute.

"No, I'm sorry, I can't stay. I just wanted to say thank you." Struggling for control, Shelby tried to focus on the view outside.

His voice was rough and seemed to have dropped an octave. "I wanted . . . I was hoping to tell you this some other time, but I took your advice."

"Advice?"

"The letter. Well, you never said exactly a letter, but it's about my wife, and what I had carried after her death." He ran a hand through his dark hair, searching for words. "You know, I should just save this for a better time."

"No, really, I want to know." Shelby leaned forward in her eagerness. Was it possible that his pain had been lifted? Could it be that easy?

Ransom fixed her with a steady gaze. "I've always been a proud man, Shelby. Always had a hard time admitting I was wrong. But I was unbelievably wrong to hold on to something in her name, something she would have forgiven." He hesitated, eyes strangely bright. "I wrote that letter and asked for forgiveness."

Stunned, Shelby felt a delighted smile spread over her face. "I'm so glad," she whispered.

"Me, too." His eyes never left her face. "I was

so angry with God, I didn't want to even acknowledge his presence in my life. I thought if he really loved us, he would have saved her. I still don't understand why everything happened the way it did, but I'm at peace. I feel like I've been swimming upstream for so long, fighting with God, and hating myself. But it was like I was welcomed home the moment I reached out." His eyes shone with joy, his face open with a happiness she'd never before seen.

Shelby's breath was caught in her throat and she yearned to wrap her arms around this amazing man. He had suffered so much, then turned away from the only real comfort in this world. His story touched her in a way that was beyond words, beyond fear.

Coming closer, he reached out for her hands. "Shelby, I need to tell you—"

As his hands touched hers, Shelby jerked back, her skin on fire. She should never have come, never have met him alone here.

His bright blue eyes went dark, confusion flooded his face.

Shelby searched around the room for some way to make an easy escape. A pack lay against the desk, heavy canvas hung with a canteen and crude metal tools. Like a drowning woman, she grasped at a new thread of conversation. "You're going away for a reenactment?"

He stared for a moment. "Right, next weekend.

Just getting a few things prepared." Ransom still faced her, eyes shadowed. "Would you like to come along? Dr. Stroud has a terrible need for assistance in the amputation tent." He smiled crookedly. "I'll probably lose a limb or two, as usual."

Her mouth opened to say yes, that she would go anywhere he wanted her to be, but in the end her words were only "No, I'm sorry. But it sounds like fun."

A deep chuckle washed over her; she felt as if she were standing in the sun on a cold day. "Liar. I was there when he first invited you. Nothing could have persuaded you to join us." He jammed his hands in his pockets and rocked back on his heels.

*Yes, but that was before I knew I wanted to be with you . . . forever.*

"Why don't you ask Tasha? Doesn't she like your hobby?" So it wasn't the smoothest reminder, but he needed to think of the woman planning their wedding, a woman whom Shelby couldn't forget.

Ransom frowned, brow creasing. "She would hate it."

"But it's good to share your hobbies, right? Especially if you'll be spending a lot of time out in the field." Shelby wished he would take another step back, far enough that she couldn't smell him.

He shook his head. "I'm lost. Why would I be sharing hobbies with Tasha?"

"Well, I'm no expert"—Shelby laughed nervously—"but marriages do well when each partner participates in the other's hobby, or at least appreciates it."

"Marriages?" He choked out the word, then started to laugh. "What does Tasha have to do with—How on earth—?" Astonished, he tried again. "You can't possibly think I would marry her."

Shelby's face flushed red-hot and she fairly shouted, "But she said you were!"

"No, you're mistaken," he said, infuriatingly calm, as if she hadn't just raised her voice at him.

"I'm not," she insisted. "That day we met in the Grind, she said she wanted to get to the Purple Parasol before it closed. She has your family heirloom ring and refuses to wear it because it doesn't match anything, so she has that big diamond instead. She talks weddings constantly! You thanked me for saving you from an evening of wedding details the night we went to dinner! She called your cell phone at midnight during an ice storm!" Shelby knew her voice was rising but was powerless to stop it. She felt as if the rules of the universe had suddenly been changed without her permission.

"You are mistaken. We're related. Second cousins on my mother's side. So, no wedding."

Her head was swimming, she was at a loss. She

put her hands to her cheeks for a moment and they now felt ice-cold.

"She's a wedding planner. And she doesn't have a thing to say that's not about weddings. It gets old, fast. I gave her the family ring because I didn't need it after I proposed to Lili. She wears that ugly diamond on her right hand because she needed a big ring to show off, I suppose. And the night she called, she knew I was driving here from Oxford. She wanted the number of a couple we both knew who had just gotten engaged." Stepping forward, eyes blazing, he said, "Is that what you've thought this whole time?"

Shelby looked up, alarmed. She licked her lips. They felt swollen. Everything was moving so quickly. Just this morning she was resigned to never seeing him again, and now anything was possible. He had been engaged, an unbeliever, an adversary. And now everything was different. She felt as if every nerve ending were on fire, the diary completely forgotten. His gaze dropped to her lips, then back to her eyes, then to her lips.

Shelby took a step back, her thoughts whirling. She wanted to laugh, to scream at him, to throw herself in his arms. But she had to think first.

"I'll be right back. I need . . . to go to the bathroom," she said in a choked voice. Without a second glance she turned and retreated.

The restroom was blessedly empty. A giggle burbled up from somewhere deep inside and she held her hands to her mouth. *Not engaged, not engaged, not engaged.* She shook her head, laughter rocking her back and forth. All the times she'd rejected his flirtations, frowned and glared and fretted.

The moment under the tree at his aunt's house flashed through her mind. Shelby wiped her eyes and tried to take a deep breath, still chuckling. He must think she was the meanest woman alive.

And he was still around. Did that make him crazy or just determined?

Deciding to reserve judgment on that last thought, she washed her hands. Her reflection showed a young woman, face flushed, eyes a bit too bright, but calm and composed. *Liar,* she whispered.

As the door swung open at her touch, Ransom lifted his head. He was still in the same spot she'd left him, eyes dark with emotion, but he remained silent as she entered the room.

"I wanted to ask you to dinner. As a thank-you," she said, her voice clear, but her hands trembled. "Do you have a dish you especially like? I can make anything and Rebecca makes a really delicious orange roast chicken that—"

"Yes," he interrupted. "I mean, yes, I'd like that, and, no, nothing special. Roast chicken sounds wonderful." He still hadn't moved from his position near the desk.

"Um, how about this weekend? Maybe Friday?"

she said, trying to be casual and wishing her heart would stop hammering. She could hardly hear him over the sound. How would she ever make it through a dinner?

"Sounds great."

She nodded and turned toward the door. A last glance showed him seemingly immobilized, but his eyes were bright with some powerful emotion.

*In vain have I struggled. It will not do.*
*My feelings will not be repressed.*
—MR. DARCY

# CHAPTER THIRTY-FIVE

"I thought we were cooking tonight. I wrote down the recipe for the teriyaki tofu, remember?" Rebecca asked. She cocked her head. "I knew it. You hate my tofu. I bet if we were having cheese grits, you wouldn't have an errand all of a sudden."

Shelby grinned. "Maybe. Maybe not."

Rolling her brown eyes, Rebecca let out a sigh. "It's so much better for you than all this stuff fried in lard. I want you to live a long and happy life. Is that so bad?"

"If it involves tofu, then yes." Shelby couldn't help laughing at Rebecca's expression. "Seriously, I don't mind it. I'm actually sort of learning to like it. That stir-fry last week was tasty." Shelby paused, choosing her words. "I just need to drive out to Natchez and paint something."

Rebecca's brows went up. "Today?"

"Right." Shelby felt her face go warm. "I have an idea. . . . I'm not sure if it will work out, but I'd like to try. And I want to do this before the weekend."

"Ohhhh." Rebecca extended the syllable several seconds. "I'm getting the picture here. This might have something to do with our dinner guest?" Her smile grew bigger and bigger.

"Maybe." Shelby grabbed her keys, easel and paint set. She felt like a teenager with a crush. A hugely overpowering crush that sent her driving across the county to paint run-down buildings that once meant something to someone else a long time ago. She shook her head at the ridiculousness of it all. "I'll be back by ten."

"Good luck," Rebecca called, "and drive safely."

Shelby angled into the car and said a quick prayer. Maybe it would turn out, maybe not. But her heart was pulling her toward an antebellum mansion, several hours away, and she couldn't seem to say no.

"I can't believe you lost another set of keys," Rebecca snorted.

"They're not lost, just temporarily misplaced." Shelby sighed, admitting defeat. "Usually they turn up, but I've looked everywhere. I'll have to tell Finch and they'll have to change the locks."

"He'll make you pay for that. But I'm on my way to campus. I'll check around Chapman, in case you dropped them."

"But you said you'd be here," Shelby said, aghast.

"I never said I'd be here," Rebecca said calmly. "I said I'd help make dinner, and I have. The angel food cake is done, the strawberries are cut, you just need to make the biscuits and put the chicken in the oven." She gripped Shelby's hand. "Look at me. From what you said, there's nothing keeping you apart. You two need to talk. You really don't need a chaperone. But you better tell me every-thing when I get back!"

"I can't believe you're leaving me to do this alone."

"I bet it will be awkward for about five seconds, and then you'll be thanking me. And I like nice jewelry, FYI." Rebecca grinned and grabbed her purse from the table.

"Very funny, traitor." Shelby grimaced and headed back to the kitchen.

"Oh, and Mr. Unengaged is here," Rebecca called out, laughing, before she opened the front door.

"But I haven't even changed!" Shelby ran for the bedroom. Her hair would have to stay in its ponytail, but she was determined to wear something nicer than old jeans and a T-shirt. She grabbed the pale blue silk dress from its hanger and slipped it on. She could do nothing about her makeup from the bedroom. A pair of matching sandals and she was ready.

She emerged to the sound of voices. Ransom was laughing easily with Rebecca, who had one foot in and one foot out of the doorway.

His dark hair was still wet from a shower, and a light blue button-up shirt and khaki pants made him seem as if he'd just stepped from a Weekender's catalog.

"Hi, Shelby. I guess I'm a little early." He glanced at Rebecca. "I'm sorry you're not staying. Maybe next time?"

"Absolutely. You guys are adorable, all matchy-matchy." Rebecca gave one last reassuring smile to Shelby. "Have fun!" And with that, she was gone.

An uneasy silence settled over the room and Shelby felt her cheeks warm under his gaze.

"Come in, please sit down. I just need to wash my hands," she said, rushing into the kitchen.

"I brought you something," he called through the living room at her departing form.

She scrubbed her hands, then swiped a towel and stepped back through the doorway. Ransom unwrapped the brown butcher paper, revealing a small, wooden easel, the right size for a tabletop. Its simple design complemented the smooth wood, varnished to a warm glow.

"An easel. Tansy mentioned you liked to paint." His voice was nonchalant but his eyes betrayed him. He watched anxiously, waiting for her response.

"An easel?" She froze, the towel suspended in her hands.

He turned it over, showing her the whorls and patterns. "A monster storm last spring split an oak at Collier House. It was over two hundred years old. My aunt called in an arborist but it couldn't be saved."

"Two hundred years old?" Shelby suddenly realized she was repeating him and tucked the towel under her arm.

"I understand the usual hostess gift is wine or flowers, but I know you don't drink and I didn't know what kind of flowers."

"Tulips, I like tulips."

"Ah, I see. Well, next time—"

"I love it. It's beautiful. I don't know what to say," she said in an uncertain voice. She took it carefully from Ransom, fighting an irrational urge to hug it to her chest.

A brilliant smile broke over his features, completely changing his countenance. "It's a copy of an antique desktop easel used by Thomas Nast."

"How long did it take you to do this? I invited you on Monday." Shelby couldn't help stroking the smooth sides, her slim fingers tracing over the pattern in the wood.

"About five hours. Not as long as some projects. And a great exchange for some fine Southern cooking."

"But I've only been cooking about an hour. That leaves me four hours in your debt."

"In that case, we should count all the time I spent watching the shellac dry. That must be about another six." He pretended to solemnly calculate in his head.

His mouth quirked up on one side, and Shelby found herself mesmerized by his lips. She wondered if they were warm and unconsciously moistened her lower lip, her tongue darting out. Her eyes were unfocused. She was lost, pondering the possibilities.

Ransom was standing near her, as close as when he had handed her the easel. He softly cleared his throat and reached out to turn it over. His hands were warm where they brushed her fingers and Shelby fought to focus on his words. "See here, I inscribed it to you, the date, and my initials. Would have put something better, like the Gettysburg Address, but it wouldn't fit. Also it would have taken hours since I was using my grandfather's hand tools."

"It's really lovely. I can't thank you enough. What a thoughtful gift." Shelby leaned toward him, almost without thinking, then checked herself. She should at least give the poor man something to eat before throwing herself in his arms. She glanced down at the easel and made a decision.

"I was going to wait until later. But since we're

exchanging gifts, I think I should give you yours."

"Mine?"

"Just a thank-you for the diary. I finished my paper on Susanna Caldwell that night and sent it over to Arthur Cavendish on Tuesday. He called a few hours ago and they're publishing it next quarter."

He grinned. "That's great news!"

"That's not all. I told my friend Brooks about the diary and I had two calls from some friends of his, producers at the History Channel, and they want me to be the consultant on a documentary of her life. Things are moving so quickly, after all that time spent looking for her name."

"I knew you could do it," he said softly, eyes dark with emotion.

Shelby swallowed. "There's no way to really say thank-you, but I have something." She popped back to the bedroom. When she returned, she placed the small package in his hands.

"What's this?"

"You ask too many questions. Just open it." She grinned and waited for him to unfold the tissue paper.

Inside was a small square framed in dark wood. He held it up, his face registering surprise, then wonder.

"My grandfather's greenhouse. That's the little Russian olive tree near the corner. And you can even see the wisteria vines along the roof." He looked up, eyes searching her face. "How did you find this?"

"I drove over there on Thursday. They let me set up a spot where I could paint." She felt a blush start to creep up her cheeks. "I wanted to give you something that had meaning. I—I hope you like it." Now she knew what he had felt as she stammered over his easel.

"It's wonderful. And look, they go perfectly together." He gently placed her small painting on the tabletop easel. They gazed at it in silence for a moment, admiring the pair. "You know what they say about great minds."

The sight melted her tenuous resolve and she wished with all her heart that dinner were over, that they could skip to the good-night kiss.

She struggled to get the conversation back on track. "Can I get you anything to drink? I'm just finishing the biscuits and the chicken is in the warming drawer. My grandmama had the best recipe for fried chicken. You have to let it rest in the buttermilk overnight. And the breading has some cayenne pepper in it for a little extra kick." She knew the words were tumbling out, but the alternative was to throw herself in his arms.

Ransom watched her walk away, his blue eyes deep and steady. "Anything is fine. And that sounds like a delicious recipe."

She slipped into the kitchen and leaned her head against the stainless steel fridge. Her cheeks felt flushed and her hands trembled. She was never going to make it through the evening. This was a big mistake. He was going to think she was some sort of unstable person, babbling and running to the kitchen every few minutes.

She raised her head and straightened her shoulders. Putting her feelings aside, she turned around in time to see Ransom poke his head into the little kitchen.

"Do you mind if I help? I promise not to burn down the house." Again the quirky smile. She focused on his collar, which was unbuttoned at the top. His smooth, tanned skin looked as if he had been on vacation, rather than holed up in an office with ancient diaries. His jaw was freshly shaved, but the dark shadow of his beard was still visible.

Quickly changing tack and gazing at his right ear, she nodded and motioned to the biscuit dough. "I was going to roll that out and cut the biscuits next."

He crossed to the porcelain double sink and rolled up his sleeves. His forearms were dusted with dark hair, and their thick muscles moved under his skin as he soaped and rinsed. Shelby envisioned the hours he spent shaving strips of wood with a centuries-old lathe, the smell of fresh sawdust in the air.

The pretty tiled kitchen seemed much smaller with Ransom in it. Shelby pinched a handful of flour from the tin. As she sprinkled it on the cutting board, she wondered how she was ever going to finish making dinner with him so near.

He leaned against the counter, his posture relaxed and friendly. "My mother told me a funny story once about forgetting the baking soda. She was so embarrassed that she threw the biscuits in the trash without saying anything, but our little dog stole them out again. My dad found him chewing his heart out on what looked like a pile of tan rocks."

She laughed, surprised. "I promise I remembered the baking soda." She rolled and smoothed the dough. "My grandpa told me that one year at the farmhouse the cook had put up some peaches but they didn't seal right so she threw them out for the turkeys to eat. The next morning when she looked out, the turkeys were lying all over the pen, dead. She was fit to be tied, thinking of how much waste it was, losing all the turkeys at once. She brought them into the kitchen and started plucking. She got through two turkeys before they woke up. They were just intoxicated from the bad peaches. There were naked turkeys in the kitchen that winter."

Ransom's eyes watered from laughter. "I can just see it. They probably woke up thinking, 'I'm never going to get drunk again, ever!'"

She shook her head. "You'd think someone could have knitted them some long underwear at least. But my grandpa said he remembers them as naked and mean, acting like they owned the kitchen. . . . Can you get the butter? It's on the middle shelf. I've got to grease the sheet."

Ransom's head disappeared from view for a moment. "You keep a stocked fridge."

"Rebecca would live on takeout from the vegan place on Fourth Street, but I love to cook. We're sort of meeting in the middle. I promise not to cook cheese grits and she lets me cook something other than tofu every day." Shelby spread the butter in quick swipes and cut out the biscuits with easy movements.

"Can't say tofu or cheese grits are on my list of favorite foods, but I do love a good biscuit." Ransom moved forward and gently transferred a biscuit to the sheet. They worked silently now, laying the off-white circles in even rows. Their shoulders brushed as they moved around the cutting board.

"Now, into the oven. I'll make the honey butter right before we eat." Shelby slid the sheet into the hot oven and brushed her hair back from her brow with the back of her hand.

He grabbed a paper towel, ran it under the water and wiped down the cutting board.

"Just leave the dishes, please. I'll do them all at once later," Shelby protested as he reached for the bowl and mixing spoon. Somebody had trained this boy well.

"However you like. I'm not afraid of washing dishes. I spent a good many evenings scrubbing pots as a kid."

"I can't believe you did many dishes at Bellepointe, somehow," Shelby said teasingly.

"Oh, but you didn't know my father. He felt that bed without supper was a poor punishment. He liked to send me down to peel potatoes or scrub the dinner pots. Mrs. Torrinio, our cook, loved him for that. She had plenty of help, but she enjoyed putting me to work best of all."

"Smart man. I think kids are happier when they have some work to do. I can't imagine growing up without anything but my own entertainment to focus on."

He nodded. "You know, when Tasha was younger, she wasn't so bad. Maybe a little silly. But I think her parents let her spend all her time amusing herself." He lifted his shoulders slightly.

Shelby opened a drawer and withdrew a linen tablecloth. "No, I understand." She didn't mind talking about Tasha now and even felt a little sympathy for her. She headed for the table and he followed.

"I was really glad to hear you thought we were engaged," he said softly from behind her.

Shelby stumbled, recovered herself. "Why?"

He didn't answer for a moment as he carefully lifted the centerpiece off the table and set it on the floor. Then he placed the easel and painting beside it. Shelby spread the tablecloth at one end and he reached to grab the other.

"Well, I noticed something. You never looked at me. We could have a whole conversation and you would only barely glance at me once or twice." He chuckled and shook his head, dark hair falling over his brow. "I was convinced you hated my guts. And the more I tried to talk to you, the worse it was."

Shelby forced a laugh, which came out pitched higher than she intended. She straightened the cloth and bent down to retrieve the easel, her mind whirling.

"I was so relieved to know it wasn't me," he said, setting the centerpiece back in its place. There was a long pause. Then he said, his voice low and full of a dawning realization, "But you're not looking at me now, either."

He stepped into her line of sight and she glanced up, straight into those intense blue eyes, felt her mind start to go blank and dropped her gaze. Shelby's heart was pounding so loudly she thought he must hear it. All those times she'd tried not to look at him because she didn't want to feel the things he made her feel.

He groaned. "I'm an idiot. Since Monday, I've been telling myself you disliked me because of Tasha. But that's not it, is it?" His shoulders sagged and he seemed to come to a decision. "You know, the dinner isn't necessary. I was happy to give you the diary, to help in any way I could. And I'll always be grateful for what you helped me understand, to accept, about my wife's death."

He picked up the painting, regret and something indefinable in his eyes.

"You're an incredible woman, Shelby." He seemed to want to say more but turned to the door. "I can show myself out."

*Elizabeth. . . now forced herself to speak.*
*—PRIDE AND PREJUDICE*

# CHAPTER THIRTY-SIX

Shelby stood with her hands still on the tablecloth, mouth open. She tried to speak but nothing came out. How had this happened? One minute they were discussing naked turkeys and the next he was halfway out the door, convinced she hated him.

"Wait!"

The word came out so loudly, so suddenly, that he whirled around.

"Ransom, please. Please stop." She took a deep breath and grabbed hold of her courage with both hands. She took a step forward and then another. "I need to explain. But I'm not good at this sort of thing. I'm sorry I gave you the wrong impression."

His expression lifted just a little but he didn't take his hand from the doorknob.

"You're right. I do—I did—try to avoid looking at you. But not because I couldn't stand the sight of you." Just the thought of it made her laugh. She wanted to memorize his every expression, every line when he smiled. "It's just that when I'm thinking"—she took a step nearer, holding his gaze—"and I see your face, I forget what I want to say. Everything sort of fades away, like fog in the sun."

She was a few steps away from him now. Hope flared in his eyes but he stayed silent.

"If you ask me a question and I'm trying to answer, all I can think of is this." She reached up and touched the shadow along his jaw. His eyes went half-closed. "And this." She touched his lips lightly, outlining them with her thumb. They were firm and warm, she couldn't raise her eyes past them. He sucked in a breath.

"And this." She was inches away. Her head swam with the smell of him, clean and woodsy. Standing on her tiptoes, she pressed her lips to his, softly. He was perfectly still for a moment, then suddenly his lips parted under hers with a groan and one strong arm wrapped around her waist.

One kiss slid into another and Shelby threaded her fingers through the thick hair over his collar. He cupped the back of her head with his hand and crushed her to him. She was lost in his touch. All those times she'd wished she could touch him, wished she could taste his skin. Time seemed to slow, then stop altogether.

Sirocco wrapped herself around Shelby's legs, meowing.

"Go . . . away . . . ," she groaned, nudging the insistent cat.

"Jealous," he said, voice muffled by her hair.

His lips found hers again and Shelby clung to him, eyes closed, her senses on fire.

Sirocco stood against the backs of her legs, paws kneading Shelby's thighs.

"Ow! Dumb cat." She stepped closer to Ransom, as if that were possible, and gasped as he trailed light kisses down her neck. Her arms were covered with goose bumps, her heart was pounding so she couldn't hear anything except her own breathing . . . and a faint beeping.

Ransom flinched and made a sharp noise in the back of his throat but didn't raise his head from Shelby's skin. "Your cat just sank her claws into my calf," he growled against her neck.

Shelby reluctantly opened her eyes and thought for a moment she had gone blind from happiness because the light from the windows had gone gray. And foggy. *Smoke!*

"Ransom!" Shelby gasped, putting her hands on his shoulders.

He mumbled incoherently against her ear. The fire alarm sounded shrilly and his head jerked up. "What on earth?"

"The biscuits!" She disentangled herself from his arms and ran to the kitchen, Ransom following right behind her. She pulled open the oven door and withdrew a smoking sheet of blackened rocks. He swiftly opened the back door for her, and she set the mess on the cement step.

Shelby grabbed a towel and waved it at the shrieking smoke alarm, but it continued its earsplitting wail. Ransom stepped behind her and, reaching up, flipped open the plastic cover and removed the battery with a quick twist. The instant silence was almost as deafening.

"Well." Ransom rubbed his face with his hand and grinned. "That was quite a first kiss."

Laughter bubbled up from somewhere deep inside and Shelby laughed until she had to wipe tears from her eyes. She leaned against him and giggled into his shirtfront. "I'm telling you," she gasped, "when you're around, I lose my mind. I didn't hear the oven beep once."

"Now we know that your cat is also useful for preventing death by smoke inhalation," he said, nuzzling the top of Shelby's head. "I thought she was just good for keeping warm during an ice storm."

"She's a genius," Shelby agreed, letting herself be pulled back into his arms.

Her cell phone sounded the first few bars of a fight song. Shelby turned her head and frowned. "That's my dad. He never calls my cell. Do you mind?" But Ransom was already letting her go with a tender touch on the cheek.

Shelby flipped open the phone, her heart sinking in her chest.

"Shelby, honey?" His voice was muted, hoarse.

"Daddy?" Shelby gripped the counter behind her.

"Shelby, it's your aunt. She . . . she's had a stroke. Bessy Arbogast came over this afternoon and found her in the kitchen. She was in her nightgown but we don't know if it happened this morning or . . ." His voice trailed off. *Or if she had lain there all night.* He didn't need to say the words. "They've got her stabilized at General Hospital, but I think you should come." His voice cracked on the last word. "I don't think you should wait until tomorrow."

"Okay, Daddy. I'm coming right now." Shelby slowly closed the phone and sank into the kitchen chair. The ruined biscuits and the dangling smoke alarm evaporated from her thoughts.

She turned to Ransom and tried to explain but not all the words would come out. "My aunt is in the hospital. . . . I need to go."

Ransom stepped to the oven and turned it off. "You should pack. I'll put the dishes away." He was already headed for the living room to gather the plates.

Shelby rose slowly from the table and walked to her room in a daze. Aunt Junetta, her rock, her cheering squad. The one she was most like, her partner in crime. She sank onto her bed, unable to grasp what her father had said, the fingers of one hand tracing the pattern in the old quilt.

"Are you done?" Ransom was tapping on her bedroom door and Shelby raised her head in confusion.

“I have to get out my suitcase,” she whispered.

“Tell me where it is,” he said briskly.

“The laundry room closet.” She realized she should at least point him in the right direction but he was back within seconds.

“I wrote a note for Rebecca and left it in the kitchen. Are you packing for the week? Several days?”

She met his eyes and shuddered. Was she packing for a funeral? “I don’t know.”

“Can I help? Where are your shirts?” Ransom had moved to the closet and was pulling out a pair of slacks. The thought of him packing her underwear made Shelby sit up and shake the fog from her brain.

“Wait, I can do it. Can you get Sirocco’s carrier? It’s in the laundry room, over the dryer.” As soon as he was gone, she grabbed socks and underwear, shirts and pants, shoving them into her suitcase. With a stab of pure agony, she took a black dress from its hanger and carefully laid it on top of her clothes. Just in case. By the time she had her toiletries from the bathroom, Ransom had collected Sirocco’s dishes and food.

“Shelby, you can’t drive like this. Let me take you.” He grasped her hands and leaned close, eyes dark with emotion.

“No, I can, I just need to . . .” What she needed was to go back in time, back to before her daddy had called. She rested her forehead against his chest and let out a short sob.

"Please, let me take you." He rubbed her back and waited.

After a few moments of struggling to control her tears, Shelby lifted her head and nodded. "Okay" was the only word that came out of her mouth, but her eyes spoke volumes.

The drive was just an hour but it seemed an eternity to Shelby. Sirocco made unhappy noises in the back, wanting to escape the carrier and wondering whose car they were in. Ransom prayed with her, asking God to touch Junetta with his healing hand. The words seemed to come so easily to him, even though it had been years since he'd been on speaking terms with God. Gratitude swelled in her that there was someone to pray, to speak the words she could hardly say because tears choked her throat.

If only she had been there this weekend, then she might have found Aunt Junetta hours earlier. As they drove, Ransom gripped Shelby's hand, fingers laced together, and only let go to shift gears. The warmth of his touch was the only thing that kept Shelby from drowning in grief.

*It was painful, exceedingly painful, to know they were under obligations to a person who could never receive a return.*

*—PRIDE AND PREJUDICE*

# CHAPTER THIRTY-SEVEN

"Shelby, I'm so glad you're finally here!" Like a drowning woman Mrs. Arbogast clutched her. Nurses bustled around, pushing carts and preparing medication.

"I want to see her," Shelby said, her voice thick with tears.

"Of course. Come in—oh!" Mrs. Arbogast seemed to see Ransom for the first time, standing silently and somberly behind Shelby.

"This is Ransom Fielding," she said, and reached out for his hand. He closed his broad one around hers, and she drew strength from it.

"Will he be coming in?"

Shelby looked at him, her eyes pleading. She couldn't do this alone.

"Yes, if they'll let me." His voice was soft, his grip firm on her fingers.

They followed Mrs. Arbogast down the brightly lit hallway, past the nurses' station, and into the critical-care unit. The door was ajar, and a faint beeping could be heard from inside the room. Shelby faltered, took a shuddering breath and stepped through the door.

Aunt Junetta lay still, a large tube protruding from her mouth. Wires and small tubes led from her veins and chest. Sensors tracked every movement, but her eyes didn't flicker at the sound of Shelby's cry.

Collapsing at the side of the bed, she felt her heart break into a thousand pieces. Her beloved cooking partner, her confidant, was steps from death. Shelby knew, at a glance, that this was not something Aunt Junetta would recover from. It was time to say good-bye.

Ransom's hands covered Shelby's shaking shoulders and smoothed her hair. After a few minutes, she felt him step away, then heard murmuring voices at the door. She couldn't tear her eyes away from her aunt, couldn't wrench her hand from her frail arm.

Sometime later, Shelby turned to see her father in the doorway. She rose, fresh tears falling from her swollen eyes. "Oh, Daddy," she whispered, sobbing in his arms.

"I know, Shelby, I know." He stroked her back, voice choked with tears.

Time seemed to have lost its rhythm. It ebbed and flowed in a way that made the evening fly by, but the night hours dragged.

"Where's Ransom?" she asked, when her father came in again near nine, urging her to eat something.

"He brought Sirocco and your bag to the house and then left for Spartainville. He came to say good-bye, don't you remember?"

Shelby shook her head, grimacing. Her head throbbed from crying, she had hardly eaten all day. She saw her purse on the chair and checked her cell. Her phone was packed with messages from Rebecca, and Shelby reluctantly left her aunt's room to make a quick call.

When she returned, a somber Jennie Anne was standing at the bedside, for once not chattering at full speed. She was pale and silent.

"Shelby," her father said, "you should go home and rest. We'll call you if anything happens." He looked pale and sad, and older than she had ever seen him.

"Daddy, I don't want to leave you here alone," Shelby said, tears leaking from her eyes.

"Go home, Shelby." He kissed her lightly on the forehead. "She's my only sister. I want to wait the night with her."

Nodding glumly, Shelby took her sister's hand and her father's hand. They bent their heads in prayer.

"Give thanks in all things, for that is the will of Christ Jesus," Shelby whispered, "so I thank God for the life of this woman."

Her father squeezed her hand, nodding. "Thank you for her life and the love she gave us. Psalm 116 says, 'Return unto thy rest, O my soul, for the Lord has dealt bountifully with thee.' Let her rest in you, Lord."

"Amen." Jennie Anne sniffed and wiped her eyes with her free hand.

Shelby gave her father one last hug and left for home.

Standing at the grave site, Shelby felt numb and cold. She should never have left. She should have stayed with her aunt in the hospital. Her family huddled together as the casket was lowered into the ground. The minister's words were familiar and comforting, but murmurs of grief sounded all around her. Mrs. Arbogast wept openly into a handkerchief. Shelby's face was dry, but her eyes were filled with tears.

Later, at the Roswell home, as visitors signed a condolence book and shared their memories, she wondered whether life would ever be the same. But of course, it wouldn't. Aunt Junetta was gone, and Shelby saw her life stretch out before her lonely and dark. If only they had had a bit more time. She wished she could have introduced her to Ransom and smiled a little at how her aunt had, even then, known that he was special to her.

Her cell phone rang and Shelby didn't move to answer it in the packed room of mourners.

Ransom had called that morning and they had talked briefly. He wanted her to know he was thinking of her, asking her to call if she wanted. A message from Jolee last weekend had passed on the condolences of the department and assured her that her classes for the week were covered.

Her phone sounded again. And again. Shelby frowned, checking the display, and saw Rebecca's name. Her mother glared at her across the room and Shelby sighed, trudging outside to answer it. She was tempted to turn it off, but something about the urgent ringing set off an alarm in the back of her mind.

"Rebecca? We're having the funeral reception. Can I call you back?" Shelby felt as if the words were coming out of someone else's mouth; her face felt heavy with grief.

"Shelby?" Rebecca's voice shook.

"What happened?" Dread coiled in the pit of Shelby's stomach.

"There's a video, online. Of you in your office . . . and it's bad."

Shelby said nothing, trying to make sense of Rebecca's words.

"You're not alone. There's a man in the video, too."

"You're not making any sense. Me and a man in my office?" repeated Shelby.

"It looks like a student. Was it a student?"

She shook her head, confusion giving rise to

anger. “I don’t understand what you’re saying. *Who* was a student?”

“Shelby, this video . . . Look, go upstairs and find it on YouTube. Someone put it on Facebook, and then it got put up on YouTube, and now it’s everywhere.”

“But what is it?” Shelby glanced back into the living room, and the mourners rotating slowly around the long table of food. “Fine, tell me how to look it up.”

“Just search for”—Rebecca’s voice trembled—“ ‘Hot Professor Does Freshman in Office.’ ”

Shelby stared at the hallway wallpaper, unseeing. Her mouth opened, but no sound came out. She slowly closed the cell phone and went upstairs, her feet leaden.

Minutes later, Shelby sat with her hand over her mouth, eyes wide with mounting horror. The video was grainy; the frame shook as the cameraperson walked toward her office. The view was clearly of Chapman Hall as the intricate decorations over the top windows came into view. The oak limb that Shelby loved nearly blocked the frame, so the cameraman had to stand on something, maybe the short wall across the street.

It was night; the light inside illuminated the action as if it were onstage. A half-dressed auburn-haired woman and a young man maneuvered around the desk, sweeping items onto the floor. The woman’s face was never shown, but her curly auburn hair swept from side to side. The young man had dark hair, but he wasn't anyone she had ever seen before. Shelby felt bile rise in her throat. Everyone would think it was her, assume she had been caught in this video.

She dialed Rebecca's number with shaking hands. "It's not me, you know that, don't you? You know that!"

Her roommate let out a long breath. "I do. You would never have, could never have, done that. But Shelby, this looks really bad."

"When did you see it?"

"I just heard about it tonight. But look at the number underneath the video."

Shelby peered at the screen and gasped. Two hundred thousand views? Was that possible?

"I'm coming back. Oh, but Ransom drove me down here. . . ." Shelby's heart stopped, wondering if Ransom had seen it yet, if he would think that was her on the video.

"I'm coming down to get you. Just hold tight." Rebecca's voice was firm, decided. "And, Shelby?"

"Yes?"

"Maybe you should call Ransom."

*You will be censured, slighted, despised, by everyone connected with him.*

—LADY CATHERINE DE BOURGH

# CHAPTER THIRTY-EIGHT

Shelby stood up, legs shaking, and the phone rang again as soon as she snapped it closed. Finch's name read on the display.

She answered, struggling to keep her voice even.

"Shelby, I've just been told to set up a meeting with you on Tuesday."

"A meeting? Told?" Her head spun, trying to catch up.

He sighed impatiently. "In light of the video, you're on administrative leave, obviously. On Tuesday we'll have a meeting with the board of directors to see what happens next."

Her knees buckled and she sat with a thump on the office chair. "On leave? But it wasn't me! How can I be placed on leave for something that I didn't do?"

"Do you deny that's your office?" His voice held utter contempt.

"No, that's my office." She struggled to organize her panicked brain. "But I lost my keys, about a week ago. Someone must have found them and filmed this video while I was gone."

"You never said anything about losing your keys," he said, disbelief palpable.

"But I did, really! And that's not me. . . ." Shelby glanced back at the screen, trying to find something in the grainy footage that proved her innocence.

"We're not discussing it now. The board has taken measures. You're on leave. Tuesday at two o'clock. If anything comes up, let me know." He hung up with a snap.

Shelby sat, unseeing, for some time. Maybe she should call Ransom. But how to begin? What could she say? The image of the couple seemed burned into her brain and she shuddered.

Rebecca pulled into the driveway a few hours later and jumped from the car. Shelby stood near the doorway, bags packed. Sirocco was in her carrier, sleeping. The guests had all gone, and she had told her father that she had to get home. His pale face hardly registered her words as he sat in his study, staring out the window.

"Oh, Shelby," Rebecca said, giving her a hug in the driveway.

"Do you think—is it really that bad?"

Rebecca bit her lip. "Well, maybe it's not. I don't know everything. Sometimes people just gossip . . ." She let the end of her sentence trail away.

Shelby's heart fell like a stone. "Finch called. I'm on administrative leave, with a board of directors meeting on Tuesday."

Rebecca gasped, shock registering in her wide eyes. "They can't put you on leave without a hearing. We have to call the dean of faculty immediately. Shelby, you can't let them railroad you for some prank someone else pulled in your office."

Shelby winced at the actions on the video being called a "prank." She loaded her bags into the car, settling Sirocco in the backseat. "I don't know what to do. It's Saturday. Will the dean even be in his office?"

"Shelby, you have to call these people at home. This is an emergency!"

She felt that her mind was overloaded with grief and shock. This new development was just one more scene in a long nightmare that had started when her father called. She laid her head back on the seat and closed her eyes. "Why is this happening? Why now?"

She felt Rebecca's hand squeeze her arm. "I'm sorry. Just rest for a bit. When we get there, we can make those phone calls."

No one would return her messages. Monday arrived and Shelby reached a secretary for the dean of faculty. The older woman's voice sounded solemn as she explained that the dean would be at the meeting on Tuesday. He would call her if there was anything to discuss before then.

Rebecca was incensed, slamming napkins down on the table. She had made some soup, although Shelby wasn't hungry. "That's what Richard Angle is there for, to be your advocate!"

Shelby shrugged, stirring the soup with her spoon. Her face felt heavy with tears, but she hadn't cried since before the funeral.

"Did you reach Ransom?"

"I . . . haven't tried." She was just so tired. She knew she should be trying to explain to him, to convince him. The video had been linked to news sites and social networks across the nation. The media coverage was overwhelming. It had started with the local stations and had worked its way up. "I don't think he wants to be part of this train wreck," she said, trying to sound offhand but only managing to sound deathly tired. She couldn't imagine what he must be thinking.

"Maybe he hasn't seen it yet," Rebecca said hopefully.

Shelby snorted. "Everyone has seen it. They played a clip on the national news. Of course, they framed it as how the digital age has made it much harder to have a romantic life without your boss finding out."

There had been no discussion about whether it had been Shelby at all. Journalists had called repeatedly, but every time she denied involvement, they lost interest. They all wanted to know who the student was and what kind of grade he'd gotten in her class. The thought of it made her stomach churn. She took a sip and forced herself to swallow. "I don't think there's anything I can do except wait for the meeting."

"That Miami station was the worst, calling the Roswells the 'Rebel Family.' You told me once that your father had sided with the desegregationists and was voted out of his position as DA, but you didn't tell me about Jennie Anne's problem this year."

Shelby nodded. "When she called me, it was all about some note she wrote that the teacher found. When the station reported it, they made it sound like she'd personally attacked a professor and barely dodged a suspension. It seems they can twist it whatever way they want."

Rebecca said nothing, her face glum and eyes bright with tears.

"But, hey, on the bright side, everyone thinks I have a social life," Shelby said suddenly, a wry smile touching her lips.

"Not funny," Rebecca said, but she laughed anyway.

*Miss Bennet, I am shocked and astonished. I expected to find a more reasonable young woman.*

—LADY CATHERINE

# CHAPTER THIRTY-NINE

She sat in the chair across from Finch, who shuffled his papers in a dramatic way. His gray hair was combed nicely, and the usual murk on his glasses was wiped clean, as if he had groomed carefully for the starring role in her execution.

Dean Richard Angle wore an expression akin to that of a patient in a dentist's chair. He had brushed off her attempts to speak to him privately, and instead ushered her into the meeting room with cold impatience.

"Shelby, this is Eric Frohmeyer, Shannon Cartwright, Linda Hamlin, Bob Marnier and Jonathon Warren," Angle said, introducing the board, who all nodded gravely at Shelby. She lifted a hand, but not a single smile answered her tentative gesture of friendliness. The dean reached forward and pressed a button on the recording device in the middle of the table. He gave the date, time and people present.

"We're here to discuss your continued

employment at Midlands College, in light of the recent video that was shown on national media outlets. The video shows you in your office with a student—"

"Wait," Shelby interrupted breathlessly. "It's not me."

"Please hold any comments until I have stated the full reason for the hearing," the dean admonished her sternly.

Shelby sank back in her seat, crestfallen. This was no hearing. It was an academic kangaroo court.

"The video has made Midlands College infamous for professorial misconduct, and the board feels that you should resign. Your actions have undermined the trust that parents and students have in the community. Respect for the college has diminished, especially on the national front. People who had never heard of us before have seen the news coverage and formed a negative opinion. The damage done to the college could be in the millions, when we consider possible drops in enrollment and donations."

Shelby's eyes opened wide. So, not only was her career down the drain, but she might be held financially accountable for this farce? The dean paused, and she didn't know if there was more to come, or if it was her turn to speak.

"Miss Roswell, is there anything you have to say?"

Shelby gazed back at Shannon Cartwright, the chair of the faculty disciplinary committee. Dark hair hung on either side of her dour face. Her eyes were unblinking behind thick, old-fashioned glasses. But Shelby had the feeling that if anyone in the room was interested in hearing the truth, it was this somber woman.

"It's not me." Shelby took a breath, her heart was pounding. "I lost my keys about two weeks ago. I didn't tell anyone because I'm always losing them and they eventually turn up. My aunt had a stroke." She felt her eyes fill with tears and angrily blinked them away. "And died the next night. I've been in Flea Bite Creek for the funeral. It's not me," she finished, her voice trembling.

"There's no time stamp on the video," said Richard Angle, who jabbed his pen in the air as he spoke, voice creaking with excitement. The dean of faculty seemed to be excited to finally be a part of something other than departmental backstabbing. "I watched it several times. It could have been recorded anytime."

Shelby winced, imagining how many people had watched the video, how many times.

"And you don't deny it's your office," said Eric almost triumphantly. He leaned back in the chair and straightened his tie.

"Yes, it's my office." Shelby's heart sank at his eagerness to find her guilty.

The dean pulled a small laptop from his bag and set it on the table. "Bob Marnier has requested we watch the video during the conference, so that we are all aware of what it contains."

Shelby sat up, shocked. "Surely everyone has seen it already." *Please, God, don't let them all watch it again.*

"There's no need for that, I would think," Shannon said, raising an eyebrow in surprise.

"I haven't actually seen the video," Finch said, and shrugged as if it hadn't mattered enough to him to see what the rest of the world was talking about.

"Then we should view it," the dean sighed.

Shelby watched in horror, stomach churning, as the clip started. It was shaky and out of focus. The cameraperson maneuvered around on the side-walk, so the giant oak limb was to the right. The screen flickered in and out, the recording quality dismal. What was she supposed to do? Where was her advocate?

Shelby sat up with a gasp. For the first time since Rebecca had called, she understood some-thing vital. This was not a random prank. It was intentional. If it had been clear, it would have been harder to make everyone believe it was her. And those missing keys were not going to turn up anytime soon.

The room seemed to spin with her knowledge that someone hated her enough to steal her keys and commit this act in her office, in front of a camera. How much hatred did it take to ruin her reputation this way?

But she was finally on the way to understanding what this was all about. She leaned forward eagerly, eyes bright. There must be some clue, something she could use. She forced herself to ignore the unfamiliar black lingerie on the young woman. The board couldn't take the contents of her underwear drawer as evidence.

The red curls swayed over a too-thin back. Shelby almost opened her mouth to point out that anybody should be able to tell she wasn't the woman in the office just by body shape. But she needed hard proof. She narrowed her eyes, willing herself to disregard the hair, probably a wig, and search for anything else.

"Stop!" she yelled, and the board members jumped. Finch swiveled from the screen and fixed her with a glare, his face twisting unpleasantly.

"Go back a second, to where she lifts her arms to unbutton his shirt," she said, pointing at the little video player. The dean reached over and scrolled back a little. Shelby waited, pulse racing as they waited for the video to begin again. "Now stop," she commanded. The dean obediently paused the clip, the screen fuzzy with the image of the young woman's hair, arms and the torso of the young man.

Shelby stood, legs shaking. She began to

unbutton her cardigan with trembling fingers, face flushed.

"Miss Roswell, please!" Linda, the only other woman on the board, who had kept silent since Shelby had entered the room, started to protest, pale eyes wide. "There's no need for theatrics." Linda looked at the dean beseechingly. "Perhaps we should have brought security," she whispered loudly.

Shelby laughed, incredulous. By now her cardigan was off and she stood before them in her silk tank top. She held out her arms and turned around, so only the back of her was visible.

"Tell me what you see," she commanded.

Despite the murmurs around the room, Shelby held her place. They would figure it out, if they opened their eyes.

There was a sudden gasp and Shelby allowed herself a tremulous smile. She turned slowly, arms still raised. "No tattoos. The woman in that video has tattoos on both arms. One here"—she pointed to each grainy biceps on the screen—"and one on her wrist, that you can see later. I thought it was a bracelet."

"How do you know it's not a bracelet?" asked the dean. His face was hopeful, but wary, as if her innocence were proven too easily.

"Because I know who that is, and maybe I know why she did this to me," Shelby said, the exultation slowly fading from her voice. *Oh, Katie, what were you thinking?*

*You thought me then devoid of*
*every proper feeling, I am sure you did.*
*The turn of your countenance*
*I will never forget.*

—MR. DARCY

# CHAPTER FORTY

As she left the building, Shelby gazed up at the bright, cloudless sky. Her father had wanted to come, but she'd told him she would have to do this alone. A quick phone call from the conference room, and he was jubilant, telling her that everything would return to normal now. She wasn't so sure, but said nothing. His voice still held traces of grief, pausing where it wouldn't have before. Shelby was thankful for his sake, and her mother's, that she had been vindicated.

She yearned to call Aunt Junetta and let her know that she would be keeping her job. The emptiness ached like a wound and she blinked back sudden tears. *But she knows already,* she reminded herself.

"Shelby." That one word brought her to a standstill. His voice was low, quiet. She turned to see Ransom standing near the door, where he must have been waiting.

"Hi," she said simply.

In the awkward pause Shelby felt her face begin to flush. He walked nearer, his dark gaze fixed on her face. The kiss they'd shared flashed through her mind, as it had so many times before, but now it rocked her with a powerful need. She yearned to reach out to him, to let him fold his arms around her.

"Thank you for your help with my aunt. I'm sorry I didn't say good-bye, or maybe I did, but I don't remember it."

"You're welcome," he said, coming close to her. She noticed his eyes were rimmed red, tired. "How did it go? I've been worried."

"Really?" Shelby smiled for the first time; a fierce gladness went through her. "I wasn't sure. When I didn't hear from you . . ." She dropped her gaze, knowing it was her fault for not trying to contact him.

"I figured you would call if you needed me." His tone was subdued, almost glum. Shelby felt a shiver run down her back, as it always did when he was near her and spoke.

"It went all right. I can keep my post here, but I don't know how they can possibly fix the media hoopla." She winced at the thought of how far the lie had spread.

"They're letting you stay?" The surprise in his voice made her head snap up. His eyes were wide, shock spread over his features.

"Well, yes." Shelby frowned, confused by his reaction. "I mean, I'm sure they planned on dismissing me at first, but when I proved the woman wasn't me, they didn't really have a choice. I'm sure there'll be some censure for losing my keys and not reporting it right away."

"It wasn't you?" he asked too loudly. A few heads turned as people passed them on the sidewalk.

Shelby stared, mouth slightly open. "What did you think?"

He rubbed his hand over his face. "I didn't know what to think. It looked convincing. . . ."

Fury rose like a flash inside her. "Convincing? A skinny, tattooed girl writhes around on my desk with some kid and it's convincing? A shaky, blurred video of someone who doesn't even show her face is all it takes for you people?" Her voice trembled with white-hot anger.

"Shelby, I'm sorry," he said, eyes pleading. "You have to understand. Everyone said—"

"Right, *everyone said*. The entire nation said that it was me, and it *wasn't*. Maybe it was too much to ask, but I really thought I would get the benefit of the doubt, at least from you." Shelby's fists were clenched and her face felt tight with the effort of not screaming at him. Her eyes burned with angry tears.

"Please, Shelby," he whispered, reaching out to touch her hand, so softly.

She jerked it back. “No, Ransom. You once told me you felt like you could trust me. But you didn’t even give me a chance to explain before you believed the worst. It seems you’re the one who can’t be trusted.”

With that, she turned and walked blindly toward Chapman Hall, doing her best to ignore the whispers and murmurs of the people she passed along the way.

“Shelby, we tracked down Katie Young.” Her father’s slow drawl sounded in the receiver. Shelby clutched the phone tighter and took a deep breath. No matter what the girl had done, Shelby still cared about her.

“Is she . . . What did she say?”

“Rebecca’s friend in Miami traced the video pretty easily. Once we told Katie that we had proof, she told us how it happened. It’s an ugly story and not exactly what we thought. David Bishop conned her grandmother into signing some papers that were a bank loan, which he pocketed, just like the LeJeunes’. So, she was working three jobs trying to keep up with the payments. When he started offering her other jobs and paying her much more than she could earn by herself, she said okay.”

Shelby’s throat constricted. “Other jobs?”

“He had a group of girls he had blackmailed into being escorts and running drugs over the state border. When the attorney general started looking into his business dealings, and Bishop heard we were behind it, he decided to set you up. He told Katie that if she stole your keys and did this job, he'd repay the grandmother's loan, and they could keep the old place."

Shelby rocked back in her chair, stunned. Katie had mentioned her family's historic home, but she had never thought that David could have been involved. What Shelby thought was simple revenge was much more heartbreaking.

"That's horrible. What's going to happen to her?"

Shelby's father made a noise into the phone. "You're a sweet girl, you know that? You could be calling for her head, she tried to kill your career."

Shelby's chest tightened at the thought of what Katie had ruined—more than her career, her relationship with Ransom. But it would probably have failed in the end if he had that little faith in her, she told herself.

"It seems that there's not a lot that can be done with a video that doesn't exactly identify the victim. Other people wrote your name in the comments, but it doesn't say that on the video. So, legally, she's probably safe. We could charge her with theft because of the keys, I suppose."

Shelby gazed at the ceiling, wishing that Aunt Junetta could give her some advice right about now. She waited for the fury to take over, the white-hot anger she had felt before, but all she felt right now was a bone-deep weariness.

"That's okay, Daddy. I think she's suffered enough. Charging her with theft wouldn't repair my reputation." Shelby's voice sounded hollowed-out by sadness to her own ears.

But she had a plan, and it might just work.

"Caroline, thank you for coming down to Midlands," Shelby said, ushering her friend into the office. Jolee had been quiet when Shelby had come to pick up her campus mail early that morning. No one had knocked or called for hours. She had no idea what was going to happen tomorrow during class. But she couldn't think about that now.

"Anything I can do to help, Shelby," Caroline said, hugging her tight. "I didn't tell my mother where I was going. I'm sure you can imagine what she's been saying."

Shelby's stomach lurched a little as she tried her best not to imagine. Then she smiled a little, glad to see her friend was still alive under all that smothering. It boded well for what she had in mind.

"I need a favor, and I need it from you." For the next half hour, Shelby outlined her plan.

"You know, I think this may just work. Let me make some calls, and we'll see what happens,"

Caroline said, eyes lit from within, voice filled with excitement.

"I knew you would be game for this!" crowed Shelby, and threw her arms around her old friend, nearly knocking her off her chair.

The next morning, Shelby stepped into the bookstore to buy a copy of the *Washington Post*. With shaking fingers, she laid her money on the counter. Clutching the paper to her chest, she walked outside and sat on a bench. The front page bore the headline "Professor Rebuilds Reputation After Viral Video Sham." Caroline's byline stood out in big, bold print. The article took up half the front page and a full page in the first section. Shelby read every word, sitting on the hard bench, students streaming past. A smile crept over her face as she read the truth and appreciated the glorious ease that Caroline had with words. She made you care about the injustice and the pain Shelby had suffered, grow angry at the near dismissal, and rally for her as she tried to expose the lies.

It helped that David Bishop was formally charged with extortion, bank fraud, pandering and many other crimes. Caroline carefully avoided hinting at Katie's identity, but had given the readers enough proof that it made the scenario believable.

Shelby folded the paper and sighed. So many

things had fallen into place, and she was thankful that the persecution was coming to an end, but a persistent misery rose in her chest. Every time she thought of the moment Ransom realized she was not the woman in the video, she felt as if her heart were breaking all over again.

The surprise on his face had told her everything. Whatever connection she thought they had, or emotions that surged in her or the energy that crackled between them, none of it mattered.

If he had watched that video and thought it was her, he didn't know her at all.

*We will not quarrel for the greater share of blame annexed to that evening. The conduct of neither, if strictly examined, will be irreproachable; but since then, we have both, I hope, improved in civility.*

—ELIZABETH

# CHAPTER FORTY-ONE

Shelby trudged to the door and opened it with one quick movement. Her mouth was open to say, yet again, she was not doing any interviews. Her heart leaped into her throat when she saw Ransom standing on the step, bright red tulips in one arm.

"Please, don't slam the door." His tone was so urgent that Shelby was startled into a laugh. As if she slammed the door in his face every day.

Standing to the side, she motioned him to come in. "Come off the step. You never know who's out there snapping photos. Rebecca says that Sirocco's got her own Internet fan club now."

Ransom stepped inside but didn't sit. He held out the tulips. "These are for you."

Shelby smiled sadly and took them. In this bittersweet moment, she couldn't decide whether to laugh or to cry. You were supposed to get flowers at the beginning of the relationship, not the end.

"I wanted to talk to you, to try to explain."

She shook her head, eyes still on the impossibly bright red globes. "Ransom, there's not really anything to talk about. I think it's better if we just go our own ways."

There was a pulse of silence.

"Just hear me out, please. Five minutes and then I'll leave you alone, if that's what you want."

Five minutes wasn't long. Part of her screamed that it was too short. She wanted to drink him in, to remember every touch and breath they had shared. Instead, she shrugged and sat on the couch, waiting for him to talk.

He sat on the love seat and looked at his hands. "I only saw about two seconds of that video, just enough to know it was your office. I thought I was saving myself some grief, but it did the opposite. If I had watched it through, I would have known that it wasn't you."

Shelby sighed, wishing this conversation were already over. "Because of the tattoos?"

"No." He raised his eyes to her. "The whole thing was wrong. The way she moved, the young kid. But there was one moment I knew for sure."

Shelby waited, knowing with a dark certainty that whatever he said didn't make any difference in the long run.

"About a minute into it, right before she gets on

the desk, that girl sweeps some books onto the floor." A wry smile touched his lips.

Her eyes widened, and she couldn't help laughing. "You knew it was an impostor because she threw books on the floor?"

"Tell me I'm wrong. Tell me you toss hundred-year-old diaries off your desk every day," he dared her, grinning.

Shelby clutched her stomach, laughter bubbling up. "Not even Rebecca noticed that," she gasped.

"It was a total giveaway." He sobered, the mirth slowly fading from his eyes. "So, when it first came out, I didn't see the video, but I let myself believe what I thought was the truth by the title. I didn't know what was on it, but I thought I could imagine." He paused, running a hand over his face. "People change, Shelby. Maybe it was years old, maybe it was a terrible mistake from your grad school years here. I didn't know."

Shelby hated to admit it, but she could see his point. "Still, you should have asked me."

"And you should have called me," he shot back. "Imagine how I felt waking up to this bomb, and then not hearing anything from you for days."

"But I was in shock, and my aunt had just died," she protested. Even saying the words, as fresh and cruel as they were, was difficult. To her alarm, tears sprang to her eyes. She impatiently brushed them away with the back of her hand.

He crossed the room and sat next to her. Tentatively reaching out one hand, he clasped hers, eyes pleading with her. "I'm so sorry. This has been a nightmare in every way. And you've been so strong. I hate that I added to your grief by not giving you the benefit of the doubt."

Shelby looked into his eyes and saw the sincerity there, and the love. It shone out so strongly that her breath caught in her throat.

"If you can't forgive me, I understand. But I need to tell you one more thing." His gaze was intense, she could feel the energy coming off him in waves. "When I came to Midlands, I was an angry, grieving man. I hated that my wife had died, that our baby had died. I refused to talk to God, refused to love anybody ever again." He looked down at their hands, fingers intertwined. "You changed everything. You said things no one else was brave enough to say. I realized I was as dead as she was, inside. And she wouldn't have wanted that."

Shelby couldn't tear her gaze from his, her heart was pounding out of her chest.

He said, so softly, "I've never been at peace like I am right now. Even if you tell me to go away and never come back, I'm grateful for having known you."

She gazed at his rough hands, tracing the calluses, and thought of the little wooden easel he had made for her. He had roughened his hands making it. She thought of how love shapes a person. He had changed her permanently, and she had changed him.

"Thank you for saying that," she whispered, and bent her head to lay a kiss on that roughened palm. He caught his breath but stayed still. "But I need to tell *you* something."

He watched her silently and nodded.

"I've had a job offer from Millsaps College in Jackson. I know the head of the history department there, and we'd talked once before about it. This trouble"—here she faltered—"with the video, it made me realize that Finch has never really been on my side. Just like you said. Not when I was a grad student, not when I was hired as a professor. He went along with it because I was easy and didn't kick up a fuss and didn't care if he was only around two hours a week." Eyes clear and filled with determination, she looked up at Ransom. "I was telling myself that staying close to home meant I really valued my family and my history. And I thought I should be proud of how far I'd come from Flea Bite Creek, but that was wrong. See, being from that place, from my kind of people, and being who I am, I should have expected *more*. At the very least, a boss that believed in me. So, I've accepted the position. I think it's a good time to make the move."

Ransom said nothing at first. She could hear his breathing, slow and deep. She wanted to lay her head on his chest and inhale his scent, pretend that nothing existed except each other.

"I think you're absolutely right," he said. "When I wondered why you were here, I didn't mean to imply that Yale was better. But I saw how he treated you."

She nodded, staring at her hands. "So, you'll be heading back to home soon. I'm—I'm glad we had this time together." She lifted her eyes, willing herself to be strong.

"Shelby," he said, her name bearing all the love he felt for her. He stroked her cheek and his eyes were full of uncertainty. "I don't want to overwhelm you. The past two weeks have been brutal."

She frowned, unsure of what he was trying to say.

"But, I hoped we could . . . continue where we left off."

Her mouth dropped open. "But how? I'm leaving, you're leaving, and that video . . . Do you really think," she asked, her voice trembling, "that we can move on from that?"

He nodded, his gaze burning her with its intensity. "And about the moving—"

"It won't work. I don't want to live states away from you. And I know you've got a great position, tenured even."

"Wait—"

"Please, don't. I know the woman is always expected to follow the man, especially if he's got the kind of job you have. But I've worked my whole career in this field, and I don't want to leave the South, and my family, and—"

"Shelby." He laughed. "Wait! Maybe I should just—"

"I'm sorry, Ransom." With those words, she lifted her hand and stroked his cheek. Gently, so gently, she leaned forward and placed a kiss on his perfect mouth, her eyes filling with tears. He returned the kiss, but didn't deepen it. He sat back and removed his hand from hers. Her eyes went wide as he knelt before her on one knee.

Out of his pocket he brought a small black box. "A few days before your aunt died, I had a jeweler make this." He opened the box, and Shelby saw a gold band with a ring of multicolored stones. Her heart was pounding so loudly she could hardly hear him.

"Remember that dinner? With Tasha?"

"Who could forget?"

"You said a lot of things about women and careers and kids."

Her eyes were glued on the box, and the gold ring inside. She kept shaking her head, hand over her mouth.

"Shelby, I'll follow you. Wherever you want to teach. I can try for a position there, or I can just write. And when we have kids, I'll stay home with them."

She blinked back tears and laughed, not daring

to believe they were even discussing their future children when she was trying to say good-bye. "What if I want to stay home with them?"

"Then *you* stay home and I'll go teach. Or we can both stay home. I'll write in the attic, whatever. We'll make it work. If you want, that is."

Shelby reached out a finger and gently touched the beautiful ring. The stones were perfectly aligned and sized. Gray and green on each end, with two white stones paired in the middle.

"Yes, yes, yes," she said breathlessly, and threw her arms around his neck.

He kissed her with a passion she hadn't known before, as if his whole heart was hers to treasure.

"Don't you want to know what it says?" He laughed, kissing her hair and her eyes.

"Oh, right." Shelby tried to focus on the ring as he took it from the box with slightly shaking fingers and slipped it on her finger. "This isn't your family ring, is it?"

"No. I know Tasha doesn't really want that heirloom, but I know she won't throw it out. And I do like it . . . but I thought this ring described us better." Shelby gazed down, struggling to think clearly past the fog of joy. "Hematite, opal, opal, emerald . . . *hooe?*" she asked, pronouncing it like the pig call.

Ransom's eyes widened and he started to laugh. He laughed until tears filled his eyes. "*Hooey?* I did call you a blind hog once."

Finally, he wiped his eyes and held up her hand, pointing to the stones. “Hematite, opal, moonstone, emerald. All mined in the South.” He sobered, eyes locked on hers. “Shelby, when I fell in love with you, I was wandering, hopeless. I didn’t really care about anything or anyone, and I liked it that way. I was never going to love anyone again. You reminded me what it was like to belong, to feel safe. Now, wherever you are is home to me.”

Shelby felt tears start to trickle from under her lids, and for the first time in weeks, they were tears of joy. And looking into his eyes, she knew her heart had found its way home at last.

*It taught me to hope as I had scarcely ever allowed myself to hope before.*

—MR. DARCY

# CHAPTER FORTY-TWO

"Will you please stop crying?" Shelby hissed as Jennie Anne sniffled into her tissue. "I know people cry at weddings, but I can hardly hear."

Her sister glared at Shelby, tissue poised halfway to her swollen, red eyes. "I'm not crying from happiness! I just can't believe you're getting married before me." With that, Jennie Anne burst into another round of racking sobs, her chest heaving under her baby-blue sheath gown.

Shelby rolled her eyes and tried not to fidget. Her dress was feeling hotter by the moment, although the simple, creamy-white satin draped flawlessly over her curves. The elegant arrangement of her auburn curls with tiny white rosebuds nestled in a simple French twist would only last so long in the humidity.

The photographer had assembled the bride's family in Bellepointe's front garden, and the setting was glorious. Blooming plants and flowering trees provided a stunning backdrop to the groomsmen in tuxes and bridesmaids in long gowns. Their wedding party was small, comparatively, which is the one thing Shelby had insisted on. She couldn't believe that they had been able to reserve a spot at just a few months' notice, but their having Tasha, the world's pushiest wedding planner, had to help.

Ellie stared off to the side, the toe of one pointed shoe tapping impatiently on the grass, most likely thinking of the reception bar that would open in a few hours.

Her father glanced across at Shelby, smiled warmly and blinked back tears, for the third time. She knew what he was thinking, wishing that Aunt Junetta could have been here. Shelby resolved not to catch his eye during the service or they'd all be sobbing. He hadn't believed her when she had called with the news. But once he had met Ransom, had spent time with him, he saw how they loved and understood each other.

Her mother was in fine form, commanding them to stand this way, then that, heedless of the photographer's instructions. Shelby had let her mother and Tasha hash out the details, knowing they would enjoy the planning much more than she ever could.

Shelby glanced at the photographer and hoped he'd last through the service. He said he'd shot hundreds of weddings, but if the sweat pouring down his pinched face was any indication, none of those had anyone like her mother at the helm.

Rebecca hovered at the edge of the group. As maid of honor, hairdresser, gown fixer and the one who kept Shelby's sisters out of trouble, Rebecca had more roles than anyone else but managed to look as if she was enjoying every second of it. Shelby watched Tom, who had flown in from Miami, at her side and smiled, betting Rebecca had her own wedding on the horizon.

Finally, after what seemed like hours, the frazzled photographer declared them finished and started to pack up his gear to move indoors. Shelby took her chance and slipped away from her mother, waving a silent thanks to Caroline. Her old friend pretended to notice a spot on the sleeve of Mrs. Roswell's silk dress, and both women became absorbed in banishing the phantom stain.

"Mr. Fontana? I know we agreed to have the photos of us—Ransom and me—on the grand staircase. But I was wondering . . ." She almost stopped at the haggard look on the man's face, but then rushed on, "I was wondering if we could take a few outside, if there's time?"

He didn't pause, zipping cameras and lenses into black leather cases. "I guess, if it's not too out of the way. But we need to hurry. The service is starting in twenty minutes."

"What on earth is going on?" Ransom said, his hand outstretched, walking as quickly as he dared, eyes shut tight.

"Just don't peek. I wanted to get a few pictures out here instead of in the entrance hall," Shelby said, tugging him along the uneven grass.

"Crazy girl," he said, but his voice was filled with laughter. "Carl swore he would hunt us down if we tried to elope, so we have to come back."

Shelby snickered and glanced up at him and almost stumbled, even though her eyes were wide-open. He was heart-stopping in his tux, hair smoothed back, handsome face alight with happiness.

"Almost there," she said, trying to catch her breath.

"We only have a few minutes," the photographer called as they came into view.

"Coming," she called back, gripping Ransom's hand and steering him into the spot she wanted him. "Okay," she whispered. "Open your eyes."

Ransom opened his eyes, and realization spread over his face. He slowly surveyed the scene, taking in the overgrown bushes, the crooked olive tree weathered by storms, the old timber framework, the broken panes of glass dully reflecting the bright sun. The grass had been allowed to grow unchecked, and it stood waist high in several tufts.

She watched his face, nervously waiting for him to say something, anything.

Instead, he touched her cheek and leaned down

to kiss her lips, a kiss so soft and deep that she couldn't catch her breath.

"Okay, let's get some pictures of you two right over here," the sweating photographer barked, recalling them from the sweetness of the moment. "Although, it's sort of beyond me why you'd want to take your wedding photos in front of an old greenhouse," he muttered as he twisted the lens into place.

Ransom smiled down at Shelby, brushing a curl away from her temple. She couldn't tear her eyes from his face, so alive with hope and promise.

"Because," he said, bending his dark head down to touch his forehead to hers, "to us, it looks just like home."

# Recipes

Now, for the most important items: recipes!

A Southern book that includes so much cooking can't be complete without some recipes, can it?

## *Cheese Grits*

Ingredients

2 cups whole milk
2 cups water
1½ teaspoons salt
1 cup coarse-ground cornmeal
½ teaspoon pepper
4 tablespoons butter
4 ounces shredded cheddar cheese

Directions

Place the milk, water and salt into a pot over medium-high heat. Bring to a boil. Gradually add the cornmeal while continually whisking. Turn the heat to low and cover. Make sure you stir every 3 to 4 minutes so the grits won't form lumps. Cook for 20 to 25 minutes or until mixture is creamy.

Remove from the heat, add the pepper and butter, tasting to see if it needs any more. Finally stir in the cheese little by little. Enjoy!

# *Bayou Pie*

This is the pizza that Shelby makes for Rebecca.

INGREDIENTS
2 cups cooked chicken, diced
1 cup good BBQ sauce
1 tablespoon honey
1 teaspoon molasses
1 teaspoon red pepper flakes
½ cup brown sugar
Prepared pizza crust
¼ cup sliced red onions
1 cup mozzarella

DIRECTIONS
Preheat oven to 425° F (220° C). In a saucepan over medium-high heat, combine chicken, BBQ sauce, honey, molasses, red pepper and brown sugar. Bring to a boil.

Spread chicken mixture evenly over pizza crust, and top with the onions and cheese. Bake for 15 to 20 minutes, or until cheese is melted.

Adjust red pepper flakes if you like your bayou pie on the mild side. Don't cook this when you're angry.

# AUTHOR'S NOTE

Dear Reader,

I hope you had as much fun visiting with the characters in *Pride, Prejudice and Cheese Grits*, as I had in creating them.

This story was inspired by many different places and people, but some might recognize a few spots mentioned in the book. Pegasus Pizza is just a few blocks from the University of Oregon campus and truly does have the best bayou pie around. (I never did find out who brought such a Southern-inspired dish to Eugene, Oregon, but I send them a hearty thank you.) The Daily Grind is also a real café that serves the most delicious white hot chocolate (but does not have a waitress who knits scarves from dog hair, or at least, not that I've heard). The buildings on the Midlands College campus are lifted directly from the UO campus, and after spending years in the history building, I have to say that historic Chapman Hall is the jewel of the quad. Giving Shelby a large office in Chapman, facing the great oak, is indeed the best kind of wish fulfillment.

As for characters, Shelby and Ransom came from my imagination. They weren't based on anybody I've ever met. But if you know me, you might suspect that I have just a little in common with Rebecca, the Jane Austen fan. Just like her, I think life is so much easier to understand through the lens of an Austen book. Be sure to check out the second in the series, *Emma, Mr. Knightley and Chili-Slaw Dogs* for a whole new cast of characters (plus a peek into Shelby and Ransom's new life) set in the beauty of the South.

I hope you enjoyed your visit in Flea Bite Creek and you can connect with me through my Facebook page Pride, Prejudice and Cheese Grits.

Blessings, Mary Jane Hathaway

# ACKNOWLEDGMENTS

This book started out as a personal project for my own writing pleasure but I have had the support and assistance of many people along the way. A special thank-you to Gail Seward Anderson, who introduced me to all the best parts of the South, including beignets and real bacon. Susan Spears, Julie Hilton Steele, Christalee Scott May and many others offered their time and talent as beta readers. Their advice, especially in Southern matters, was invaluable. Many thanks to the amazing team at Howard Books, specifically my editor, Beth Adams, who cold-heartedly cuts every one of my exclamation points. Also, a big thank-you to assistant editor Katie Sandell, who allows me to send her long, rambling e-mails about all sorts of minutiae. Thank you to the Howard Books team members for helping in the publication of this book—all editors, proofreaders, copyeditors and cover designers! Last but not least, to my husband, Crusberto. He has sat patiently through innumerable BBC adaptations of Jane Austen's novels (along with Mrs. Gaskell's *North and South*) and still does not understand why grown women swoon at the sight of a man in a cravat.

# READING GROUP GUIDE

## *Introduction*

Shelby Roswell is a woman on a mission. As a professor of Civil War history at a small college in the South, her sights are set on becoming a tenured faculty member, with every publication and course evaluation an important addition to her portfolio. But it appears her plans will be foiled when Ransom Fielding, a handsome visiting professor in her department, publishes a review of her new book that has the potential to destroy both her hopes for tenure and her reputation within the department. The battle lines are drawn, and the stage is set for a modern-day version of *Pride and Prejudice* with a Southern flair.

## *Topics & Questions for Discussion*

1. What did you enjoy most about *Pride, Prejudice and Cheese Grits*? Which character was your favorite? Why?

2. Based on the description of each character in chapter one, how would you describe Shelby

Roswell and Ransom Fielding? Which one were you most drawn to initially?

3. Discuss the role that assumptions play in creating conflict between characters throughout the book and the relationship between assumptions and prejudice. How have assumptions impacted your relationships in the past?

4. Compare and contrast Shelby Roswell with Elizabeth Bennet in Jane Austen's *Pride and Prejudice*.

5. Which character(s) from Jane Austen's *Pride and Prejudice* does Shelby's roommate, Rebecca, resemble? What role does Rebecca play in Shelby's life and in the story?

6. In what ways is the vocation of Civil War historian an apt metaphor for the developing relationship between Shelby and Ransom?

7. How does David Bishop differ from Jane Austen's Mr. Collins? How did David Bishop's involvement in the video scandal add a different dimension to his character?

8. In what ways does Ransom Fielding demonstrate the beneficence and generosity

of Mr. Darcy's character in Jane Austen's *Pride and Prejudice*? Contrast his actions with Mr. Darcy's.

9. What is Shelby Roswell's fatal flaw throughout the story? In what ways is it the reverse side of her greatest strength? What is one of your qualities that can be both a gift and a curse, depending on how it is used?

10. In what way was Shelby's experience with the disciplinary committee at Midlands an experience of "the shoe being on the other foot" for her, in terms of making judgments about others? Have you ever had an experience where you received unfair treatment? How did the experience impact you?

11. Describe some of the key catalysts that contributed to the transformation in Ransom's character throughout the story. Describe the changes you observed.

12. On page 378, Shelby "thought of how love shapes a person." How were both Shelby and Ransom shaped by their growing love for each other?

13. What is the difference between making judgments about a person and prejudice? Can

you make judgments without becoming prejudiced? Describe some examples of both that are illustrated throughout the story.

14. How does the description embedded in the stones of Shelby's engagement ring reflect the journey that Shelby and Ransom have each taken throughout the story? In what ways were each of them on a personal quest to find "home"?

15. If you could spend an afternoon with one character from this story, who would you choose? Why?

# About the Author

Mary Jane Hathaway is the pen name of an award-nominated writer who spends the majority of her literary energy on subjects unrelated to Jane Austen. A homeschooling mother of six young children who rarely wear shoes, she's madly in love with a man who has never read a single Jane Austen novel. She holds degrees in religious studies and theoretical linguistics and has a Jane Austen quote on the back of her van. She can be reached through the Facebook page Pride, Prejudice and Cheese Grits.

**Center Point Large Print**
600 Brooks Road / PO Box 1
Thorndike ME 04986-0001 USA

**(207) 568-3717**

**US & Canada:**
**1 800 929-9108**
**www.centerpointlargeprint.com**